The Chinese President

A Rory Mack Steele Novel, Volume 8

Eugene Lloyd MacRae

Published by CreateSpace, 2013.

THE CHINESE PRESIDENT

First edition. December 11, 2013.

Copyright © 2013 Eugene Lloyd MacRae.

ISBN: 139781927767016

Written by Eugene Lloyd MacRae.

Chapter 1

LOUISVILLE, KENTUCKY

ASSASSINATION. That was his specialty. Jun "Danni" Kang had been working undercover in the United States for the Peoples Republic of China for the last fifteen years. Moving to America, attending and graduating from Stanford University had given him legitimate friends and contacts, allowing him to blend in perfectly. Chang ran a small computer business with ten employees. In actuality, they were a cell of eleven men who engaged in various forms of espionage. Political, military and industrial espionage was a necessary part of their daily lives. But the spying part was boring. Clean-up was their specialty. And it wasn't boring. What if U.S. government agents were getting too close to the operation? The team terminated them in 'accidents'. If a scientist, who was critical to American military abilities couldn't be turned, he fell off a balcony. If a politician, passing sensitive information to China suddenly got cold feet, Kang happily involved himself personally. He eliminated the target with pleasure. Which is why Chang was excited on this rainy April morning. It was specialty time for him.

Kang stood patiently under his umbrella on the street corner across from the KFC Yum Center. He listened to the patter of the rain on his umbrella. It was soothing in a way. And the air smelled so clean.

The crowds were moving a little faster this morning, everyone wanting to get to work without getting too wet, so he watched carefully, in case his target was moving faster than normal as well. A few people grumbled when they had to walk around Kang, but he stayed in position. The businessman should be heading this way any minute and he refused to miss him. Two minutes passed. Three minutes. There he was, half a block away and heading this way.

The target stopped and pick up his morning coffee from the street vendor on the far corner as usual.

Kang felt his pulse quicken in anticipation.

The target took a sip, nodded his head in approval, then turned and began walking in Kang's direction again.

The same routine every morning, thought Kang. That's how you get mugged, robbed or raped. The bad people know where you'll be at your most vulnerable every time. And a target's routine was also a great tool in helping an assassin know where to strike.

The target waited calmly for the light, sipping his coffee. A few moments later, the light changed and the crowd started across the street, their shoulders hunched up against the rain. The target stepped off the sidewalk, walking like he didn't have a care in the world.

Kang moved over to stand beside a large concrete planter. He closed the umbrella in preparation. As his target approached this side of the street, Kang gripped the umbrella in his right hand. He discretely pressed a small button with his thumb and a tiny needle filled with hydrogen cyanide protruded from the top of the umbrella. It was an old method of assassination but it worked well in a crowd.

The target stepped up onto the sidewalk, nodding at a couple of other businessmen passing by. He passed the concrete planter like he did every morning.

Kang fell in step behind as the businessman walked past. Kang increased his pace and jabbed the tiny needle point into the back of the man's thigh.

The target turned, confusion etched on his face as his hand went to the area where he had felt the pinprick.

Kang just nodded as he walked past. The target would be dead in a little over ten minutes. Kang felt no remorse. The man had been the owner of a business that was caught spying on China. He now worked part-time for a charity agency, but no longer owning the business didn't absolve him. This was the song and dance of spy vs spy.

Chapter 2

LOUISVILLE, KENTUCKY
8 Years Later
"GET THE BACK-UP AND KILL HER!"

The man in the black, pinstriped suit was used to voices being distorted electronically. To him, there was no mistaking the venom behind the words. Yet, considering all he had done over the years, it still surprised him, considering who the target was, "She just left with her friend–"

"Then kill them both! No loose ends. But get that back-up first."

IT WAS 2:00 AM AND Candy Jossel and Wendy Symonds were giddy like two young schoolgirls. Connor Harrison Lane had just been elected President of the United States and they had been part of his campaign team. Two months out of college and they both felt like their future was set. Next stop was Washington DC and an opportunity to get really involved in changing the world. Walking down a sidewalk in Old Louisville arm in arm they sang 'We are the Champions' by Queen. Neither young lady saw the tall man in the blue suit with his jaw set hard until they nearly bumped into him.

"Oops, sorry Mister," Candy giggled.

Wendy laughed, grabbed Candy by the elbow and turned her around, "I think you've had too much celebratory wine young lady."

Candy giggled again as they began walking in the other direction, "Could be–"

Both young women stopped quickly. They clutched at each other's sleeve. Another hard-faced man in a black, pinstripe suit stood on the sidewalk blocking their way. And this one was holding a Beretta Nano handgun equipped with a silencer.

The man took a step and looked directly at Candy. "You made a backup disk earlier. Where is it?" he demanded.

"We don't know what you're talking about," Wendy said in a small shaky voice.

Candy stared at the gun. She gave her head a small shake no.

The man in the rear stepped forward. He grabbed Wendy's red leather purse.

"Hey," Wendy yelled. She took a step towards the man to grab her purse back but she was shoved backward roughly.

Rummaging through the purse, the man then uttered disgust and threw the purse to the sidewalk - lipstick, an extra pair of earrings, a pack of tissues, and a pack of gum tumbled across the cement.

Wendy grumbled as she moved forward to pick up her stuff, "Hey? Watch what you're–"

But the man pushed her back again and then lunged forward and grabbed Candy's black leather handbag.

Candy glanced at her friend as the man began rifling through her handbag, "If - if you're looking for money–"

She was cut off when the man threw the black leather purse to the ground in disgust. It rolled off the edge of the sidewalk and dumped some of its contents on the street. The man sneered as he looked at his partner, shaking his head no without a word.

Now it was the partner's turn - he spoke in a low, ominous voice as he brandished the weapon, "I want the backup disk and I want it now. Do you understand me?" When he didn't get an answer he calmly turned the gun towards Wendy's right leg and fired. The silencer muffled the shot but Wendy's scream echoed off the brick buildings and down the side alley. She fell to the sidewalk writhing in pain.

Candy yelled, "Wendy!" and dropped to her knees beside her friend. She reached for the wound, intending to stop the blood - then she cried no when she was ripped away from her friend and hauled roughly to her feet by the man in the blue suit.

"Where is the backup disk?" he demanded to know. He shook Wendy like a rag doll and she whimpered. The man with the had gun stepped forward and waved it under Candy's nose, "Do you want me to shoot your friend again?"

Her eyes wide with fear - Candy opened her mouth to speak - a crackling sound filled the air.

The gunman screamed and fell to the concrete sidewalk, his weapon clattering into the street.

Still frozen in fear, Candy looked down to see Wendy holding a pink colored Taser in her hand

Wendy's voice was filled with pain and tears rolled down her cheeks as she yelled, "Run Candy! Get help." She grimaced and rolled towards the other man and lunged at him with the Taser.

But he saw it coming and the man twisted away, lifting one leg and barely avoiding the defensive weapon.

Sensing he was off balance Candy hit him hard with her shoulder, driving him back

The man stumbled back, his foot twisted on the edge of the sidewalk and he keeled over- landing half in the street - grunting hard as his head hit the pavement.

Candy tore her arm away from his grasp, jumped over him and took off for the entrance to the dark alleyway. She turned as she ran - looking back at her friend.

Wendy saw her turn to look back and she shook her head, crying out, "No, Candy. You need to run." She lunged at the man half in the street with the Taser but he saw it coming again and rolled away from her thrust. He scrambled around to his knees, looking for the weapon the other man had dropped.

Candy turned and ran hard down the dark alley. The smell of vomit, urine, and garbage was overwhelming and she gagged. Desperately peering into the darkness as she ran, Candy looked for a hiding place or a back door–

A muffled shot sounded behind her.

The sound hit her like a blow to the stomach and Candy stopped, looking back, "Wendy–?"

The pounding of footsteps told her someone running for the entranceway to the alley.

Candy turned and ran. Her right leg ran into something in the dark and she fell hard. The breath was knocked from her lungs. The clatter of metal garbage cans falling around her body was like a beacon in the dark to the men chasing her. She knew she had to get moving. Candy struggled to roll over and get her legs moving again. Her leg shot out to the side and she fell. Garbage and wet cardboard made the footing treacherous as Candy fought to get to her feet.

Footsteps were now pounding down the alley towards her.

Candy finally got her feet underneath her and she ran blindly. A thin, upright light appeared ahead on the right and she ran for it. An exit door slightly ajar offered hope. Desperately shoving her fingers into the slight crack between the door and the casing, she pulled hard. It barely budged. Rusty hinges protested as she put her foot against the door casing and pulled in desperation. The door grudgingly moved with a dull grind of metal. Candy grit her teeth and pulled harder, creating a larger crack.

The footsteps pounded closer.

Candy desperately thrust her body at the tight opening. She pulled her breath in and squeezed her body into the crack.

The footsteps were right there!

Pushing hard, Candy finally tumbled through into the darkness beyond. Catching her balance, she turned and grabbed the inner panic bar of the door, pulling desperately. It wouldn't budge this way either. She set her foot against the door casing again and pulled with all her might. The door grudgingly pulled shut with a groan and the lock clicked in place.

Someone pounded several times on the other side of the door. Muffled yelling and cursing filtered through.

CANDY JOSSEL FOUND herself in a dark hallway that extended along the back of the building. She extended her arms and felt for objects in the darkness. Afraid to trip over something in the dark, she began shuffling her feet and her escape down the hallway was so slow she cursed herself. Her heart pounded in her chest. Candy was positive the men would hear it and track her down. She concentrated on slowing her heart rate. But now she could hear her own raspy breathing. Fear was rising in her stomach. How long before they found her? A splash of light appeared up ahead. The splash of light grew larger and she was able to see the floor. She moved faster, heading for the beacon of possible safety.

The sound of distant sirens reached her ears.

That was good. Someone must have alerted the police. As she approached the splash of light, Candy realized that the illumination was coming from an adjoining hallway to the right. Was it a way out? She peered around the corner and down the hallway. There appeared to be a door at the far end. Candy headed for it. She passed a few doors on the left and the right as she walked. She gingerly tested each doorknob, in case she needed a place to hide, but every door was locked. The air was musty and she had the impression she was inside an old, beat-up apartment building. Probably even abandoned, she thought. Everything was silent around her.

But the sirens outside were getting louder.

She spotted a large front door with heavily frosted glass just ahead. Candy took a few quick steps and reached down for the door handle. Slowly pushing the door open a crack, Candy peered out. She wondered if the two men would be waiting for her. But all she saw was a dark, empty street. She pushed the door open more.

There was a screech of tires and then sirens exploded across the front of the building as two police cruisers flashed by the front of the building.

Startled, Candy pulled the door closed. She could hear the police cars screeching around the corner at the end of the block on the right. Candy knew she had to go back and check on Wendy but she was too afraid to even step out of the building. Candy chastised herself. Wendy was dead because of her lie. Because Candy had decided to protect someone else instead. Tears filled Candy's eyes as she thought about her best friend lying on the sidewalk.

CANDY GATHERED HERSELF and pushed the door open a crack.

Five people were walking past the front of the building. A skinny young man, wearing his ball cap backward, came running up behind them, "Yo bro. What's all the noise about?"

A tall young man with a cornrow hairstyle shrugged, "Don't know. Something is happening around the block."

"Well, let's go," the skinny young man said with exuberance and he skipped past them.

Candy took a deep breath and stepped out of the old apartment building, falling in behind the five people. She used them as a shield as they headed for the end of the block. There were several nightclubs and bars along the street and people started pouring out of them and heading towards the crime scene as well.

Candy kept an eye out for the two men. Young men and women, in their early teens and 20s, fell in step behind her. She felt safer in the noisy crowd. Turning the corner at the end of the block Candy could see flashing lights. Several police cruisers were parked in the area where she and Wendy had been attacked. A Mercy Ambulance Service vehicle and a paramedic truck were parked nearby.

Optimism filled Candy's heart. Maybe they were already treating Wendy. Candy saw a number of police officers just ahead, instructing a very large crowd to keep back. Candy slipped through the buzzing crowd, watching for the two men. Looking between the bodies of several bystanders, Candy could see a figure covered with a blanket lying on the sidewalk. Her hands flew to her mouth, stifling a cry. A blood pool extended out from the covered figure on the left. And a river of blood drained along the edge of the sidewalk to a street drain. Hot tears fell from Candy's eyes. Pushing herself closer through the crowd, she approached the edge of the yellow police tape. Candy opened her mouth to yell for a policeman—

The two men were across the street.

The blood froze in her veins.

The two men were *inside* the cordon of yellow police tape.

How could that be?

They didn't look to be under arrest. They were simply talking to another man, who had a gold police shield hanging from the top pocket of his suit coat.

Candy was about to yell out to arrest the two attackers when she spotted something else. The ground seemed to sway under her feet.

A heavy-set man caught her arm, "Are you okay, lady?"

Nodding, Candy steadied herself. She couldn't believe it. The two men *also* had gold shields hanging from the top pockets of their suit jackets.

The two men are police?

Candace Ella Jossel's body began shaking. Fear made breathing difficult. She backed away from the yellow crime scene tape, bumping into several people.

"Hey lady!" one woman yelled when Candy stepped on her foot accidentally.

"Sorry," Candy whispered. She lowered her head, afraid the sudden confrontation would attract the wrong attention. Her heartbeat increased as she glanced back at the two men beyond the yellow tape.

They *were* looking in the direction of the yell.

Candy turned and slipped quickly through the crowd. Just ahead, a young couple was talking with others about the activities taking place in the crime scene beyond the yellow tape. Just beside them was a baby carriage and Candy spotted a Louisville Cardinals basketball jacket and ball cap sitting inside. The young woman was holding the baby in her arms. Candy discreetly bent at the knees, picked up the cap and jacket and slipped away. As she moved away from the back of the crowd, she put the ball cap on, slipped the large jacket on and zippered it up to cover the top half of her yellow dress. She glanced back, wiped a tear from her eye and whispered, "Sorry Wendy."

Candace Ella Jossel put the collar up, slipped her hands into the jacket's pocket and moved away from the crime scene as quickly as her shaky legs could carry her.

Chapter 3

CANDY JOSSEL SAT HUNCHED at the lunch counter, her hands around a hot cup of coffee. She had used the five dollars she had found in the jacket to pay for it, having lost her purse and everything else at the crime scene. Despite being surrounded by early morning workers eating their breakfast, the rich smells of bacon, toast, and scrambled eggs barely registered with her. In the midst of their lively conversations, she grieved for her best friend, trying to make sense of the encounter that had taken place only a few hours before. She and Wendy had gone from two people, who had the world by the tail, to one dead and one living in the blink of an eye. And the one that was living was filled with grief, remorse, and guilt.

"Hey Harry, can you turn that thing up," someone yelled from a table over on the far side.

Candy watched as a man behind the counter turned around and pointed a remote control up to a 60-inch high definition television high on the wall behind him. She felt the blood drain from her face as she realized that was *her* picture in the top right-hand corner of the screen. 'CNN breaking news' was scrolling across the bottom of the screen and a white-haired announcer with a white beard was talking.

"CNN is following the latest news about a murder that has taken place in Louisville, Kentucky. A murder that involves staff members at the campaign headquarters of newly elected President, Connor Harrison Layne. Our CNN reporter, Barbara Partner is in Louisville, Kentucky right now. Barbara, can you tell us what is happening there?"

A dark-haired female reporter was holding one hand to her left ear as she tried to listen to what was being said to her among the din and noise coming from the large crowd around her. She finally spoke into the microphone she was holding in her right hand, "Yes, Carl. I'm having trouble hearing you. As you can see there is quite a crowd around me right now. I'm in front of the campaign headquarters of Connor Harrison Lane, who was just elected President of the United States last night. Louisville police found the body of Wendy Allison Symonds sometime after 2 AM last night in Downtown Louisville. She had been shot dead. She was a volunteer worker here, working on the presidential campaign of then Kentucky Governor Connor Harrison Lane. We have a brief clip of Lane as he spoke about an hour ago at 7:30 AM."

The picture shifted to a scene of Connor Harrison Lane, surrounded by a sea of reporters and microphones. Lane was a tall politician with salt-and-pepper hair. He didn't quite have movie star good looks, but the confidence he exuded made him an attractive candidate for both men and women. Right now though, Lane looked very tired and he spoke with a hoarse voice, "Both myself and my staff want to extend our heartfelt sympathies to the family of Wendy Symonds. She was a wonderful young lady–"

"President Lane, how will this affect your presidency?" one of the reporters yelled.

Lane turned and looked at the reporter with some anger in his eyes, "This is not about me. This is not about my presidency or my campaign or my staff. This is about a wonderful young lady who lost her life under tragic circumstances. This is about her parents, her family, and her loved ones. This is about those who knew her and were better for it. I'll do everything I can to help her family and loved ones through these trying days to come."

Another reporter shouted, "How about the shooter - Candace Josse? She's reportedly another member of your staff. Is that true? What can you tell us about her?"

A coldness rushed over Candy. They think I'm the shooter?

Lane ignored the question. He turned and pushed his way through the sea of reporters trying to get him to give them more information or some juicy sound bites for their next newscast.

The scene shifted back to Barbara Partner in front of Lane's campaign headquarters, "As you can see Carl, I don't imagine President-elect Lane got any sleep last night. He looked tired, haggard and worn. There is no doubt these tragic circumstances have overshadowed what was a marvelous campaign. One that led him to become president of the United States. Back to you, Carl."

The scene shifted back to the white-haired CNN announcer, "Thank you, Barbara. The picture you are seeing on your screen right now is the campaign headquarters' photo of Candace Ella Jossel, the alleged killer of Wendy Allison Symonds, Although the Lexington police are not saying anything official, our inside sources tell us they have the murder weapon, a 9-mm Beretta Nano. And they found a fingerprint from the alleged killer, Candace Ella Jossel, on the barrel of the gun."

Candy's hand began to shake when she heard that statement. Something was wrong. Something was despairingly wrong. She had never touched that gun. At least, she didn't remember ever touching the gun. What was happening here?

The CNN reporter continued and the picture shifted to a picture of a six foot tall, athletic woman, pushing her way through a crowd while he spoke over the scene, "This is Keira Blaze Jossel, the campaign manager for Connor Harrison Lane in his run-up the presidency of the United States. She is also the older sister of the alleged shooter, Candace Ella Jossel."

Candy could barely breathe as she saw her sister stop in the middle of the crowd and turn to look at one of the reporters who asked if she had been responsible for the hiring of her sister.

"Yes, I hired her," Keira Jossel said sharply. "I was trying to help her. I didn't think she'd do anything like this." She turned and took a step away. Then she stopped dead in her tracks, turned back and looked at the crowd of reporters, "I don't think she did this. I'm sure–" Keira Jossel shook her head and turned away, pushing herself through the crowd.

Candy was stunned. Even her sister thought she had done this. Who was she going to turn to now? The whole world was closing in on her.

The scene shifted back to Carl Power, the CNN reporter, "Candace Ella Jossel was hired fresh out of college along with Wendy Allison Symonds to work in the campaign headquarters of Connor Harrison Lane. They were both considered bright young minds, although sources tell us that Candace Ella Jossel had been a troubled teen, involved in drugs quite a bit, in reaction to the death of her father, Warren Howel Jossel. Mr. Jossel had been the driver of the vehicle involved in an accident ten years ago that took the life of his wife and two middle daughters. Candace Ella Jossel survived that accident and we have been told it affected her quite a bit. Older sister, Keira Blaze Jossel, was not involved in that accident and she was working for Kirby Booth Wilkinson, the Ambassador to China at that time. Keira Jossel hired both young women...."

Candy's entire body was shaking as she slipped from the counter stool. She kept her face down, hoping no one would notice her under the Louisville Cardinals ball cap. She could barely get one shaking foot in front of the other as she walked across the diner floor and out the door to the sidewalk. Stuffing her hands into the Louisville Cardinals jacket, Candy moved to the left, ducked into a doorway and out of sight - and stared down at her feet. What was she going to do now? They thought she was a killer. They thought she had shot her best friend. Maybe if she called the police? The cruel memory of the crime scene came flooding back to her. Three policemen, all standing together on the other side of the yellow police tape, talking calmly. And two of *them* were the attackers. The police were in on this somehow, there was no doubt. She was being framed for murder.

Chapter 4

STEPPING OUT FROM the shelter of the doorway, Candy felt exposed and vulnerable. Turning left - she had no idea where she was going - she just needed to walk. Staying close to the buildings, she watched for the police, ready to hide in a doorway again. A half block later, she stood at an intersection. Without a real plan - she simply crossed the street and kept on going north. It seemed as good a direction as any right now. Over the next two blocks, he tried to come up with a plan - but she had nothing. She had no idea how she could clear her name - where to go—

A police cruiser with two officers crossed the intersection just ahead, heading west.

Instead of turning into a doorway, Candy panicked. She turned to her right and crossed the street, intending to go in the opposite direction. She heard the screeching of tires as she stepped up onto the sidewalk.

The police car backed up swiftly into the middle of the intersection and screeched to a stop. The officer at the wheel turned in his seat, looking at her.

Candy kept walking toward the corner - she knew if she ran now it would definitely look suspicious. She kept her head down but her eyes up, watching, hoping they would just go away.

Another officer stepped out of the passenger seat and looked over the top of the cruiser at her. The officer at the wheel picked up his radio and began talking into it.

Candy knew they had made her. She almost laughed. Using that term, referring to herself like that seemed so unreal. She had no choice. Reaching the intersection, she sprinted around the corner and took off down the street.

The shout went up from one of the officers, "Stop! Police!"

As her feet pounded down the sidewalk, Candy heard the screeching of tires, and the wail of the cruiser siren started. The roar of the engine, heading in her direction, confirmed they were after her. She desperately looked for a way out.

A well-dressed woman had her hand on the door handle of a dress shop just ahead of her. The woman pulled the door open and stepped inside.

Candy darted into the open doorway, just as the door was slowly closing, jostling the woman aside, heading for the back of the shop.

"Hey! Were not open yet," yelled the woman.

Candy wasn't listening. She was looking for an exit sign as she ran, starting to panic at the fact she didn't see one. She cursed herself, wondering just how stupid she was to get trapped inside here. She ran through a set of curtains into an area where an older woman was working with fabric at a cutting table. The woman looked up in surprise as Candy ran past her. Spotting an exit sign over a door to the right, she slid to a stop, turned and headed for it. Without a moment's hesitation, she slammed her body into the emergency bar to push the door open. The emergency alarm for the store went off and she found herself in a back alley. Candy turned to her right and began running down the long, dirty alleyway. She passed several doors but didn't bother trying them. Candy was headed for escape at the far end of the alleyway. But halfway there, escape was suddenly blocked off.

A police cruiser screeched to a stop across the end of the alley.

Candy's heart raced faster as she slid to a stop.

"Stop! Police!"

Turning on her heels, Candy ran ten feet and stumbled to a stop again.

An officer stood outside the exit door, back at the dress shop. He began running towards her.

Spinning back around back, Candy saw the police cruiser had backed up and was now making the turn into the alleyway. She was trapped. Frantically looking for a way out, she ran toward the police car, heading for the nearest back doors she could see. She tried the first one - it was locked. She tried the next one - the same. She swore. The cruiser was coming closer. The next door mercifully opened and Candy rushed through, barreling down a long hallway, her footsteps echoing off the walls. Making a couple of blind turns, Candy realized she was inside another old apartment building. But this one was occupied. She could smell breakfast cooking and low voices inside the apartments she passed.

Fast footsteps started echoing somewhere behind her.

Candy kept running, looking for a way out or a place to hide. She made a right turn and spotted a glass door at the far end of the hallway. She ran for it. Her shoes slid as she put on the brakes and she slammed into the door, rattling the glass. She flapped the pain from her right hand, reached down with her left and pushed the door open. As the door closed behind her, she found herself on a small landing in front of a dirty sidewalk.

There were a few people walking on the street but no sign of a policeman.

Running down the three steps to the sidewalk, Candy looked up and down the street, desperately trying to determine the best escape route. Candy tried to calm herself, tried to slow her breathing as she walked quickly across the street and headed for the double-door entranceway to an old Romanesque style office building. She didn't want to attract attention, but she had to find someplace to hide before the policeman chasing her caught up. Or before the policeman in cruiser appeared around the corner.

Candy bounded up two steps and pulled open the right-hand door, just enough to squeeze inside. She softly pulled it closed it behind her. The glass in the double doors was frosted and she couldn't see outside. She had no way of knowing if the police officer chasing her had seen her come inside. Turning, Candy walked quickly across the small lobby area, looking for signs of a back exit. There was a hallway to the left and the right. But she could see barred windows at the far end on each side. There was another hallway just ahead past the office directory on the wall. Candy took the hallway straight ahead. She spotted a door at the far end. Halfway there, Candy turned and looked back, listening intently for someone coming into the building behind her. Everything was quiet. She hurried on. Reaching the exit door, Candy cautiously opened the door just a crack. Her heart sank.

A police cruiser with lights flashing and siren wailing slid to a stop in the back alley, right outside the exit.

Pulling the door shut, Candy turned and headed back towards the front of the building. She crossed the small lobby area and stopped dead in her tracks.

The dark outline of a police officer painted the frosted glass of the left entrance door. He was obviously standing on the steps on the other side.

Candy could see him talking into a microphone. The sound was muted but the words were unmistakable.

"Yes, sir. The suspect is inside the Lee Building. My partner is parked in back."

They knew she was in here! Candy turned to look for another way out. The small elevator beside the directory had a sign that said 'out of service'. There was a stairway with a wooden railing on her right. Candy ran for it and bounded up the steps two at a time. She had to find a place to hide. Reaching the second floor, Candy ran down the hallway, checking doors on either side. They were all locked. Candy reached the stairway landing at the back of the building. She looked down over the railing, holding her breath and listened. Everything was quiet. She looked up and decided to try the third floor. She moved up the stairs, trying to move quieter this time. Reaching the top floor, she moved down the hallway, trying every door. All locked. Candy tried to twist a few of the doorknobs but wasn't strong enough to break anything lose. Candy headed down the hallway towards the back of the building. She twisted every doorknob and pushed and pulled on every door. She couldn't find a single hiding spot. Reached the landing for the back stairway, Candy anxiously looked over the old wooden railing. Everything was quiet. She was trapped, with no way out and no place to hide. But something struck Candy as odd. No one was pursuing her. An ominous dread fell over Candy Jossel.

Chapter 5

CANDY STOOD AT THE TOP of the landing on the third floor of the old office building. The building was quiet and the police had not come in to arrest her. Did she elude them after all? Candy took the ball cap off and stuffed it into the right pocket of the Louisville Cardinals jacket. Hearing only the sound of her own breathing, she stepped down on the first step, as close to the wall as possible. The building was old and she wanted to keep the stairs from creaking. She had seen that in the movies one time. Hopefully, it would work in real life. Coming to the turn in the stairs, Candy stopped dead in her tracks. She had heard something below. Or was it her imagination? She tried to maintain control of her breathing, listening for the slightest sound.

A stair creaked somewhere down below. There was another squeak. Someone was coming up the stairs.

Candy turned and moved as quickly and quietly as possible back up the stairs. Reaching the top landing, Candy slowly turned to look over the railing.

A man with brown hair and wearing a blue suit appeared on the stairs, moving in slow, fluid movements.

Candy's breath became ragged and noisy.

The man stopped, turned and looked up at her.

She recognized him as the man her and Wendy had bumped into last night. But this time, he had a gun in his hand. That was why the police hadn't come in to get her. They were waiting for these two guys to arrive and finish her off.

The man began climbing the stairs again, his cold, hard eyes never wavering from her face.

Turning on her heels, Candy took a few steps towards the hallway - she stopped dead.

The man in the black, pinstripe suit, the one who had shot Wendy in the leg, was standing ten feet. And he was holding the same long-barreled handgun.

Candy backed up - her eyes on the gun - until she was stopped by the old wooden railing. She turned to dart down the stairs - and froze.

The man on the stairs had reached the top step. He now stood to her right, holding his gun steady at her chest.

She was trapped. Candy looked from man to man - her eyebrows pulled in tightly when she realized both men had gold badges hanging from the top pocket of their suit jackets. They *were* the police - and they were going to kill her. Her mind whirled, trying to make sense of it.

The man who had shot Wendy in the leg spoke first, "Same question as last night, where's the backup you made?"

Candy swallowed as she looked at the gun and then back up at the man's face, her voice weak, "Why - why did you shoot Wendy? She didn't do anything to you. You're the police for gosh sakes. Why–?"

The man snapped his answer, "Because *you* didn't cooperate. It's *your* fault. All you had to do was give us the backup–"
"I don't understand. Why–?" Candy asked again.
The man on the step spoke in a weary tone, "Just shut up, sweetheart and give us the backup. Then it will all be over and we can all go home."
Candy considered what he said. We can all go home? But Wendy couldn't go home. And Candy doubted she wouldn't get the chance to go home either. She slid away from the man on the top step, but the wall was right there. It was over.
Suddenly the man in the black pinstriped suit grimaced and screamed in pain. He dropped his gun as he tried to hold his right side. A moment later, he fell to the floor.
Behind him was a tall man with black hair, dressed in a black leather jacket and blue jeans. The man moved quickly, took two steps and drove his fist into the other gunman's jaw.
The gunman in the blue suit fell backward, landed on the steps below, upside down, and slid heavily down the staircase. His gun dropped to a step and bounced over the side, disappearing, two echoes bouncing off the wall as it struck a banister and then the floor below.

The tall man turned, walked back and kicked the gun with the long barrel down the hallway.

Candy watched it, spinning like a top as it slid along the floor. She looked back to the tall man. His hand was extended towards her as if he expected her to take it. Candy hesitated.

"It's up to you. But once he recovers, I can't guarantee your safety," the tall man said. He spoke in a low, reassuring voice as he indicated the first gunman still rolling on the hallway floor in agony.

Candy looked up into his silver-blue eyes. He looked so calm in the middle of all this craziness. She hesitated briefly again. Then she reached out and took his hand.

The tall man led her part way down the stairs where he stopped and bent over the gunman lying motionless on the worn, wooden steps.

Candy whispered, "Is...is he dead?"

The man checked the pulse in his neck, "No, he's just out cold." He lifted the gold shield dangling from the man's top pocket in the palm of his hand and examined it briefly. Then he dropped it and led Candy past the body and down the stairs.

"Who...who are you?" Candy asked as she struggled to keep up with his long legs.

"My name is Rory Mack Steele. I work as a private investigator for Highlander Investigative Services. I came in to see a client who said he would be here an hour ago, but he hasn't shown up yet. I was in a small washroom and overheard those men talking to you when I came out."

Candy remembered all the locked doors. He must've been behind one of them.

REACHING THE MAIN FLOOR, Rory led Candy to the back door of the building. He put a finger to his lips for quiet as he reached for the doorknob. Opening the door just a crack, he took a quick look outside. He closed the door carefully and shook his head no. Taking Candy's hand again, he led her to the front entrance. The frosted glass in the upper portion of the double front doors reflected movement outside. Rory pushed the door open just a crack and peeked out. "Police cruisers guarding both entrances," he whispered as he carefully pulled the door shut.

"We're trapped," Candy whispered.

Rory nodded, "Looks like it." He walked part way down the hallway on the left, trying a few office doors but they were all locked.

"I already tried all the doors. Everything is locked," Candy said as she followed closely behind.

"You tried all three floors?" Rory asked as he pointed a thumb at the ceiling.

"Uh, huh."

Rory nodded. No surprise there. It was still too early for working hours.

"And the windows at both ends of this hallway are barred," Candy added. She crossed her arms and hugged herself.

Rory was quiet, his eyes looking around. They were definitely in a tight spot. He took a deep breath and let it out slowly, thinking. Then he turned and led Candy back to the front entrance area.

"What are we going to do?" Candy asked as she looked toward the stairs. Her voice was scared and squeaky. "They're going to come...."

Rory turned and looked at the front door. Then he looked down, tugging on his lower lip, thinking. A moment later he held a finger up, "I have an idea." He pointed to a spot about ten feet in front of the doors, "Lie down there."

Candy's eyebrows went up, "Pardon?"

"Lie down lengthways right here on the edge of the rug," he instructed her.

She looked down. There was a rug about ten feet square in front of the door, She looked back up, "You want *me*...to lie down on the rug?"

"Yes."

Candy crossed her arms, "I'm not sure exactly what you have in mind."

"What I have in mind is getting you out here, before those men upstairs recover enough to come after us. Are you interested in getting out of here alive or not?"

Candy bit her lip and shrugged, "This doesn't make any sense but..." Candy sat down on her hip on the edge of the rug. Carefully keeping her yellow dress down, she lay on her back on the rug.

Rory bent over, "Scoot up a little more this way so your shoes are on the rug as well."

Her forehead wrinkling, Candy looked up at him for a moment and then complied. She held her dress in place as she lifted her knees and pushed herself up, her shoes slipping on the floor a couple of times before she got all of her body on the rug.

Rory noted the bill of the ball cap sticking out of the pocket of the jacket and he tried to push it back in. But it wouldn't go. "Okay," he said, "cross your arms across your chest."

Candy looked up at him, her face a mask of confusion. She finally complied reluctantly.

Rory stepped back, bent down, gripped the edge of the rug, yanked it upwards, and began to roll Candy towards the door.

Candy squeaked in surprise as she was rolled up inside the rug.

Once he had her safely hidden inside the rolled up rug, Rory hoisted it up, draping her over his shoulder, "Wow, that's heavy."

"I heard that," was the muffled reply.

Rory grinned. She was scared but still feisty. That was good. It was easier working with someone who was feisty and willing to fight back. He took a deep breath, pushed open the front door and stepped outside. A young officer standing on the sidewalk turned to look at him.

"Good morning officer. Is something happening out here?"

The officer looked surprised, "What are you doing in there? It's supposed to be blocked off–"

"Night janitor," Rory replied cheerfully. He shifted the rolled rug on his shoulder, "Gotta take this one to get cleaned." He patted the rug in the area where her bottom would be, "You can't believe what people track into this building. No one likes to wipe their feet outside anymore. You would think people would have more respect for clean things–"

The officer was annoyed with his talk. "Get moving," he said with a wave of his hand.

Rory gave the officer a big grin and a quick salute, "Yes, sir. Have a good day officer." Rory patted the rug again and then began whistling 'Hi Ho, Hi Ho, it's off to work we go,' as he walked up the street with his bundle over his shoulder.

Chapter 6

RORY WALKED CALMLY along the sidewalk, giving the impression he wasn't in any particular hurry. At the corner, once he was out of the view of the young officer, he began moving a little faster. Hustling across the empty street, Rory angled to the right and onto the sidewalk. As he passed the entrance to the alleyway on the other side of the street, he took a discrete look. The police cruiser was still parked in the alley outside the back door. Which meant the two men he had left incapacitated back inside the building still hadn't raised the alarm. So far, so good.

Moving across the next street and past several old buildings, Rory finally ducked into a narrow alleyway. Gently laying the carpet down on the pavement, he slowly unrolled it.

Candy squeaked inside as she was unrolled. She looked annoyed as she finally appeared, lying on her back on the rug, looking up at the buildings on either side of the alley.

Rory held out his hand and lifted her to her feet.

"You patted me on the ass," she protested as she straightened her yellow dress out.

"Really?"

"Yes, really. *Twice.* I really don't know you and I would appreciate it if–"

"Okay, the next time you're in a rug I'll be more careful," he said with a wink.

Candy gave him a stern look.

"But right now, we need to move," Rory said. He held his hand out.

Candy's eyebrows lifted, "I'm not a little girl you know."

"I know. But it's easier and faster to lead you away from here without having to talk."

Candy grudgingly took his hand and let herself be led to the far end of the alleyway.

Before stepping out of the alley, Rory peered around the corner of an old brick building, looking both ways, "It looks clear. Let's go." Stepping out, he led her farther away from the office building, the two men, and the police.

Candy continually looked behind them as they moved down the street.

After walking two blocks, Rory pulled her into a doorway set back off the street.

"Did you see someone?" Candy whispered in alarm.

Rory shook his head no as he looked back down the street, "Just want to make sure we aren't being followed."

Candy nodded her head but didn't appear to relax her guard.

"What's your name?" Rory asked after a few moments of watching the street. When she didn't answer right away, he glanced at her. He had the impression she still wasn't sure if she could trust him. He couldn't blame her, considering what she had gone through back there. He looked back down the street, "Okay. From here on, I'll just call you Rug Burn."

Candy's eyes fluttered, "I... I don't think any of this is funny...."

"No, I imagine not," Rory said. He didn't press her any further. There were a few people on the street, but nothing set off alarm bells. He took Candy by the hand again and they left the shelter of the doorway, once again moving away from the two men and the police presence back at the old office building.

After a few moments of walking in silence, Candy spoke up, "My...my name is Candace Jossel. My friends call me Candy."

Rory nodded, "Okay, Candy Jossel. Nice to meet you." He led her around a corner and down the sidewalk with a purpose, "Can you tell me why those men back there were trying to kill you?"

Candy blinked and hot tears filled her hazel eyes. Actually hearing it said out loud obviously hit her hard. She looked up into Rory's silver-blue eyes, "I... I don't really know."

Nodding as he considered her answer, Rory asked, "What about this backup they were asking about? What's that all about?"

Swallowed, Candy then licked her lips and her voice was just above a whisper, "I...I don't really know...."

Rory stopped dead in his tracks and looked down at her, "Really?"

Candy pulled her hand hard from his. "No! I don't."

Rory looked down at her for a brief moment, "Okay, then. I guess you don't need my help. I hope things work out okay for you." He turned, looked in both directions and then stepped off the sidewalk.

CANDY WATCHED HIM WALKING away across the street. She looked up and down the sidewalk, suddenly feeling very vulnerable. She definitely needed help. Confusion swirled in her head. She couldn't go to the police because it was the police who were after her. It was the police who had shot Wendy. It was the police who had framed her somehow. She felt like collapsing right there in the street as she thought about her best friend, lying dead under that blanket. But left on her own, she would probably be dead sooner or later as well. But...if she trusted this man...and answered his questions, would she be betraying her own sister? She couldn't do that. Confusion swirled through her mind. Right now she had no one else to turn to...and he *had* helped her to escape. "Wait," she called out finally. She stepped off the sidewalk into the street and headed for this Rory Mack Steele on the other side of the street.

RORY LOOKED BACK AT her over his shoulder. Then he stopped and turned around, waiting. An engine roar made him look to the left. A large, dark car was headed right for Candy at high speed. He looked back. She had no idea it was about to run her over. Candy Jossel didn't have any more than a few seconds to live.

Chapter 7

CANDY WAS HALFWAY across the street when she saw Rory charge off the sidewalk, his face a mask of hard determination. She froze in fear. Was he going to hurt her? His arm hit her hard as it wrapped around her body. The breath was knocked from her lungs as she was forced backward. Her heels scraped along on the pavement. Candy opened her mouth to scream.

A large, dark car flashed passed her in the street, the engine screaming like the banshee of death.

Terror struck Candy's heart. The car would have run her over if Rory hadn't intervened. She heard the tires squealing.

The car spun around and began sliding backward. Smoke poured from the wheels as the car tried to gain traction. It stopped its backward momentum. The tires continued spinning and squealing. The car shot back in their direction.

As Candy's feet settled back on the pavement, she realized it wasn't a near accident.

The car was now aiming to run them both over on the sidewalk.

"RUN!" RORY YELLED AS he took her hand and moved them away from the onrushing vehicle.

Candy ran for her life alongside Rory. He steered her to the right, into an alleyway. The 2-1/2 inch heels on her black pumps were very narrow and she slid easily on cardboard and debris on the pavement. Only Rory's strength kept her up as she ran.

The car's tires squealed as it swerved and drove into the alleyway entrance behind them.

Candy stopped and pulled her hand out of Rory's.

"We have to keep moving," Rory yelled as he slid to a stop and reached back for her.

"I know, I know," she yelled as she slipped her pumps off. Candy began running hard with one black pump held in each hand. She was moving faster now but she could hear the roar of the engine behind her. It was getting closer.

Rory suddenly stopped, ripped open a door, grabbed Candy's elbow and thrust her through the open doorway.

Candy spun around, falling to the floor on her back, her yellow dress flipping high up her thighs.

Jumping through the open doorway, Rory landed on top of her.

The vehicle chasing them smashed into the open door, ripping it from its hinges as it shot past.

Candy looked up into Rory's silver-blue eyes. "C-can you get off of me, you big lug?" She modestly began pushing her yellow dress back down to cover her legs.

Rory smiled down at her, "Are you sure?" Before she could answer, Rory jumped up and pulled Candy to her feet, "Let's go."

Candy turned and started running ahead of him down a short hallway. She ran past a room on the right, the sound of clattering dishes reaching her ears. The smell of breakfast cooking filled the air. Candy burst through a set of swinging doors. She stopped dead.

Rory followed behind, stopping dead in his tracks as well.

They were in a large, jam-packed restaurant. No one paid any attention to them. The early morning sun was streaming through the restaurant windows. The buzz of conversation filled the air. Busy service staff moved passed Rory and Candy, heading down the hallway towards the kitchen.

Someone at the far end of the hallway yelled, "Hey, what happened to the back door?"

Candy looked back and then at Rory. She was ready to run.

Rory made a discreet motion for her to stay calm. He took her by the elbow and they began moving slowly through the crowded tables towards the front entrance and the street. Rather than go right outside, Rory stepped to the side of the door, stretched his neck and looked out the window. He didn't see the car, police or any evidence of the two men he had put out if commission earlier. All he saw was an early morning crowd of enthusiastic tourists outside.

A couple of young women, just heading out the front doors of the restaurant and Rory had an idea. He looked down at the bill of the cap, still sticking from Candy's pocket. "Is that a Louisville ball cap? Like the jacket?"

Candy nodded.

"Put the cap on," Rory said.

"Why? Do you see the men or the car?" Candy asked in alarm. She stretched her neck to look out the windows.

"No. But we have to hurry. Put the cap on," Rory said. As she did, he pulled her in behind the two young women as they opened the front door.

Candy complied, slipping it on, pushing her hair back behind her ears.

As soon as the two young ladies were outside on the sidewalk, Rory reached out and tapped one of them on the shoulder, "Excuse me?"

Candy watch the two young ladies look back at them cautiously.

Rory put on a big smile, "Sorry to bother you. My girlfriend here said *everyone* we meet here will be a Louisville Cardinals basketball fan. That can't be true, right ladies?"

"Uh, huh," said one of the young women, still cautious.

"Seriously, you're Cardinal fans?" Rory said, sounding surprised.

The other woman raised an eyebrow, "This *is* Louisville, you know."

The first young woman shook her head, "I 'spose you're one of those stupid Kentucky Wildcat basketball fans. That would figure...." She rolled her eyes.

Rory shook his head, pretending to be deflated as he gave Candy a rueful smile, "I can't believe it. I guess you win, babe." He made a show of digging into his pocket and pulling out a wad of bills. He counted off $100 and held it out to the young lady, "Here you go. I have to give you $100 and you get her cap and jacket as well. Then I have to buy her a whole new set."

The young woman looked at her friend, "Is he for real?"

Bug-eyed, the friend said, "If I was you, Jamila, I'd be taking that before he turns into a pumpkin or something."

Jamila snatched the money, stuffing the cash in her blouse.

Rory lifted the cap from Candy's head and passed it over.

Snatching that as well, Jamila glanced to the jacket as she put the cap on her head, wondering.

Rory glanced to his left down the sidewalk. The tourists were on the move. He bent down and whispered in Candy's ear, "Hurry up and give her the jacket."

Candy hesitated for just a moment, then slipped the Louisville Cardinal's jacket off, handing it over to the young lady.

"I should have known you'd win again," Rory said loudly as he put his arm around Candy. "Thanks, ladies."

"No, thank you," Jamila said, She hustled to put the jacket on.

"You got one dumb boyfriend," the other young lady said. "Good thing he's rich and good looking. Otherwise, you'd have to dump his ass."

"Ain't that the truth," Candy said with a shake of her head.

Rory turned her away from them.

Candy whispered to him, "*What* are we doing?"

"Sending those guys on a wild goose chase if they show up," Rory explained. He guided Candy down the sidewalk and into the crowd of tourists who were now boarding a Toonerville II Trolley.

Candy nervously fidgeted as they waited for the people ahead of them to board the trolley. When it was their turn, Candy eagerly grabbed the bar at the side of the stairs and pulled herself aboard.

Rory followed right behind Candy. They moved towards the back and sat side-by-side on a trolley seat.

The gold and green, motorized trolley began moving down the street.

The dark car appeared again, screeching around the corner. It swish-tailed out of control for a moment, then straightened out and headed for the front of the restaurant. It slid to a stop outside the front door. Then it suddenly took off with a roar in pursuit of the young lady down the street wearing the Louisville Cardinals cap and jacket.

"They went for it," Candy said in relief as she watched the car drive in the other direction.

"For now," Rory said realistically. "Now, why don't you tell me what this is all about?"

Chapter 8

CANDY CLEARED HER THROAT, obviously still reluctant to open up despite the fact Rory had saved her again, "In all honesty, I really don't know what it's all about. And that's the truth."

"Okay. Why don't you start with this backup that they're looking for?"

Candy lowered her head, and smoothed down her dress, "I'm... I'm not really sure."

"I thought you were going to trust me?"

"I know. It's just...." Her voice fell away as she looked at the people around them. The other passengers were engaged in conversations of their own, looking at the sights and discussing the buildings and landmarks they were passing.

Rory watched her struggling with some inner turmoil. She definitely wanted to talk but something was holding her back, "It's just what? What are you afraid of?"

There was a slight shrug of her shoulder, "I don't know. I guess I'm just afraid of letting my sister down if I say the wrong thing." She looked out the window.

"Why don't you just start at the beginning with the easy stuff? Who are you and who is your sister?"

It took a moment before she turned her head, toward Rory, her eyes down, "As I said before - my name is Candace Jossel. My sister is...Keira Jossel." She looked up at Rory. When he didn't react she added, "She's the campaign manager for Connor Harrison Lane?"

Finally registering, Rory's eyebrows rose, "You mean the man who was just elected President of the United States?"

Candy nodded, "I'm part of the campaign team."

"So that's a good thing, right?"

"Yeah." The yeah didn't sound too enthusiastic.

"Okay. So how did you end up going from being part of the campaign team that was victorious last night - to being a wanted fugitive with two men trying to kill you?"

"You haven't been watching the news, have you?"

Rory shook his head, "No. Not really. Other than hearing about the election results, I ate a quiet breakfast. Tell me what happened."

Tears shimmered in her eyes, "Wendy Symonds and I were celebrating after the victory last night. We were just walking down the street, minding our own business, when those same two men stopped us, pointing a gun at us. They shot Wendy in the leg and I froze. When she was lying on the sidewalk, she hit one of them with her Taser and yelled for me to run. I did. I left my best friend behind and they killed her." She squeezed her eyes shut for a moment as hot tears rolled down her cheeks. "I went back after...I was going to talk to the police but...somehow they set it up to make it look like I shot Wendy. The police have been pursuing me ever since."

Rory nodded as he watched her. Tears continued to roll from her eyes. "So, why did these men stop you in the first place? What did they want?" he asked.

Candy wiped the tears from her eyes, "I really am being honest when I say I'm not really sure. This whole thing is turning out to be a nightmare."

Rory narrowed his eyes as he looked at her. His brow furrowed in thought.

"Are...are you going to turn me in now?" she asked quietly.

Rory pursed his lips, "Since something doesn't seem to add up here, we'll say no for now."

"For now? What does that mean?"

"It means for now." Rory moved on to another subject, "The man back in the office building said he was asking you the same question as last night - where was the backup. What was he talking about?"

Like before, Candy was very reluctant to say anything.

Rory waited patiently for her to open up.

Candy sniffled and wrung her hands together, "Last night, when the election was going on, the computers in the campaign office went down. Everybody was out working to get the voters out. Everyone was calling in looking for names and directions. But we couldn't give them anything because everything was down. There were people calling from all over the state. From all over the country...."

"Who's in charge of the computer system?" Rory asked her. "You must have had tech support?"

Candy nodded her head sadly, "Yes, but the head of IT and his people were all out with everyone else, helping to get the voters out. It was a stupid oversight. And only my sister and the head of IT usually had access to the mainframe at the campaign headquarters anyway. Something had to be done. No one was answering their cell phone, so I went into the office with the mainframe computer and got it running again. I have a Bachelor of Science Degree in Computing and Business and the whole election hinged on us getting things going again–"

"If only two people had access, how were you able to get in without a password?"

A flush of embarrassment crossed her cheeks," I guess I accidentally saw the IT manager put in his password."

"Accidentally?"

There was a slight shrug, "It just happened. I saw him type in g-u-a-n-d-i–"

"Guandi?"

"Yeah. I instantly recognized it from a Chinese kid who was in our grade school. All the guys in those days were into martial arts and this kid had these Chinese charms that his father gave him. He always talked about the one for Guan Di, the Chinese God of War. Anyway, I was surprised when the head of IT was into the system and the word just stuck with me."

"The guy used that for a password? He wasn't using eyeball retina recognition or some other fancy technology to keep the system locked up? I thought all computer nerds did stuff like that?"

"What can I say? The IT manager is a Chinese descendant and even the smartest professional resorts to easy things to remember for passwords. He simply used something from his own life that he could easily remember. It sure helped me when I needed it."

Rory nodded in understanding. "Okay. Was this Wendy with you when you went in there to get it running?"

Candy shook her head no as she soaked up the tears on her cheeks with the sleeve of her dress.

"So I'm assuming you made a backup?"

Candy nodded her head, "Yeah. I figured if it went down again or we lost everything, we would be in real trouble. So I made a backup of everything on the mainframe computer."

"So, where is this backup now? Do you have it?" Rory asked.

Candy shook her head vigorously, "No. I left it in the room. There was no need to take it. As long as it was there, we could get things running again if necessary. But the computer system kept on running, everything ran like clockwork and we won the election."

"Why didn't you simply tell those men that–?"

"I wish I had," Candy said forcefully. "Maybe Wendy would still be alive." Candy pounded a fist on the seat and the words spilled out of her, "But I was afraid they were trying to get information to hurt President Lane. And I didn't want to hurt him or my sister. I was a real screw-up after our parents died. I was into drugs and...my sister hired me as part of the campaign team after I got out of college. She was helping me to get a second chance and I didn't want to let her down. When Wendy pulled the Taser and stunned the man with the gun...I just left her there...I was trying to protect others but because of me...."

Rory shook his head no and squeezed her hand, "No, it's not your fault. Someone else decided to shoot Wendy. In my experience, people like that would have probably killed you both anyway, even if they had gotten what they wanted."

Her body shuddered at the thought, "I... I never thought about it that way...but I still feel so guilty."

Rory's brow furrowed for a moment, "How did those two men know you had made a backup in the first place?"

Giving it some thought, Candy then shook her head slowly before she looked up at Rory, "I have no idea. There were a couple of dozen people manning the phones when I went in there - but I went in alone. Wendy stayed on the phones, trying to reach the IT manager in case I couldn't get the computer system running again."

"Did you tell anyone that you had made a backup after you came out?"

Candy looked down the trolley aisle, thinking as she watched a few people get off. "Not that I remember. I don't know how they knew," she finally said. "Everyone was so busy once the system was back up and running. Wendy and I were in charge of coordinating everything. Wendy was working so hard, she was so cheerful...." her voice trailed off as tears filled her eyes again.

Rory looked up and stared out the trolley window as he said in a low voice to himself. "And why would two agents from the Secret Service want a backup with that information?"

"The Secret Service?" blurted Candy. She looked around nervously at the people nearby, then lowered her voice to a whisper, "Are you sure?"

Rory nodded, "Remember the man lying on the stairs? Remember how I looked at the badge hanging from his top pocket?"

Candy nodded.

"That was a Secret Service Special Agent's badge," Rory said. His eyes narrowed as he stroked a finger along his jaw, "The Secret Service is tasked with guarding the nation's top political officials, including presidential candidates. Have you ever seen those two men before? They must have been assigned to Lane's campaign."

Candy shook her head vigorously no, "The first time I ever saw them was on the sidewalk when they stopped us. And then they were talking to the local Louisville police at the crime scene-"

Rory as he looked at her, "They were?"

Wendy nodded.

"Are you positive?"

"Yes," Candy confirmed. "I saw them on the other side of the crime scene tape. That's why I ran. I was going to talk to the police when I realized the two men who had stopped us and shot Wendy were talking to a Louisville police detective. I saw them all standing around with their badges hanging out of their upper pockets. I thought they were all Louisville police. And then, when the Louisville police chased me into that old office building, they never came in to get me. Instead, it was eventually those same two guys who showed up, asking for the backup again. I just thought they were Louisville police detectives as well."

"Well, they weren't. The Louisville police must have called them in," Rory concluded. "And we didn't see any police cruisers searching the streets for us after I carried you out. Instead-"

"That black car that nearly ran me down. The one that chased us," Candy said as she completed Rory's thought, "It must have been those two men in the car."

Rory nodded and they rode in silence, thinking things over.

"Do you have any idea what information they wanted to get from the backup?" Rory asked after a few moments.

Candy shook her head slowly no, "I'm not totally sure about everything that was on there. I know they were a lot of e-mails and the names of campaign contributors along with lists of potential voter names and–" She blinked her eyes several times.

"What's wrong? What is it you think they want?" Rory asked her.

"It's...it's what won the election for Governor Lane," Candy said. "That has to be it."

Rory narrowed his eyes as he looked at Candy, "I don't understand. You mean the election was rigged?"

"No, no," Candy replied quickly. "Nothing like that. It's demographics. My sister was a whiz-bang at mathematics and demographics. She had voting trends broken down into segments of the population. Even down to specific neighborhoods in cities across the country. It's been done before but not nearly as detailed as Keira did it. For a long time now the voting split in the country has pretty well been 50-50. But we were able to shape the campaign to concentrate on specific segments of the population that would give us a voting edge."

"You mean you could promise a guy on Elm Street in Des Moines he would get the new refrigerator he needed in return for his support? That kind of thing?" Rory asked.

"Yeah, pretty well," Candy said.

Rory cocked his head as she did some thinking, "But...the election is over. It would be another four years before they could use it–"

Candy shook her head vigorously, "There are a number of Senatorial elections coming up. Right now, President Lane's party holds the edge in the Senate. But if the opposition could get their hands on this information...."

Rory shrugged, "So. That just means both sides have the same information. It simply means it would be a level playing field–"

"Not really," Candy said. "Each Senator pretty well runs his or her own campaign. And since not everyone in the party sees eye to eye with Governor...I mean...President Lane...he's not necessarily going to share the information with them. Keep in mind there were other people trying to get the party nomination for President, running against Lane. And they'll do it again in four years. There are a lot of big egos in politics. And not everyone wants to work together, even if they're supposed to be on the same side."

"So...you think some senator wants this information then?" Rory asked her.

"Or the leaders of the other party," Candy said. "If they could focus on specific by-elections and win, they could swing the balance of power their way. They could impede every single thing President Lane tries to do. And they wouldn't have to steal the computer or break into it. All they need to do is get the backup I made and they have all the information at hand." She looked at Rory in earnest, "We need to let my sister know. We need to go to the campaign headquarters."

Rory considered her request for a moment. He shook his head, "I wouldn't recommend it. That could be very dangerous. Why don't we just call her–?"

Candy shook her head emphatically no, "We *have* to go there. We *have* to let her know."

"After the election win...and the problems of last night...she might not be there," Rory reasoned.

"Then we'll find her," Candy said firmly. "But we also have to secure the backup."

"Are you sure? Those men still think you have the backup on you. They could have someone waiting to intercept you before you get inside."

Candy gave him a determined look, "I'm going. I have to. You don't have to come if you're afraid. But I can't let my sister down."

Chapter 9

RORY FOLLOWED CANDY out from the alleyway between two old buildings. The sidewalk on this side and the other side, along with the street itself, were still littered with confetti, banners, and signs from the obvious victory celebration. Across the street sat at an old brown brick, ten-story building that looked like it had seen better days. A sign in a window on the first floor identified the space behind the doors as the Louisville campaign headquarters of Connor Harrison Lane.

"I don't see anyone over there," Rory said.

Candy didn't say anything as she stepped off the sidewalk, heading across the street. Rory followed behind Candy as they dodged traffic and stepped up onto the sidewalk on the other side. Candy moved into the doorway and twisted the doorknob on the double doors. It didn't open. Candy gripped the doorknob with both hands and twisted and shook it, the door rattling, "What's going on?"

Rory moved over to one of the large side windows and peered in between large pictures of Lane, "It looks empty."

After jiggling the doorknob a couple of more times, Candy walked over to peer through the window as well, "That can't be. It was just here yesterday."

"The election is over," Rory said. He took a step back and looked up at the building. "They must've closed it down since they didn't need it anymore."

Candy walked over to the doorknob and jiggled it again, "It can't be. It just can't–"

Rory put his hands on her shoulders, "It's empty, Candy. There's not much you can do."

She stopped jiggling the doorknob but Candy pulled roughly away from Rory's hands, clearly frustrated. She had tears in her eyes and wiped the back of her hand under her nose, "They probably had to close it down fast because of all the media attention. I should have realized it. It's all my fault."

"Not everything is your fault, Candy."

"Yes, it is. It's *all* my fault," she said bitterly. "They would probably still be here celebrating if it wasn't for me."

Rory put his hands in his pockets. He looked up and down the street and monitored the traffic, "What do you want to do now?"

Candy didn't say anything. She just twisted the doorknob again, shaking it and rattling the door. Letting out a frustrated breath she peered through the window into the empty space again, desperately hoping to see someone appear. Cursing under her breath, Candy went back to twisting the doorknob and jiggling the door. Then she pounded on the door frame with her fists, "Hello? Hello?"

Rory watched her twist and shake the doorknob several more times again. He genuinely felt sorry for the young woman. She'd gone from the immense high of victory to the low of seeing a friend die and have someone trying to kill her. "Do you have a safe place you can stay?" he asked. "You can't stay here on the sidewalk all day–"

"Yes I can," she said forcefully. "I have to. I have to let my sister know. Maybe someone will come back." Candy used her fingers to take the tears off her cheeks. "Do you have a cell phone?" she asked Rory after a moment.

"Yes."

She held out her hand, "Can I use it please?"

Rory reluctantly pulled a tiny cell phone from his left pocket, "Who are you going to call?"

Candy held her hand out, "I have to call my sister. I have to let her know–"

"Are you sure that's wise? Keep in mind those men *are* Secret Service. They could be monitoring all the calls going in and out for Lane's people. If those men find out exactly where you are–"

Candy jerked the cell phone away from Rory's hand, "I *have* to let my sister know that someone is after the information in the computer system. I have to."

"I can't keep you safe if you keep putting yourself in danger," Rory reminded her.

"Keira *has* to find that backup and make sure the system is secure. The rest doesn't matter." She began punching numbers into the cell phone.

Rory raised an eyebrow at her loyalty to her sister. He gently placed a hand on her elbow, "Okay. But let's not stay out in the open here." He guided her down the sidewalk and moved her into a recessed doorway for more protection, "At least stay out of sight and safe while you call."

Candy nodded as she listened to the cell phone ringing. "Sis! It's me–"

Rory monitored the people and the traffic passing by as he listened to the one-sided conversation.

Listening for a few moments, Candy then spoke urgently, "Listen, I didn't do it. I'll explain everything later–"

Rory watched as tears filled Candy's hazel eyes.

Candy ran her fingers through her messy, brown-two-tone, rock-chick hairstyle, "I know, I know. But the most important thing is that someone is after the demographic information in the computer system. That's right. I went to the campaign head-quarters but–" She chewed on the end of her thumb. Then her face brightened. Nodding several times at whatever she was being told, Candy finally said, "Okay. Okay. I'll do that. I'll watch for him. Thank you so much, sis. Uh-huh. Bye."

"What's up?" Rory asked as he watched her slip the tiny cell phone inside the right pocket of her yellow dress. He doubted she even knew she was doing it; she was so focused on what she needed to do for her sister.

Candy wiped tears from her eyes and smiled at Rory, obvi-ously relieved, "My sister says she believes I didn't do it. She wants me to come in and she'll get the best lawyers available. Keira said we'll fight this thing–"

"I didn't hear you mention anything about the backup," Rory said. "Just about the information..."

Candy blinked her eyes a couple of times when she realized he was right. "I...I didn't get a chance to." Then she seemed to dis-miss it as a problem, "But that's because my sister was more con-cerned with my welfare. I can tell her when I see her–"

"See her?"

"Yeah. She wants me to go to Cherokee Park. She's going to send her assistant, Lance Washburn, to pick me up there. There's a hill in the center of the park and I can watch people coming so someone else doesn't sneak up on me."

Rory bit his lip as he considered her plan, "That could be very dangerous. Someone could still catch us unawares–"

Candy looked up into Rory's silver-blue eyes and shook her head, "No. You can't come with me. My sister said I had to go there alone."

"I can't let you do that," Rory insisted. "If those men show up again–"

"My sister told me to go alone. *That's* what I'm going to do," Candy said firmly. "It's not up for discussion."

Rory considered her plan for a moment, then he spoke softly, "Okay. How about if we compromise? You let me go with you over to the park, to make sure you get there safely, and then you go in alone."

Candy looked at him for a moment and then took a deep breath, letting it out, "Okay. Truth is...I'm scared."

Rory nodded, took her by the elbow and escorted her down the street towards Cherokee Park. This time she seemed to be happy with the gesture. But instinct...and years of working cases against bad people...told Rory this was a bad idea.

Chapter 10

CANDY JOSSEL STOOD on Baringer Hill in Louisville's four hundred and nine acre Cherokee Park. The sun was warm and birds sang happy songs high in the trees. There weren't many people in the park today but Candy still felt extremely vulnerable and very much afraid. She could see a small family in the distance off to the right, trying to fly a kite. And there had been a young couple with two large greyhounds over on the left. But the dogs had bounded happily over the grass, barking as the couple climbed the hill hand in hand behind them, and they all disappeared over the crest. Other than that, she was totally alone and totally isolated. She kept her gaze in the direction of the 2.4-mile long Scenic Loop roadway; positive Lance would come from that direction. Every so often she would check in the other directions, but so far no one had appeared from anywhere to climb the hill towards her. Then a figure in a blue suit appeared from over a small knoll dead ahead. He was walking in her direction. The person had the long-legged, loping gait of Lance Washburn. But she waited for a few moments to be sure. It did seem to be him though. Her hands shook slightly as she raised them over her head and she signaled in his direction. After a moment, the figure raised his arms and signaled back in a similar gesture. Candy immediately felt relief. She couldn't help but smile as she began to walk down Baringer Hill to meet Lance. After a few steps, Candy heard a low roar off to her right. She glanced down the hill in that direction as she continued moving down the hill towards Lance.

A dark vehicle shot over a low ridge. It bounced a couple of times as it landed on the grass and then tore up the hillside, heading in her direction.

Candy froze. It was the same large car that had tried to run her down earlier. The two men had found her! She looked down the hill to see Lance Washburn running in her direction. But the car would get to her long before he did. Candy looked back at the car tearing up the hillside towards her. There was no place to run and no place to hide. It was over.

CANDY HEARD A SMALLER growl to her right and she turned quickly to look. A blur shot up over the hill, - flew twenty feet- and landed with a bounce right beside her. It was Rory Mack Steele. On a Honda CRF250X dirt bike.

"Get on," Rory yelled over the noise of the dirt bike.

Candy hesitated as she looked back towards Lance.

Touching her elbow, Rory urged her to jump onto the bike behind him.

Candy finally reacted. She straddled the bike in her yellow dress, wrapped her arms around Rory's waist and held on tightly.

Rory twisted the throttle. The bike slid sideways as the rubber knobs on the back tire ripped through the grass and into the dirt.

Candy screamed as her body leaned and she held on tightly, the momentum threatening to throw her off the dirt bike.

After an agonizing moment, the back tire gained traction and they shot back up the hill in the direction Rory had come from.

Glanced to her left, Candy yelled, "Look out."

The dark car ripped up grass and dirt as it veered directly for the dirt bike.

Candy's dress was pushed high up her legs as the dirt bike roared over the crest of the hill. The bike went airborne and Candy closed her eyes tight and screamed.

Landing hard, the bike bounced several times on the other side. Grass and dirt broke away and the bike fishtailed. Rory fought to keep it straight as it bounced up and down.

Squeaking as her butt bounced hard on the seat, Candy fought to stay on.

The Honda fishtailed in the other direction, then straightened out and shot down the hillside, toward a line of trees.

Candy looked into the mirror on the dirt bike's left handlebar and caught a glimpse of the dark car soaring over the crest of the hill behind them, the motor growling in pursuit of them.

The dark car bounced hard several times as it landed. It twisted sideways, straightened out, accelerated and pursued them with a roar down the hill.

A gunshot rang out. Crack!

The bike's mirror shattered.

Candy screamed and ducked her head instinctively.

Crack!

A bullet tore a groove in the aluminum handlebar just beside the shattered mirror.

Rory began zigzagging to throw their aim off.

Candy fought hard to maintain her hold around Rory as the bike swung back and forth.

Crack! Crack! Crack!

The bike reached the bottom of the hill and roared between two large Bald Cypress trees.

Candy instinctively pulled her shoulders in, trying to make herself smaller, afraid she would scrape against the trees on either side if she didn't.

Crack! Crack!

Bullets tore into the bark of the tree on their right and wood splinters exploded into the air.

Candy screamed.

Rory steered the dirt bike to the left and used several larger Hickory trees as cover.

Crack!

A bullet slashed across the side of the tree, leaving an ugly gash.

Slowing the bike just a bit, Rory turned right and steered slowly through a thick line of small bushes. He hoped their pursuers wouldn't be able to follow them.

The car's roar sounded right behind them.

On the other side of bushes, Rory applied the throttle again. The bike did a wheelie.

Candy screamed, holding on for dear life.

Rory let off on the throttle, the bike settled back down and gained traction. They shot across the grass between another stand of trees.

Candy glanced back. She couldn't see the dark vehicle.

THE MAN IN THE BLACK, pinstriped suit sat behind the steering wheel. They were parked on the Scenic Loop. The Cochrane Hill Road was just to their left.

"Considering the direction they were headed, I imagine they'll end up on I-64," commented his partner in the blue suit.

The man in the black, pinstripe suit narrowed his eyes as he considered the suggestion. A cell phone rang and he pulled it out of his breast pocket, "Yeah."

"What were you two jackasses doing, Blacker?" The electronic distortion did little to hide the anger behind the voice.

Blacker glanced at his partner, "We thought it best—"

"I don't pay you to think! If you would've waited until Washburn had her in the vehicle, we would have both her and the backup. Now we have neither."

"We didn't anticipate her having help," Blacker answered in defense.

There was a brief silence on the phone. "Who helped her to escape?"

"We have no idea who he is," Blacker said. "But Conroy is positive it's the same man who attacked us at the office building." He looked over at his partner, who nodded in agreement.

"Why is he still helping her?"

Blacker looked at his partner, "We have no idea."

The voice on the other side of the call was angry and spit out the words, "Are they lovers?"

Blacker raised an eyebrow, "We have no indication their paths have ever crossed before this."

There was another period of silence on the phone. The voice was calmer now, but there was no mistaking the intent behind the voice, "I need you to find them fast. Get the backup. Then kill them both. No loose ends, Blacker. Make the bodies disappear."

Blacker nodded as the caller ended the conversation. After a moment of thought, he punched in another cell number.

"Yes?" answered Lance Washburn.

"Are Kittner and Arquette still with you in the park?"

"What the hell were you doing?" Washburn yelled. "I was told to—"

"Enough!" Blacker said sternly. "I already have new orders and they don't come from you. Send Kittner and Arquette Eastbound and through the subdivision to I-64. Tell them to cut straight through the park, if necessary. I'm heading north to Lexington Road. Once they get there, they are to call me. We'll catch the man and woman in a pinch."

"But—"

"Do it *now*!" Blacker closed the call, threw the cell phone on the dashboard and angrily floored the gas pedal. The vehicle ripped off in the direction of Lexington Road and I-64.

Chapter 11

A NUMBER OF PEOPLE YELLED at Rory as he drove the dirt bike hard through Cherokee Park. Rory ignored them. Etiquette and park rules went out the window when someone was trying to kill you. They finally emerged at the three-way junction of Cherokee Park Road, Scenic Loop and Beals Branch Road. Rory stayed to the right of Beals and drove into the trees that ran parallel to the edge of I-64. Rory maneuvered slowly around trees and bushes, trying to stay hidden as long as he could, angling left towards the highway. He finally stopped and let the dirt bike idle just passed the tree line, alongside the busy highway, cars, and trucks zipping passed. Rory could see Cochran Hill Tunnel off to their left. He raised his voice and gestured to the right, "We'll head that way–"

Candy's voice was shaky and barely audible over the sound of the traffic."Wait. We have to call my sister first. We have to let her know what happened."

Rory glanced back, "Are you sure that's smart?" He looked down at Candy's bare thighs wrapped around him.

Candy got off the dirt bike, self-consciously pushing her yellow dress back down around her knees. She already had the cell phone in her hand and began pushing buttons, "We *have* to. She has to know."

Rory turned the bike off, pushed out the kickstand with his heel and got off the bike. He placed his hand on the phone, preventing her from dialing, "Think about this for a minute. How did those guys know you would be in the park?"

Candy looked at Rory and then her face took on a look of anger, "Do you think my sister had something to do with that?"

"No," Rory said calmly. "But keep in mind those guys appear to be Secret Service. As I said before, the Secret Service would have a guard detail for Lane. That means those guys could have access to all the phone lines, including the ones your sister is using. They can easily monitor for calls coming in from you."

Candy licked her lips as she stared at Rory and considered what he was saying. "But...we can't let them get the information...or the backup...my sister has done so much for me...I can't let that happen...."

"I don't think it's just about the backup," Rory replied.

Candy blinked a few times, "What...what do you mean?"

Rory gave her a hard look, "Which one of those guys back there just asked you for the backup?"

Candy looked confused, "I...I don't know what you mean? They...they never talked to me. They just appeared–"

"And they started shooting at us," Rory said. "They had no idea if you had the backup on you. They had no idea if you had decided to hide it somewhere for safekeeping *before* you went to the park. If that was the case, if they had killed you, if they had killed both of us, they'd never find the backup. How would they get that information you were talking about then?"

Candy looked into Rory's eyes and considered what he was saying.

"So they want the backup...or Candy Jossel dead, so you can't talk about what you know," Rory reasoned.

Candy face turned white, "But...but I don't know anything. I don't–"

Rory looked into Candy's hazel eyes, "But they think you do. That means there's something else on the computer system they don't want the world to know about. When you made the back-up, *for the entire system*, you copied that information. For all they know, you saw whatever it is they're trying to hide. So they need the backup and...or...they need to silence you."

Candy had a hard time swallowing and her face was a mask of fear as she realized the truth.

A loud growl sounded over top of the other vehicles on the highway and the dark vehicle ripped out of the Cochran Hill Tunnel, heading in their direction.

"Jump on," Rory yelled as he straddled the dirt bike and hit the electric starter.

Candy barely got herself seated before the Honda took off. She nearly flipped off backwards before she caught the side pockets of Rory's black leather jacket.

The studded tires of the Honda tore up the grass as Rory accelerated. They dug into the soft shoulder of the roadway and then created a line of black rubber on the pavement as the bike rocketed away, trying to fit into the traffic.

A large tanker truck swerved to the left to miss them as they cut in front, black smoke billowing as the heavy tires shredded on the pavement.

The dark vehicle accelerated with their prey in sight.

Rory accelerated almost instantly to 70 mph.

Candy's yellow dress was pushed high up on her thighs, baring her legs. Her face was a mask of fear as her body leaned backwards, only her frantic grip on the pockets kept her on the bike.

The dark vehicle began to gain on them.

Now Rory began weaving in and out of traffic, trying to gain some distance. When it didn't look like it was giving them enough distance from their pursuers, Rory simply rode the dotted white line between two sets of cars. Drivers in the lanes on either side honked their horns and yelled. Rory ignored them as he accelerated but by bit.

The dark vehicle rode the bumper of the last car in the left lane and honked.

Applying more power, Rory leaned forward to keep the front wheel down. The Honda dirt bike zipped ahead of the two lines of cars and shot into an underpass.

The dark car began weaving back and forth, the drive leaning on the horn as it looked for a way past the two lines of cars blocking his pursuit of the dirt bike.

The dirt bike emerged from the underpass. Rory had planned to steer back into the trees on the other side of the underpass but there were none. Instead, they were now passing a line of houses on the right. There was no quick and easy route of escape. Rory looked around the long curve ahead, trying to spot for another way out of this chase. If he could get off while the dark car was still trapped behind the vehicles, he reasoned they might get a chance to disappear. He slowed the bike just a bit, positioning himself to thread between another two lines of cars coming up.

Candy pulled hard with her arms, trying to get upright and get her arms around Rory.

Car horns started blaring behind the bike again.

Rory glanced back to see the dark vehicle riding the outer shoulder of the highway, kicking up clouds of white dust. They were trying to pass the blockade and it wouldn't be long before they did. Rory heard a deep growl up ahead of them.

A large, red SUV roared through the emergency turnaround up ahead between the divided highways, sending up a cloud of dust. Its tires squealed as SUV swerved onto the road and headed straight for the Honda, driving against the traffic. Cars honked their horns and swerved out of the way.

Rory and Candy were trapped in a pinch.

Chapter 12

THE ROAR OF THE DARK VEHICLE'S ENGINE was coming closer from behind. The large, red SUV up ahead was closing the gap fast. On the passenger side, an arm, holding a handgun appeared, aiming at the dirt bike.

Rory looked for a way out. *Now what?* Spotting trees coming up ahead on the right, Rory yelled over the noise of the engine, "Hang on." He twisted the throttle of the dirt bike to full speed.

Candy screamed as the acceleration drove her back. She frantically held on to Rory's pockets, her yellow dress flapping out behind her.

Veering off the road, Rory drove over the soft shoulder, down into a gentle ravine, then shot up the other side and plunged between two large Tulip trees. Candy let out a scream as they whipped by closely on either side. Rory heard tires screeching back on the highway behind them but he had others worries. He suddenly emerged on the fairway for Hole Number 3 on the Seneca golf course. He was headed directly for a group of golfers.

The golfers scattered in all directions just in time, cursing and yelling obscenities.

The dark vehicle and the red SUV maneuvered off the highway and found a way through the trees to pursue the Honda dirt bike.

Rory roared down the golf course fairway, narrowly missing a golf cart and another group of startled golfers. A five iron barely missed his head, thrown by a red-faced golfer screaming at him as the Honda shot past. Rory accelerated up a slope, turning in his seat to check on the pursuers. His movement tore Candy's hand away from his right pocket and she fell backward, windmilling her arms as she fought to stay on.

Rory cursed when he saw the dark vehicle and the red SUV tearing up the fairway as they accelerated in pursuit.

The first set of golfers was running for the trees, scared out of their minds as the vehicles shot past them.

Slowing the bike, Rory reached back and grabbed the side of Candy's clothing, pulling back up behind him. As she wrapped her arms around him, he turned his attention finding a way out of this chase. He turned right at the end of a small sand bunker and then twisted the throttle hard, applying full power.

With the sudden acceleration, Candy lost her grip and swore - she squeezed her knees against the sides of the seat as her upper body leaned back.

The Honda zoomed across the open ground, headed for the putting green for hole number 5.

On the green, four women turned at the approaching roar - and promptly ran screaming, abandoning their putters.

Driving across the green, the front wheel of the Honda ran over a Scotty Cameron putter one of them left behind and it banged up against the back wheel before being spit out.

As the bike dropped down a slope on the far side of the green, Candy was thrown forward this time and slammed into Rory's back. She grunted with the blow but threw her arms around his waist again.

Rory almost lost control with Candy's weight shift. The bike fishtailed and he slowed, straightened the bike out and then accelerated again, aware the sound of the pursuing vehicles was coming closer. They had lost ground when he had slowed. But Rory also realized, despite being on a dirt bike, he had no real advantage over the open ground. His pursuers were faster. And they *were* going to catch up fairly quickly.

Four more angry golfers scattered as Rory crossed the 7th fairway. Time to use the nimbleness and the smaller profile of the Honda, he thought. He turned left, heading for a stand of trees. Rory cut his speed in half and edged into the trees.

The two pursuing vehicles ripped across the grass, heading right for the dirt bike.

Rory accelerated the Honda around a large tree, putting it between them and the pursuing vehicles.

Crack! Crack!

Bullets ripped into the bark of the tree, shocking torn pieces into the air.

Candy pressed her face into Rory's back and held on tighter.

Rory maneuvered through a stand of large Oak trees. He looked back to his left.

The red SUV skirting to the left along the tree line.

He glanced back to the other side.

The dark vehicle was heading to his right along the tree line.

Rory realized they were going to try and put him in a pinch again. Once he emerged from the safety of the trees–

Crack!

Bark exploded off a tree to the right of the dirt bike.

Rory instinctively ducked and nearly lost control of the bike, sliding sideways

"Watch out!" Candy yelled.

The dirt bike was heading directly for a huge tree. Rory applied power, put a foot out to shift the weight of the bike and veered to the left, the dirt bike barely missing the tree before plunging into a line of scrubby bushes. Rory held his right arm against his face as thin branches whipped him. The Honda dirt bike suddenly burst out of the trees, shot across a lawn and barely missed the corner of a large, brick house.

Candy screamed as the bike fishtailed hard to the left.

Rory fought to get the bike under control. He straightened it out, digging ragged grooves across the green lawn. A moment later the dirt bike plunged back into the trees. Rory drove back and forth, weaving between the trees. He spotted a possible way out of their predicament. He turned hard to the left, putting the Honda into a slight swerve.

Candy screamed as she fought to stay on.

Rory accelerated through the trees, heading for a road he could see just ahead.

The bike burst out of the trees and shot between two houses, plowing through a line of flowers.

Off to the left, the red SUV shot out of the trees. It swerved onto Seneca Park Road and the engine roared as it headed straight for the dirt bike.

Rory accelerated to full speed...but he didn't take the road...instead he drove straight across it...heading for a slight hump next to Bear Grass Creek.

Candy realized what he was going to do and she screamed, "Noooooooooooo!"

The CRF250X Honda dirt bike's suspension was jarred as they hit the hump and then the bike soared into the air.

Candy screamed all the way over the water.

The Honda landed hard on the other side and bounced several times.

Rory almost lost control - the bike skidded one way and then the other. The rear wall of a two-story red brick house loomed menacingly dead ahead. Rory slid the dirt bike to a sideways stop.

Candy fought desperately to stay on the bike.

Crack! Crack!

Bullets buried themselves in the red brick wall of the house.

Candy screamed when shards of brick exploded near her head.

Rory accelerated around the corner of the house - dodged a set of garbage cans- and headed for the front yard.

Crack!

Driving hard across the lawn, Rory headed for the road in front of the house. He slowed to steer onto the roadway and then accelerated, moving away from the creek. He had no idea how quickly their pursuers could get around that creek and catch up so Rory kept his speed up as much as possible. The roads were twisty through the subdivision and they nearly crashed a couple times, but Rory had no choice. He had to keep moving as fast as possible. When he was finally able to steer onto a long stretch of roadway, Rory accelerated and took chances, zipping in and out of the traffic. He ran through two stop signs. A red light appeared ahead. He kept his speed up.

"Look out!" Candy yelled.

A large transport truck was going to T-bone them.

Rory cranked the throttle, accelerating and bringing the bike up into a wheelie.

Candy screamed.

The transport truck's horn blared loudly...and missed them by inches.

Within moments, they reached another major roadway and Rory drove southbound. He kept his speed up until they reached the entrance to the Henry Watterson Expressway. Here, Rory slowed the bike, pulling to the edge of the highway. He stopped and looked down the highway behind him. There was still no sign of the dark vehicle or the red SUV. Rory brought out the kickstand.

Swinging her leg off the dirt bike, Candy's hands were shaking as she pushed her yellow dress back down.

"Are you okay?" Rory asked as he got off the Honda. She nodded but Rory could tell she was completely shaken. Rory took in a deep breath and let it out, trying to calm himself after the adrenalin rush from the chase.

Candy voice was hoarse from all her screaming, "They definitely *are* trying to kill us, aren't they?"

Rory could only nod, "Yeah. Considering there are no Louisville police cars chasing us, we can safely assume they don't mean to take us prisoner."

Candy blinked several times and licked her lips as she thought about her predicament. "So...so what do we do now?"

Hands on his hips, Rory considered the question. He looked back down the highway and then turned and looked in the other direction. He looked down, thinking.

Candy put her shaky hands to her lips, closing her eyes, "If...if you want to leave me, I can understand. There's no reason for you to—"

Rory held his hand out, "Do you still have my cell phone?"

Candy opened her eyes and pulled the cell phone out, handing it across to Rory, "Do you think maybe you could take me to a hotel or somewhere where I could stay before you leave me—?"

"No need to do that," Rory said as he used his thumbs to work the browser on the cell phone. "There's a Jaguar dealership just west of here," he said after a few moments. "Let's head there first."

"I... I don't understand."

"Well, we definitely can't stay anywhere in Louisville right now. Sooner or later, they're going to catch up to us. We also need to go on the offensive." He put the cell phone in his pocket.

"What...what do you mean? How do we do that?"

"We need to figure out what it is they're trying to hide," Rory said. He stroked his chin, "We need to figure out what's on that backup. That might be our only leverage. Do you know where everything went when they closed up the campaign headquarters?"

Candy thought for a moment, then she looked up at Rory, "My sister said they packed everything up. It's being moved to Washington, DC."

"Do you know exactly where?"

"I...I think so," Candy said. "The IT Manager has an office somewhere in Washington..."

"Then we need to go to Washington DC and find that backup," Rory said. "*And* what they're trying to bury along with you. They won't be looking for us there."

Crossing her arms over her chest, Candy licked her lips, "Why...why are you helping me? I mean, I appreciate it but...you don't really know me and...."

Rory nodded, "That's true. Would you prefer I didn't help you?"

Candy wrinkled her forehead, "N-no, I don't mean that...I just...."

"Those guys tried to kill me, too. I take that a little personal." He narrowed his eyes as he looked back down the road, "And right now, I want to know *why*." After a moment, he shrugged and then straddled the dirt bike, "Hop on. It's a ten-hour drive to Washington from here and we need a better vehicle. You've been flashing too much leg and attracting too much attention already."

Candy blushed as she straddled the bike behind Rory, "I wouldn't be showing so much leg if you drove slower."

Rory grinned, "Fat chance of that happening." He gunned the engine and the CRF250X Honda dirt bike accelerated to 70 mph with Candy screaming hoarsely all the way, her yellow dress pushed up high on her bare legs.

THE ELECTRONIC VOICE *on the other end of the cell phone was irate, "You better have something good for me, Blacker, after you lost them again!"*

Torion Blacker sat behind the steering wheel, smoothing the wrinkles from his black pinstriped suit as he spoke in a clipped, even tone, "Our people on Louisville PD were able to come up with some information. One of the buildings across the street from the campaign office had an ATM with video that they were able to access after-hours."

They were sure to stay under the radar?" the electronic voice asked.

"Yes. Using facial recognition software and a number of government databases, we were able to figure out who the man is. Our friend is Rory Mack Steele. Government records show him to be a Canadian citizen with dual U.S.-Canadian citizenship. His family runs a private investigation firm out of Toronto, Canada as well as in New York City. He's ex-military. Ten years in the Canadian Army."

"A Mickey Mouse outfit. He shouldn't be a problem," the electronic voice said.

"I'm not so sure. His military Regiment was the Black Watch. But his last seven years indicates he was attached to CSOR, the Canadian Special Operations Regiment. Whatever he was doing was and still is highly classified–"

The electronic voice hissed with anger, "So penetrate the shield if you need to. We've done that before. I don't need to tell you that, do I?"

Blacker gritted his teeth, "No you don't. But in this case, *whatever* he was doing is not even being shared with their friends at the Pentagon."

The electronic voice emitted a low growl of frustration.

Blacker glanced at his partner who only shook his head, "I was able to gain access to his psychological profile," he continued. "This man is highly intelligent, resilient and very tough. And there was one additional trait that tells me where we might find him, along with Candace Jossel."

"What trait is that?"

"He will never, ever give up."

There was a brief silence. "Which means he'll want to know what's going on. And since the last point of contact for the woman he is so chivalrously protecting was Lane's campaign headquarters—"

"He will be following it to Washington, DC," Blacker said with a nod.

"Are you sure? We can't go on a wild goose chase."

"Once we found out who he was, we accessed his credit cards. He just made a purchase at a Jaguar dealership. We have the license plate. The vehicle was last seen heading eastbound on I-64. We can track them and—"

"Do it. Kittner and Arquette can stay behind, in case they double back. Just find them both and kill them," the electronic voice said. "I no longer care if we get the backup. Just find the two of them and make them disappear...forever. Do you hear me?"

Blacker looked at his partner as the call ended, "Your wish is our command."

His partner gave a slight nod of his head as he pulled out his own cell phone. "I'll call ahead to our friend at the mortuary. Get him to delay a couple of funerals so we can double-bag the caskets."

Chapter 13

THE TRIP FROM LOUISVILLE, KENTUCKY was tiring for two people who were already low on energy from the constant tension of running for their life. Rory and Candy used a truck stop outside Charleston, South Carolina to try and recharge their energies. They grabbed some fast food and tried to get a few hours of sleep in the parking lot. But every noise kept them both awake. Before they left, Rory picked up a pair of oversized sunglasses and a large straw hat to disguise Candy as best as possible. There was little else to work with for women's clothing at a truck stop. Once they were underway again, Rory kept a constant eye out for pursuit as they drove towards Washington. He was worried what government resources the Secret Service agents might bring to bear on them. But there had been no sign of the dark vehicle or the red SUV. And they weren't stopped by any of the state trooper vehicles they passed. So far, so good. Candy finally fell asleep in the front seat, clearly exhausted from the tension. Nearing Merrifield, Virginia, Rory left I-66 and took I-495, the Capital Beltway, southbound. His plan was to time their arrival to avoid the early morning rush-hour traffic. But the local traffic report said the volume was heavier, with a traffic accident backing things up. So Rory took I-395, a more direct route into Washington.

WASHINGTON, DC

Rory kept his brand-new Jaguar XK R-S at the speed limit along the Henry G Shirley Memorial Highway. He didn't want to attract the attention of any police cars patrolling the area. As the skyline of Washington appeared just ahead of them, he reached over and tapped Candy on the shoulder.

Candy stirred in her seat, wiping the sleep from her eyes, "Are we there yet?"

"Just about," Rory said.

Stretching her arms, Candy yawned - it was quickly cut off when she realized her yellow dress had ridden quite high up her bare legs, her underwear nearly on full display. She pushed the dress back down as she glanced at Rory.

"All my sightseeing was out the window," he said with a smile.

"Yeah right," she said as she sat up. She combed her two-tone brown hair with her fingers, "I must look a mess."

"Yep."

Candy laughed. Then she stretched in her seat to look out the window on Rory's side, "Is that...?"

Rory glanced to his left, "The Pentagon? Yeah."

"Wow," Candy whispered. She sat back in her seat, a sadness on her face, "I thought I'd see it once Lane won but...not this way. Wendy and I had talked about it..." Her voice trailed off, obviously reliving the painful moment of her friend's death and all that had happened after.

Rory looked at the famed building. The huge parking lot on the edge of the interstate was filled with cars. "I'm sure you'll get to see it up close once we get all this cleared up for you."

"I know," Candy sadly replied. "But somehow it won't be the same...."

Rory nodded, knowing what it was like to lose somebody. You never get over not being able to share experiences with loved ones you've left behind. Within moments the Jaguar was crossing the bridge over the Potomac. The GPS voice told him to stay to the left so Rory merged into the traffic.

Candy leaned over and began a search on the GPS. After a moment she shook her head, "Lee Park Yim is the name of the IT manager. But I don't see any business with a combination of that name at all."

"No problem," Rory said. "We'll stop and get a room and a bite to eat first."

"A room?" questioned Candy with a little mirth in her voice. "Aren't you assuming a little too much, Mr. Steele?"

"All right. A room with *two* bedrooms and *two* separate baths. Is that better...Ms. Jossel?"

"Maybe," Candy replied.

"Women," Rory said as he shook his head. "Anyway, once we get settled in, we can do an Internet search and see what pops up. There has to be something. Even if we only find his house or an apartment that gives us a place to start."

Candy sat back in her seat, "Okay. That makes sense." She was quiet for a moment then asked softly, "Can we go by the White House?"

Rory thought about it for a moment, then shook his head, "No. As much as I'd like to - if someone recognizes you - no, I don't think it's a good idea. We have enough people after us already."

Candy nodded her head half-heartedly.

"Be patient. We'll get this whole thing cleared up and you can be in the White House in no time."

"Well, I won't really be in the White House," Candy said.

"But you still have friends in high places that can get you in, right?" he asked with a smile. He needed to keep her spirits up. Candy returned his smile and nodded her head but she wasn't very cheerful. He couldn't blame her. He had her do a GPS search for places to stay and chose the Embassy Suites in the West End area. It was slow going as Rory steered through the Washington, DC traffic to their intended lodgings. Candy donned her large, oversized sunglasses and straw hat disguise in the parking lot before they went inside to get a room. Rory asked what they had available and he had to settle for the two-bedroom presidential suite.

"I hope you're not expecting me to pay for that," Candy whispered as they waited for the young lady behind the counter to enter the information in the computer, "I know you're helping me but...."

"Don't worry, this is just how I roll," Rory. We can talk about some kind of payment plan for your half later." Despite the oversized sunglasses, Rory could see her blush.

Candy shook her head softly, "I still can't get over the fact you're actually helping me,"

"Well, the first time I saw you, you were in trouble. And you've been in trouble ever since. So you need help."

"But...you could still walk away...."

"That's not how my granny brought me up," Rory said simply.

The young lady handed Rory a small envelope, "Here is your key card, Mr. Steele. We hope you and Mrs. Steele have a pleasant stay here,"

Rory took the key card and thanked her. He began walking towards the elevators across the lobby, Candy at his side.

"Mrs. Steeel?" Candy whispered. She lifted the sunglasses and looked at him.

"Wouldn't want to ruin your reputation, now would we?" Rory winked at her. Then he turned his attention to the people around them, looking to see if anyone was watching them. Nothing looked out of place. Halfway across the lobby, Rory realized Candy was no longer walking beside him. He looked back in concern. She was standing back near a sofa and a couple of easy chairs grouped in front of a fireplace. It was apparent she was staring at something. Rory walked back to her, "Anything wrong?"

Candy barely looked at him. "The newspapers," she whispered.

Rory looked down at a stand holding stacks of newspapers. They all had pictures of Candy under sensational headlines.

The Washington Post: Presidential Staffer Commits Murder.

The Washington Times: Member of President's Team Sought For Murder.

The Washington Examiner: Lane's Victory Marred by Murder.

The New York Times: Murder Stains Presidential Win.

Rory gently placed his arm around Candy's shoulders and urged her to move away. She resisted.

"I've ruined everything for them," she whispered sadly.

"You didn't do it, did you?"

Candy glanced up at him, "No, but..."

"Then somebody else is responsible, not you," he reasoned.

"I know," she said, not sounding too convinced. Then she glanced around nervously, "What if someone recognizes me?"

"Just walk confidently with me. It's what I call hiding in plain sight." Rory urged her to move towards the elevator with him. "C'mon, If you slink around, you gather more attention to yourself. Just keep in mind, you're not a murderer."

Candy swallowed and looked like she was about to cry, "The problem is, the public thinks I am."

Chapter 14

RORY HAD THE CONCIERGE deliver a fully equipped laptop to their room. After both of them had a shower and a bite to eat from room service, they began an Internet search for the office of Lee Park Yim, the IT Manager for Lane's presidential campaign run. Like Candy had already said, there was nothing obvious with his name attached to it. Using various parameters in a Google search, Candy finally found a company called TechCom IT Consulting with the name of L Yim attached to it. It had a main floor office on 12th Street NW, above G Street NW. Using the phone numbers on the company website, she also found a possible location for Yim's house.

Rory gave it some thought and then said, "Let's head to the address for that TechCom. The business is a more definite connection to our man. And at this time of day, he should be at work. What do you think?"

Candy agreed with the plan and donned the oversized sunglasses and straw hat disguise again. Jumping into the Jaguar, they started the slow trip across town through the busy Washington traffic. Finding a parking spot opposite Macy's Downtown Metro Center, they walked up to the address Candy had written down on a piece of hotel-stationary. It was nearly 4 o'clock. Figuring the office would close by five, they took a table next to the window in a Starbucks across the street and waited. Several coffees and sandwiches later, they were still waiting. Even when the sun went down there were still lights on in the office. And they could see someone move across the front window from time to time. They waited another hour.

Candy returned to their table with another two mugs of coffee. As she set them down, she glanced at the business, her frustration showing, "Is he going to work all night?"

"Looks like it," Rory said.

Candy took her seat again, shaking her head, "This is ridiculous. The guy's a workaholic,"

Rory glanced over towards the coffee counter, "Yeah. And I'm not sure we can wait in here much longer. The servers over there are beginning to get suspicious. It looks like we're a couple of bad guys casing a joint or something."

"Well, aren't we?"

"You're a wanted fugitive but you're obviously a novice crook. You don't confess to a crime that easily."

Candy wrinkled her nose at him, "Very funny. " But her glance over to the server, and then to the other tables, indicated her worry, "But you're right. They are beginning to wonder. And I'm really going to look suspicious if I keep these sunglasses on after it's dark out."

"True. Time is definitely running out on our present plan." Rory looked back across at the office for a moment and then asked Candy, "Did you mark down that house where we thought this guy was living?"

"Uh-huh." Candy dug into the right pocket of her yellow dress, pulled out a piece of paper and unfolded it, "It was up in an area called...Woodley Park."

Rory nodded, thinking, "Was this guy married?"

Candy gave it a moment's thought and then she shook her head, "No. I don't think he was. Why?"

"Because if he's here in his office," Rory said, "then his house should be empty."

Straightening up in her seat, Candy asked, "Do you think we might find something there?"

"It's worth a try," Rory said. "We can always come back here, after midnight if necessary, to check out his office."

AN HOUR LATER THEY were parked, with their lights off, on Thompson Circle, looking at the house. It was a dark brick, English Manor style single-family residence.

Rory frowned as he looked at the 13,000 square foot house."Are you *sure* this computer guy lives here?"

Leaning forward, Candy squinted, "That's the right house number. And it was the only address with the name L Yim attached to it."

Rory shook his head, "No, this can't be right. That's gotta be a $7 million house."

Candy considered the house for a moment and then said, "Well, he was the IT Manager for Lane's campaign. He took care of all the computers, making sure they were all running, that kind of stuff. And this is Washington, DC. And since he has an office here...."

"Yeah, I guess he must be making a pile of money. It still doesn't feel right, though."

Candy gave it another moment's thought and then said, "Well, no matter how he can afford it, at least it looks like our luck is changing. Unlike the office, it looks like there's no one home here. That part is good, right?"

Rory nodded in agreement, "Yeah." Then he turned in his seat and looked at the three other houses on the circle. "The problem is, if we park here, we're too conspicuous. There are lights on in that house on the right. I'm sure they'll call the police if we stay parked here. They'll probably see us walking up to the house as well."

Candy stretched her neck, "It looks like there are some woods in the back of the house. Maybe we can find a way to sneak in from the back way."

"I think you're right." Rory started the Jaguar and slowly drove around the circle and back out to Woodland Drive. He turned left. After a bit of driving the streets in the area, Rory finally found a suitable parking spot on Norman Stone Drive, south of the circle. He nosed the Jaguar into some trees in the Woodland-Normanstone Terrace Park, leaving it all but hidden in the darkness.

RORY AND CANDY MOVED across the road and into the trees in the space between two fancy homes. They moved as quietly as possible to avoid waking anyone. Reaching a steep incline, they began a slow climb through the trees towards the back of Yim's house. After twenty minutes of hard climbing in the dark, they entered the backyard. The house was dark and quiet. There was an arched, double doorway in the back of the house. Rory and Candy moved cautiously across an angel stone patio, afraid to bump into something in the dark.

Reaching the doors, Rory knelt in the darkness and pulled a small set of lock picking tools from a pocket. "Keep an eye peeled," he whispered to Candy.

"W-what are you doing?" Candy whispered nervously back. She looked into the darkness around them.

There was a slight snick sound and the door opened.

"How did you do that?" Candy asked. She stretched her neck to look into the dark house.

Rory didn't say anything. He just slipped inside, letting Candy slip in behind him and then he shut the door carefully behind them. Standing in the dark, they could vaguely see they were inside a large family room filled with a few pieces of furniture. A large LCD screen on the far side dominated the room.

Rory whispered to Candy, "Assuming they brought the computer stuff here, any idea where he might keep it?"

Candy was silent for a moment and then she whispered back to him, "How would I know? I've never been here before."

"Okay. Let's see if we can find an office or a study," Rory whispered. "Let's go this way." Moving left towards an archway, they crept quietly across the back of a long, dark sofa. They moved through the archway into a sparsely decorated dining room. Rory slowly led Candy through the lower floor of the house, cautiously exploring every room. They found a kitchen area, a living room, and a sun-room along with a few other spaces that were empty. But they found no study or computer room anywhere. Moving without a word back to the central staircase in the foyer, Rory and Candy slowly crept up the stairs. Exploring the second level, they found several bedrooms, a bathroom, and a linen closet. But still no sign of a computer or computer equipment anywhere. They moved back to the staircase.

"Should we go up there?" Candy whispered. She indicated the stairs going up to the next level.

"I guess we'll have to. But if we go up there, it's not going to be easy to get out if someone comes home." Rory thought for a moment and then said, "But no risk, no reward I guess. Right?"

Candy swallowed nervously and nodded. After listening intently to hear if anyone was near the house, they slowly crept upwards. They found a large master bedroom on the right-hand side of the third level, a large bathroom, and an empty room. There was one last room.

Rory opened the door so they could see inside. In the darkness, they could see a number of cardboard boxes stacked against the wall on the left. And directly across from them was a large desk with a computer on top. "This looks like his study," Rory whispered back over his shoulder.

Looking past him, Candy whispered excitedly, "That's the computer from the campaign office in Louisville."

"Are you sure?"

"Yes. Positive," Candy said.

Rory led her into the room and across to the computer on the desk.

Candy tapped Rory's arm and gestured to the stack of cardboard boxes, "I don't see any writing on them but maybe those boxes in the corner are from the office as well. My sister said everything was packed up so...."

"Could be," Rory said. He pulled open the top drawer on the desk and rummaged through some items. He pulled out a small box cutter, "Why don't we go through those boxes and see if we can find that backup you made that seems to be so important to somebody."

"But if we open them up, won't that alert Yin that somebody was here?"

Rory shrugged, "Someone is trying to kill you. How much more trouble can we get in? Are they going to chase us any harder?"

"The man has a point," Candy said.

The first thing Rory did was go over to the window and pull the curtains shut, "We'll need some light in here to search. Why don't you close the door? The less light that gets out the better."

Candy went over and shut the door, flipping the light switch on before heading over to the boxes. She slid one over to Rory as he joined her, "You take this one and I'll take the next."

Rory knelt down, slit the tape along the top of the box and then handed the box cutter to Candy, "So, what exactly am I looking for?"

Candy watched Rory open the top of the box, "We need to find a 512 MB USB flash drive...shaped like a Tampon."

"Pardon?" His eyebrows went up.

Candy blushed, "It was a joke gift from Wendy. We figured no one would touch it - and we were right. At least none of the guys would get near it."

"I don't blame them," Rory said. He shook his head as he knelt there looking at the box.

"It's white and this long," Candy said. "With one end round, one end flat, with a long string tail–"

"I know, I know," Rory said. He took a deep breath and started digging.

Candy couldn't help but smile as she slit the tape on the box in front of her. She opened the flap and began digging through its contents. They were searching boxes number seven and eight when Rory cleared his throat. Candy looked up to see Rory holding the USB flash drive up by the string tail.

"You found it!" Candy said as she jumped up to take it from Rory.

"Uh huh," Rory said. He was quite willing to let her take it from his hand.

Candy gripped the round end and popped it off to reveal the metal end post of the flash drive, "We can take it back to the suite and plug it into the laptop. Then we can see what's on here...what someone wants to kill me for."

Rory nodded, "Right. Put it in your pocket where it'll be safe."

Candy had a very pleased smile on her face as she put the cap back on the USB drive. She slipped it into a zippered compartment in the pocket at her waist on the yellow dress.

Rory gestured to the computer, "Now, why don't you start that thing up and let's see what we find."

Candy looked at Rory with a confused look on her face, "But...we have the backup. Wouldn't it be safer–?"

Rory interrupted her, "Keep in mind what happened at Cherokee Park. They were ready to kill you, whether they were able to get their hands on the backup or not."

Her face went somber, "I know but - aren't we taking an unnecessary chance?"

"I know how scary this is," Rory said. "But maybe it also relates to something they *think* you saw when you were making that backup. We need to take advantage of this opportunity. We'll just take a few minutes and see what pops up, okay?"

.Candy relented reluctantly and walked over to the computer. She sat down and stabbed the button to turn the monitor on. It sprang to life. Her brow furrowed and she looked up at Rory who stood by her shoulder.

"What's wrong?"

"The computer is already running. He just had the monitor turned off."

"Why would he do that?"

Candy thought about it for a moment, "I'm not sure. I guess it's not unusual for offices to keep their computers running but...most people turn them off at home...."

"Well, he is a techie, that's his job I guess."

Candy nodded and then asked, "What should I look for?"

"I'm not really sure what we're looking for. Is there anything that stands out just looking at the monitor?"

Leaned close to the screen, Candy looked over all the icons. She shook her head, "No. Nothing stands out."

Rory rubbed the stubble on his chin, thinking, "What would be on the backup?"

Candy looked to the side for a moment and gave it some thought. Then she looked up at Rory, "Usually you just back up important program data, documents, e-mails, correspondence, pictures...."

Rory nodded, "Okay then, we can sift through those things later on the backup. For now, just use those computer skills of yours to look over anything else. Maybe something pops up."

Candy turned back to the monitor, picked up the mouse and began to sift through the contents of the hard drive.

After a few moments, Rory walked over to the door of the study, cracked it open and listened for the sounds of anyone in the house. Then he walked over to the curtains and peeked out. Nothing seemed out of place, everything was quiet. He moved back to the door of the study again, listening intently for the slightest sounds. After letting her work for fifteen minutes, Rory was about to tell Candy to stop when he saw her stiffen in her chair.

She had a look of horror on her face.

He stepped to her shoulder and looked at the monitor, "What's wrong? What did you find?"

Chapter 15

CANDY JUST SAT THERE, her hands at her face, not saying a word. Then she spoke in a hesitant voice, "I...I can't be sure. I'm...I'm not as good at computing as Yim is...and I could be wrong."

"Just tell me," Rory said. "What did you find–?"

"No. I'm not going to say anything to hurt anybody. I don't want to hurt Yim," Candy said defiantly. "It wouldn't be right. I know him. I'm probably wrong. In fact, I know I'm wrong. He wouldn't–" She began typing away on the keyboard and then clicked on an icon with the mouse. A screen opened up and they were looking at another desktop. Candy put a hand to her mouth, "O-M-G."

"What is it?" Rory put his hands on her shoulders. "Candy?"

Candy shook her head defiantly again and shrugged his hands off her shoulders. "No, it can't be–" she insisted. She closed out the desktop screen and clicked on another icon. Another desktop popped up on the screen. Candy let out a little cry.

"You *need* to tell me what you're looking at," Rory insisted. "Do you hear me? What are you seeing?"

"Yim–" She cut herself off, shaking her head again.

Rory knelt beside her and looked up at her, "If I'm going to help you - if I'm going to help *us* stay alive - you need to tell me what you're seeing–"

Candy blurted it out, "Yim has back doors into the computer systems of Lane's opponents."

Rory looked at the screen and then back at Candy, "When you say back doors...?"

"Yim has penetrated their computer systems somehow - illegally - without them knowing about it. He is - he's spying on Lane's opponents for the Presidency." She had hot tears in her eyes. Moving the mouse across the screen, she clicked on another icon and up popped another window. Candy let out another little cry of despair.

"What's wrong?" Rory whispered gently.

"Yim was spying on people in Lane's party as well as the opposition," Candy said in a small voice. She moved the mouse to an icon and double clicked it. A number of files popped up. Candy scrolled through them. "That's all the correspondence and e-mails for Senator Dirkett. He ran for the party nomination against Connor Harrison Lane. Yim has installed key logging software as well. Every keystroke on Dirkett's computer is recorded, every movement of the mouse...."

"So...you're saying Yim was spying on the opposition for Lane?" Rory asked her.

"Not necessarily," Candy said.

"What do you mean?"

"If it *was* for Lane then it should end here. But Yim has all the data from those back doors, plus everything on *this* system, being funneled to a third-party. In fact, it's siphoning every kind of data from their systems, through this system, and filtering it to an outside computer right now. In real-time," Candy explained.

Rory looked at the screen and then back at Candy, "He's sending the data to someone besides Lane? To who?"

Candy looked back at the computer screen, "I'm...I'm not sure..."

"Can you figure it out? We need to know where the info is going–"

She swore under her breath, "I can't believe...."

Rory placed a hand on her shoulder, "It's okay. I know you're upset. You don't want it to be Lane. Just stay calm. We'll get through this, alright?"

Candy took a deep breath to compose herself. "I can't believe Yim would do this. My sister trusted him," she said in anger. She called up Google and did a web search. Navigating to a website, she downloaded a file. When the download manager asked 'Run/ Download' she clicked run.

"What are you doing?"

"Installing software to analyze the data going through Yim's router," Candy said. Next, she double-clicked an icon and the new program began running. "Okay. There's the I.P. address," she said after a moment of examining data on the screen. She went back to Google and did an IP-Whois-Lookup. "There it is," she said, pointing at the screen. Her hand flew back to her mouth, "Oh no! ZongChi Technologies Limited."

Rory narrowed his eyes, "Where have I heard that name before?"

Candy looked at Rory, still kneeling beside her. Tears filled her eyes before she spoke, "They're a Chinese manufacturing and technology company with a large branch office set up in the

United States. They are one of the largest in the world...if not *the* largest. They manufacture, install and service computer infrastructure and telecommunications equipment."

It instantly dawned on Rory, "I remember now. They were in the news recently. They've been trying to get government and business contracts. But they've been accused of being spies for the Chinese government."

"That's right," Candy confirmed. "And right now, with what Lee Park Yim has set up, they've been able to spy on the leading American politicians–"

"How many?" Rory asked quickly.

"I'm not sure. There are so many," Candy answered she scrolled through a long list of icons on the computer screen. Then she froze and looked at Rory.

"What's wrong?"

Candy licked her lips, "I just realized...the worst part of this whole thing is, with Lane's win, they have a back door into the Presidency of the United States. A Chinese company has a front row view into the Oval Office at the White House."

Chapter 16

CANDY WAS ROCKING SLIGHTLY on the chair in front of the computer as Rory stood beside her. Both of them were in shock at what they had just uncovered. At what it meant for the United States. The Chinese not only had a front row seat into every aspect of the American government, they could actually manipulate it for their own ends.

Rory suddenly realized something. "If this computer is filtering things right now, then someone may know we're here."

Candy nodded, "That's true–"

"We better get out of here now," Rory said urgently. He reached down and turned the monitor off.

"But we can't just leave it here, filtering the info," Candy protested. She turned the monitor back on.

"Unfortunately we have to," Rory insisted. He reached down and turned the monitor off again.

"But we could wipe out this hard drive and stop what they're doing–"

"I highly doubt they don't have another computer system filtering the information," Rory said. "And even if they don't, they have all the back doors in place they can access from a new system. Right now, the possibility is they don't know we're here.

Those men only *think* you know something. Once they *know* we've seen this, who ends up coming after us before we can alert the authorities? And how do you prove what you know? We don't have time to make copies—"

"But—"

"We already have enough people trying to kill us," Rory said sternly. He stopped her hand halfway to the monitor again, "Right now our first priority is to stay alive so we *can* tell someone. Let's go."

Candy stood up with tears in her eyes and grudgingly allowed Rory to guide her towards the door.

"But we *have* to let my sister know about this," Candy whispered.

Rory flipped the light off and opened the study door.

"We have to," Candy repeated in a more urgent whisper.

Rory put a finger to his lips as he guided her over to the stairs. Even in the darkness of the house, he could still see her anger and frustration. They moved down to the second floor quickly. Rory paused at the top of the second landing, listening intently. Then he guided Candy back down to the main floor.

"We have to let my sister know," Candy repeated again as they moved into the back family room.

"Later," Rory said in a low voice.

"We have to," Candy insisted in a louder voice. She resisted his efforts to lead her to the back door.

"We'll get to that—"

Candy yanked her arm out of Rory's grasp and moved away from him quickly.

"Where are you going? Candy?" Rory saw her pick up something from a small table. He moved quickly across the room and snatched the land-line phone from her hands, "Are you crazy?"

She protested as Rory set the phone back in place, "Give me that back. We need to let them know."

"We need to get out of here first." Rory took her elbow and escorted Candy firmly to the back door.

Candy tried to wrestle her arm away from Rory, "Then we should call the police."

"We won't be able to help anyone if we get arrested."

"We just tell the police what Yim is doing and they arrest him, not us," Candy insisted in frustration. "Why aren't you listening to me!?"

"Do you remember what happened the last time we had contact with the police?"

"But we have to do something," Candy hissed.

Rory opened the back door and peered outside. Still not seeing anyone, Rory guided Candy into the darkness behind Yim's house. "Do you really think it would be the police who showed up? Or those two men?" he said in a harsh whisper.

Candy spoke loudly, "They're back in Louisville. And my life isn't important–"

"Yes, it is," Rory insisted in a louder voice himself. "And so is mine."

"But–"

Rory shushed her again and found himself shaking his head in frustration. He guided Candy across the angel stone patio and into the trees. Candy was obviously miffed but stayed silent on the climb back down the steep incline. It was more difficult going downhill in the darkness and they had to be careful not to trip. Both of them were puffing hard when they finally reached the bottom of the incline.

As they moved between the two large houses, Candy started her insistent demands again. "Rory, we have to phone my sister right now," she hissed.

"Just give it a rest for now," Rory said. "We'll get to that." He led her past the trees to the edge of the road.

"But the longer we wait, the more information they get," Candy said in a louder voice.

Rory put his hands to his lips to shush her again. He led her across the road toward his hidden Jaguar.

Candy let out a low growl of frustration.

Just as they reached the gravel shoulder, Rory felt a sting on the left side his neck. Rory's hand automatically went to his neck. He felt a thin object stuck in his skin.

Candy whimpered and her left hand shot to her neck as well.

Rory turned to her.

Candy dropped straight down to the gravel.

As soon as he took a step to help her, Rory's legs dropped out from under him. He fell hard to the gravel. He was face-to-face with Candy.

Candy's hazel eyes were wide open, frozen in surprise.

Rory tried to move but he couldn't. All he could do was stare at the woman across from him, lying on the gravel shoulder. He heard a car pull up on the roadway somewhere below his feet.

A moment later footsteps crunched on the gravel shoulder.

Rory watched as a pair of men's shoes walked to the left of Candy's head. Hands reached down and gripped her shoulders. Someone must have been down at Candy's feet because he saw her lifted up off the gravel shoulder. The pair of men's shoes shuffled past Rory's face as Candy was carried towards the road. A few moments later, Rory heard footsteps crunching across the gravel towards him again. He felt a hand brush on his neck, removing whatever was there. As he was picked up by the shoulders and feet, Rory tried desperately to move but couldn't. He was carried onto the road where he was placed into the back of a vehicle, lying down and facing Candy. What was happening? He heard a door slam shut at his feet. The vehicle rocked slightly to the left as someone got into the driver's side up front. Then the vehicle dipped a bit the other way as someone got into the passenger side. The vehicle started and within moments they were driving down the road. The street lights they passed gave him a glimpse of the vehicle he was in. He and Candy Jossel were paralyzed and riding in the back of a funeral hearse.

Chapter 17

RORY TRIED TO KEEP TRACK of all the turns they made, trying to visualize in his head where they were being taken. But after a while, it became totally useless. Every so often he would see Candy's hazel eyes staring back at him. He could tell she was scared. Rory tried desperately to get a single muscle to move but nothing worked. The fact that he was aware of his surroundings, that he could feel everything but couldn't move a muscle was significant. That meant whoever had taken them prisoner had used something like Curare to paralyze them. The sting in the neck probably meant it was delivered by a very tiny metal dart to their necks. Candy, at her lower body weight, had succumbed to the effect of the drug first. And since they weren't dead, that meant a low dosage had been used. That told him the effects were going to wear off eventually. But would it be soon enough?

They had been traveling at a good rate of speed for a while when the hearse finally slowed and came to a stop.

Rory figured they were at their final destination and he was still unable to move. He silently cursed.

Voices! Someone was talking to the driver about an accident up ahead and having to take a small detour.

That was good, thought Rory. The longer it took the better.

The hearse turned left and started moving again.

Rory estimated they had been traveling for maybe another 15 minutes before the hearse came to a stop. He heard the doors on the driver's side and then the passenger side open and close.

A moment later, the back door to the hearse opened up and he watched helplessly as Candy was pulled out and disappeared.

A few minutes later, he felt himself being pulled out of the back of the hearse as well. He fought desperately to move a muscle. But nothing happened. He was placed on his back on a gurney, his head turned to the left. He saw a line of evergreen shrubs a few feet away.

The gurney started moving.

Rory could hear the wheels rolling along a concrete walkway. There was a bump, the gurney tilted as it went up a ramp and then was pushed through a doorway into a building. The walls were a sterile white. Several closed doors zipped past. Rory had the impression he was being pushed down a long, white hallway. There was a bump and they went through a set of swinging doors There was a smell in the air and he tried to place it. Formaldehyde? That would make sense since they had been in a hearse. Then his blood ran cold. *What are these guys planning?* He tried to calm himself. The fact he could smell meant the drugs were wearing off. *But how long...?*

The gurney jerked to a stop and was turned right. Rory felt a bump again. The gurney was pushed through another set of swinging doors. Rory could see he was now in a large, well-lit room. He could hear the footsteps of whoever was pushing him echoing lightly off the beige and white walls. The scent of formaldehyde was under another smell...burnt sandalwood? He wasn't sure.

The gurney stopped moving and he saw Candy Jossel again. She was 50 feet ahead of him, lying perfectly still on her back on another gurney. Her yellow dress was pushed high up her legs and sat near her hips and he wished he could push it down for her.

A man was passing his hands over her body, searching her. Again, he tried to move a muscle, desperate to help her. Nothing was working. Now he felt someone behind him patting his body, searching him as well.

The man searching Candy made a sound of disgust.

"Find something?" The voice was right behind Rory.

The man searching Candy shook his head, "Nothing you want to know about."

Rory' line of sight to Candy was cut off as someone in a black pinstriped suit stepped in front of him.

The person bent over and looked into Rory's eyes.

It was one of the men who had been chasing Candy from the start. He was the man Rory had punched in the kidney back in Louisville when this first started.

"Surprised to see me?"

Rory was. The man in the black pinstriped suit was the last person he had expected to see. Kentucky was at least a ten-hour straight drive from here. Even if they had been alerted by the computer system back in Yim's house, there was no way they could get to Washington, DC this fast. How had they been able to track them here?

"You should have left things alone, Steele," the man said in the black pinstriped suit.

Another surprise. How did they know who he was? Then he remembered. Pinstriped suit and his partner were Secret Service.

They had the resources to figure out who he was. That still didn't answer how they had managed to track them here. But it upped the ante. Rory would have to up his game to match theirs. *If* he managed to survive.

"Now, before we take care of you, we want you to see what's going to happen to your lady friend over there." The man in the black pinstriped suit stepped back and allowed Rory to see Candy again. Two men were lifting her off the gurney. A third man pulled the gurney away and Candy was carried another five feet away to a small conveyor. And sitting on the conveyor was a casket! The third man stepped around to the casket and opened the lid. Rory could see an old woman lying in the casket. Candy Jossel was placed in the casket on top of the body and it was closed. Rory strained to move but it was futile.

The man in the black pinstriped suit stepped back in front of Rory and looked at him again, "She's all ready for the crematorium. That's what that big shiny box is at the end of the conveyor. It gets up to 1800°F. In a couple of hours, she'll be nothing but bone fragments. We'll scatter those over the Potomac. Kind of patriotic, don't you think?" The man's smile never reached his eyes.

Rory heard a loud whump as the crematorium started up. He tried desperately to move. He couldn't imagine how scared Candy must be right now. Rory concentrated as hard as he could to move a single muscle.

The man in the black pinstriped suit nodded. He reached out and wiped a bead of perspiration from Rory's forehead. "I can see you trying, Steele. I can see it in your eyes. Like I told them, you'll never give up. That's why we have to get rid of you. But because of all the trouble you caused us, your death won't be that quick. In fact, you'll have a *lot* of time to think about it." The man stepped back as another gurney appeared in front of Rory. There was something on top of it. Rory was picked up and he saw what was on the other gurney. Rory realized he was staring at another casket with the lid up. A small, elderly man, dressed in a black suit lay inside! They placed him on top of the dead body and closed the lid.

Chapter 18

RORY HAD BEEN around dead bodies before, but lying on top of one was a new experience. And being inside the casket added to the creepiness. With the lid closed, he could smell the chemicals used by the embalmer, mixed with the Elmwood of the casket. He heard muffled instructions outside the casket from the man in the black pinstriped suit.

"We'll take this one out back. You guys finish everything in here once the box is hot enough."

"She's gonna scream like hell," a gruff voice said

"No. She's paralyzed like I said. She'll feel it but her vocal chords won't let her say a thing. Too bad, that would've made things a little sweeter."

Rory felt anger and a surge of adrenaline coursed through his veins. Rory strained to move his muscles. The coffin he was in started to roll. He felt a slight bump, which meant it had gone through the swinging doors again. Part of him concentrated on moving a muscle while part stayed aware of where they were taking him. If he could get out, he had to be able to find his way back to Candy. He could feel a right turn and then the smooth vibrations of the wheels rolling on the floor. That meant he was being moved down the hallway again, away from the direction they came in. He felt his right arm twitch a little. More adrenaline coursed through his veins. The drug was starting to wear off. But would it be soon enough?

Rory concentrated and strained harder to move. He heard something scraping and sliding across the top side of the coffin. *What was that?* Another twitch of his arm. He felt the casket moving down an incline now. Then the wheels started to clack. They were on some kind of flagstone or walkway. Rory felt his body move. But was that him or was that the bounce from the rough surface they were rolling over? Rory didn't hear any slight echo from the clattering wheels. Were they outside the building?

Rory concentrated, trying to move his shoulders. There! Movement. The clacking stopped and the wheels hissed like they were moving over grass. They *were* outside! Where were they taking them? Even if he escaped, how would he know where Candy was? Rory desperately concentrated to get his body cooperating again. A little movement in his fingers meant it was working. But would it be soon enough? The casket stopped and there was silence. Rory listened. He heard the whine of an electrical engine and then the casket was being slid. It bumped to a stop then moved in a herky-jerky motion in one direction, then in the other. Rory heard another electrical whine and it felt like the casket was being lowered. Rory realized they were using a forklift, probably to get the casket over an open grave.

"Okay, it's on the lowering device. Get the front end loader with the dirt and we'll finish this off."

They were going to bury him alive!

Rory didn't have much time. He concentrated harder - his hands moved - then his arms and he felt elation. They were sluggish but he was able to lift his arms and place his hands on the lid - his hopes died again - he was too weak to do anything. He tried his legs. They moved a little. But with the body underneath him, there wasn't enough room in the coffin to get any leverage against the lid. He felt the casket start to lower. Then he heard the rumble of a gas engine and knew the loader was about to be moved into place, beside the mound of dirt that would be beside the open grave. That wasn't good. He didn't have much time left. Rory calmed himself for a moment to think - he realized even if he could push harder against the lid, it wouldn't do him any good. The casket would be closed using a catch-lock. It was about eight inches from the top end. But now he had another problem - how could he unlock the casket to get out?

Rory concentrated and worked to rotate his body on top of the old man. He felt the old man's waxy skin against his cheek but he did his best to ignore it. He had to think. Sometimes people were buried with mementos or favorite objects. He hoped it would be the case with this old gentleman. Rory struggled to shift his arms towards the man's chest. It was slow and awkward. He concentrated on his hands and fingers as he began to search the man's pockets. He felt something on the inside top pocket of the suit. He slid his hands inside and felt a ring. Probably his wedding ring. Nothing else. Rory slowly moved his hands down to the side pocket. Nothing. He felt something a little higher up on the waist. There was a small pocket with a pocket watch inside. No good. He struggled to roll over and began checking the other side. He ran his fingers over the side pocket. There was something there. Rory slipped his hands into the pocket and felt for the objects inside. There was a thin chain with a small cross at the end. The problem was it was too thick. It would never fit into the crack. He kept searching. His fingers felt a strange object...toenail clippers? There was another small object that felt like a heart-shaped locket. Damn. People were buried with all kinds of mementos but this one had nothing he could use. He rolled onto his back and tried to push against the lid. No good. Then it struck him. Rory rolled back over and reached in for the toenail clippers. Crap! Still no good. There was no small file on this one. Wait. He pulled up the cutting lever and flipped it over to lie flat. It might work. He rolled over onto his back and reached up for the area where the catch-lock should be. He slid the lever into the crack between the lid and the side, sliding it gently back and forth, feeling for the catch-lock. The coffin bumped against the bottom of the grave and his numb fingers dropped the clippers. Rory cursed, rolled over and searched for the clippers. There it was. He picked it up and rolled back over, hearing the hiss of his clothing against the silk material at the top of the casket. The sound was chilling, but he had to will himself to move slower. Then he heard hisses underneath the casket. They were removing nylon, webbing straps used to lower the coffin. He couldn't afford to lose any more precious time.

Carefully moving the cutting lever into the crack, he moved it back and forth several times, ten to twelve inches from the top of the casket. C'mon! C'mon! Time was running out. Finally, he heard a little snick. He pushed the lid open and looked up. Against the background of stars in the sky, he saw the outline of the loader's bucket as it moved over the open grave. Rory's body was still sluggish as he shakily got to his feet. He felt bad at having to stand on the old man's body but it put his head level with the top of the grave. He concentrated on getting his muscles to cooperate. Someone stepped up to the open grave. Rory stepped on the left side of the casket, grabbed the left ankle and pulled. A man let out a startled cry as he fell into the grave. Rory heard a grunt as the man landed hard on top of the old man in the open coffin. Rory quickly stepped on the fallen man's body, reached up, grabbed onto the edge of the grave and pulled himself up. He rolled away from the open grave and struggled to his feet again.

"Blacker!" The call came from down in the grave.

The door to the loader opened and someone leaned out, "What the hell are you doing, Conroy?"

Rory saw it was the man in the black pinstriped suit.

The Secret Service Agent's eyes went wide when he realized it was Rory. But he was too late to do anything about it.

Rory threw a punch with all his weight and rage behind it and the man in the black pinstriped suit sagged, tripping the lever for the bucket.

It slowly tipped and dirt rained down into the open grave.

Rory heard a scream for a moment and then silence.

The man in the grave was buried alive under the dirt.

RORY TURNED AND STAGGERED away from the loader. He saw the back of a building and thought of Candy. His legs were still a little rubbery as he moved over to the electric forklift. Rory pulled himself into the driver seat. He turned the key. It started and the wheels spun grooves in the grass as he pushed the accelerator down. Making a sharp turn, Rory headed towards the building across the grass. He saw a wide loading door up ahead. He shot up the ramp and pushed through heavy PVC strips hanging from the top of the wide doorway. That was what he had heard scraping over the top of the coffin. Which meant he was heading the right way back to Candy. He found himself in a large area where they must load and load the coffins. Straight ahead was an open doorway. He passed through and drove down a long white hallway. He desperately looked for the swinging doors that would lead him to Candy. He reached a set that had a sign over the top of them that read 'Crematorium'. Rory turned the forklift left and barged through the swinging doors into the room on the other side. There were three men in the room and Rory caught them by surprise. He blasted through the closest man with the front of the forklift, rendering him unconscious and knocking him to the side. The other two men were beside the casket that was now halfway inside the roaring flames of the huge crematorium. The men were still frozen at his unexpected entrance. Rory accelerated and drove the forks between the legs of the man on this side of the conveyor. Rory spun the forklift to the left, using the fork to rip the man's leg out from under him. The man screamed as he clutched his knee and fell to the floor where he passed out from the pain.

The other man leaped over the end of the conveyor and ran towards Rory.

Rory spun the forklift around to face him. Jabbing the button to lift the forks, Rory accelerated two feet forward to meet the man, then jerked the forks left. He caught the man in the neck, snapping his C-4 vertebrae and killing him instantly. Rory spun the forklift right and drove quickly to the end of the conveyor. Leaning over, he banged the control button with the side of his fist to reverse the conveyor.

The casket slowly began backing out of the licking flames.

Rory wheeled his vehicle around and drove alongside the conveyor. Stopping dead, he turned the forks towards the conveyor and the casket.

The top half of the casket was in flames.

Rory positioned the forks, drove forward and slipped the forks under the casket. Lifting it up from the conveyor, Rory backed the forklift slowly away from the conveyor, making sure he didn't tip the casket over. He lowered it to the floor, then pulled the forks away, letting the casket slip off and come to rest on the floor. Leaving the forklift, Rory ran to the casket. Ducking low to avoid the flames, he unlocked the catch-lock and opened the flaming lid.

Chapter 19

CANDY'S EYES WERE FILLED WITH TERROR. But she didn't make any attempt to get out of the coffin. Which meant she was still paralyzed. Rory noticed her breathing was labored as well. The drug was affecting her lungs. He had to act fast or he would lose her. Her yellow dress had ridden high up her thighs and Rory gently pulled it back down, reassuring her, "Don't worry. Everything is going to be okay. Let's get you out of there."

There was no sign of relief from Candy's eyes.

Rory gently scooped his arms under her and lifted her off the old woman and away from the flaming casket. But his muscles were still weak and he nearly dropped her. He wouldn't be able to carry her very far. Rory cursed under his breath, then caught himself. If he showed frustration, that could worry Candy. She already had enough trouble breathing. But he had to act quickly before someone else came after them again. Maybe the man in the black pinstripe suit was already on his way back inside. Thoughts whirled through Rory's mind. A plan formed, but would it work? Rory turned and gently laid Candy across the forks. Her hips sagged between the forks. He jumped back onto the forklift, carefully lifting the forks just a little off the floor. Candy didn't fall through to the floor. That was good. But he would have to be careful. He lifted her a little higher, then turned the forklift slowly. He drove across the room to the swinging doors. Slowly pushed his way through, Rory anticipated someone attacking them. But there was no one in the hallway.

Rory turned left and carefully drove up the white hallway, which he was sure would take them to the front of the building. Hopefully, the hearse they had been brought here in would be still there. This escape in slow motion was agonizing. He looked back over his shoulder to see if anyone was coming after them. So far, so good. Pushing slowly through a set of swinging doors, Rory saw a doorway up ahead. The door had been propped open and left that way. Moving through it and down an incline, they were finally driving on a long walkway outside the building. Rory looked into the dark ahead, hoping to see the hearse that had brought them here. There it was. As he got closer, Rory was surprised when he saw his Jaguar parked behind the hearse. Someone had driven it here. Rory surmised they would have used a crusher at a nearby scrap metal yard to get rid of it...after they had cremated Candy and buried him alive. He wouldn't forget this. Within moments, he had the partially paralyzed Candy Jossel lying across the backseat. Getting in, Rory started up his GPS and within moments he was driving fast for the nearest pharmacy.

RORY PARKED IN THE darkness behind a closed pharmacy in a strip mall. He draped his shirt over his head and tied the arms across his lower face to create a make-shift mask. No need to have the police using security surveillance footage in the pharmacy to put out an APB on him. They had enough people chasing them already. Using a broken piece of concrete, Rory smashed in the front window of the pharmacy. As the burglar alarm sounded, Rory ran behind the pharmacists' counter and searched for what he needed. He found an IV kit quickly. Now he needed a physostigmine, a parasympathomimetic alkaloid that would counteract the drug in Candy's system. At least, he hoped it would. He was working on old memories here but he had no choice. He tried to slow his own breathing as he searched through the various drugs in stock in the back. He cursed. The print on these packages was so small and in the dark...Antilirium...that was it! Rushing back around to the Jaguar, Rory used the back way out of the strip mall to make a getaway. As he drove, Rory spoke to Candy, still lying paralyzed on the back seat, to reassure her. Ten minutes later, Rory pulled into a larger mall area and parked. Rory got into the back seat and set up an IV drip into Candy's left wrist. Rory held the bag up, letting the drug drip into the wrist vein.

After a few moments, Candy's ability to move her fingers was an encouraging sign. She made a small movement with her head. The fear in her eyes began to dissipate.

"Are you okay?" Rory asked her.

Candy nodded her head. It wasn't much of a movement but it was encouraging.

Rory pushed her yellow dress back down her bare thighs.

"Always the gentleman," Candy whispered. Her voice was hoarse.

"I don't like my women paralyzed when I try to take advantage of them," Rory replied with a smile.

"I thought that *was* when you were supposed to do your kinky stuff," Candy whispered.

"Now you tell me."

Candy gave him a weak smile, "I'd like to sit up if I could...."

Rory nodded as he set the IV bag in the back window, then helped her up. Candy slowly pulled her legs around and got them on the backseat floor. Then she put a hand to her forehead as she sat there. After a few moments, she massaged the back of her neck.

"Do you still have the thumb drive?" Rory asked her as he held up the IV bag again.

"Yes," Candy said. She slowly slid her hand down to her pocket and pulled out the Tampon shaped flash drive. "He did find it but...."

"He thought it was real," Rory said with some amusement.

Candy nodded and then got angry. "That pig felt me up," she hissed. "He stuck his hands up my dress...feeling between my legs. It was humiliating."

"I'm sorry you had to go through that," Rory said. "If I could have gotten free earlier..."

Candy shook her head slightly, "No. It's not your fault, At least we're not dead. I could feel the heat of the flames...and lying on that dead body...." She shuddered.

"How about if we head back to the hotel and get cleaned up?" Rory said to change the subject.

Candy nodded. Rory took the IV needle out of her wrist vein and helped her to get into the front seat. It wasn't long before the GPS unit guided them back to their two-bedroom Presidential unit at the Embassy Suites. Rory retrieved his Baby Eagle 9915 RL Polymer 9mm handgun from the lock box in the trunk and then walked slowly with Candy up to the room. Once inside, Candy sat heavily in a large easy chair. She stayed there, head back and eyes closed, obviously exhausted and obviously shaken at nearly being cremated alive.

Chapter 20

RORY SET HIS GUN DOWN on the coffee table and stepped into his bathroom. Running the shower as hot as he could take it, Rory leaned against the wall, allowing the water to massage his neck and his back. He felt bone weary. He wasn't sure if it was an after-effect of the Curare or his constant struggle against the paralyzing effects that has done him in. It didn't matter. He felt tired and sore. Rory admonished himself as he let the hot water do its work. Letting his guard down had nearly cost them their lives. He had underestimated the Secret Service men being able to find them. He had assumed they were working on their own, that they wouldn't have all the resources of the government to use. He was wrong. He couldn't make that mistake again. He wouldn't.

Grabbing the soap and lathering up, Rory scrubbed away the smell of the crematorium and the formaldehyde as best as he could. A few minuted later he thought he could hear talking. He listened intently. Was that the television? He turned the shower off and listened, wiping soap from his face. He could hear somebody speaking in low tones. He stepped out of the shower. Taking two steps, he pulled the bathroom door open a crack. Nothing. Everything was quiet. He peeked out. He didn't see Candy...and the television didn't appear to be on. He heard the door to Candy's bathroom close. After listening for another moment, Rory closed the door and stepped back into the shower, rinsing the soap off. Turning the shower off, Rory stepped out and reached for one of the large white towels. Toweling the water off, he slipped on his gray boxers and walked out into the living room. Everything was quiet. He wondered if he was just being paranoid and hearing things. Shrugging it off as his imagination, Rory walked over to the coffee maker. A good strong brew was in order. His hand stopped halfway to the coffee packet and his blood ran cold. A low voice out in the hallway sounded familiar. Rory turned and moved quickly to the coffee table where he picked up his handgun. Slipping silently over to the peephole in the door, he looked out into the hallway. The man in the black pinstriped suit, the man called Blacker, walked into his view. He was followed by several other men. Rory turned and made a dash for Candy's bathroom. He grabbed the knob and threw the door open.

Candy - dressed only in a yellow brassiere and panties - turned with a surprised look on her face, "Excuse me!"

Rory grabbed her wrist and pulled her out.

"What are you doing–" Her question was cut off when someone placed a key card in the suite door and it opened partway, held in place by the chain and bolt across the door.

"We have to get out," Rory whispered urgently. He pointed towards the curtains on the wall opposite the door.

Candy dashed across the room.

Someone began hammering away with a shoulder on the other side of the door, trying to break away the chain and bolt.

Candy ripped open the curtains and was confronted by a glass wall that looked out on a hallway. She desperately looked for a latch to open patio doors but there was nothing. She looked back at the door, panic rising. "Rory–" she whispered harshly as she pointed at the glass wall preventing their escape.

Rory picked up his wallet, slipping it into the waistband of his gray boxers in front. Grabbing the car keys, he pushed them down beside his wallet in his boxers. Dashing across the room, he held his gun out to Candy, "Hold this."

Candy's hand shook as she gripped the gun butt gingerly. "What now. We can't get out," she said in wide-eyed fright.

Rory turned and grabbed a large porcelain lamp from a table. Years of military training and investigative work had taught Rory one important thing. A thing every person staying in a hotel should always do. Check out every avenue of escape in case of fire or some other emergency. Rory knew this hotel was built around a large central atrium and all the inner rooms had a back glass-wall, covered by curtains. The curtains could be opened to let light in but there was no sliding, patio-style door. The hallway on the other side looked down over the central courtyard, ten flights below. It was presently their only hope of escape. Rory threw the lamp hard and it smashed through the window, taking out the entire pane from floor to ceiling and creating an emergency exit.

Candy handed the gun to Rory and then took a couple of steps back. Two quick steps and she leaped across the broken glass and into the hallway. Her bare feet went out from under her and she let out a cry as she landed hard on her butt.

Rory ran and jumped.

Candy turned on her hip to her left to get up. She screamed.

As Rory was in the air over the broken glass, he realized two men were rushing towards them from the left in the hallway.

The men reacted to Rory's appearance, bringing up their weapons.

But Rory reacted quicker, due to Candy's scream. He soared over the glass, dropped to his knees and brought the gun up.

Crack! Crack!

Their aim had been high and the bullets whizzed low over Rory's head. He pulled the trigger twice.

The two men dropped backwards, each with a bullet to the chest.

Rory was up quickly and grabbed Candy's hand. She was frozen with fear and he had to pull hard to get her up and moving again. They heard the door smash open back inside the suite. Leaping over the fallen bodies, Rory looked down and noted no blood. That meant the men were wearing body armor. He would have to keep that in mind. Rory and Candy ran in their underwear, passing a number of rooms before reaching a corridor that connected this outer hallway to the inner one. Rory slid to a stop. "This way," he said as he pointed down the corridor.

Candy slid to a stop and ran back to Rory.

Crack! Crack!

Two bullets buried themselves in the wall.

Candy ducked and yelped.

Rory grabbed her hand again and pulled her to her feet. They both ran hard, their bare feet slapping on the black and gold marble floor, echoing off the walls. The pounding of running footsteps sounded behind them. Halfway down the corridor, Rory made a change of plans. He slid to a stop and turned Candy to the right into a stairwell. Going down, they took the stairs two at a time. Reaching the next landing, Rory heard footsteps pounding on the stairs above them. He realized it was too risky to use the stairs all the way to the bottom. That would leave them open to a gunshot from above. Rory guided Candy back inside to the connecting corridor on this floor and turned right. In a few moments, they found themselves in the inner hallway where they slid to a stop.

"Which way?" Candy asked frantically.

The bank of elevators was a dozen hotel doors down on the left. Rory pointed at them and they ran hard in that direction.

As soon as they reached the elevators, Candy jabbed the down button over and over.

Rory lifted his handgun and looked back down the hallway, ready to fire.

They could hear the pounding of shoes heading in their direction.

It was a nerve-racking wait as Candy jabbed the down button repeatedly, "C'mon, c'mom."

"It isn't going to come any faster," Rory said as he kept watch.

"You don't know that–"

The elevator doors finally started opening. There was a woman inside the elevator car.

Rory slipped the Baby Eagle into the back of his underwear before he slid into the elevator car behind Candy.

Candy pushed the button for the main floor and moved back into the corner of the car to stand beside Rory.

The woman's eyebrows went up as she looked over Rory and Candy's attire.

"Going to use the pool," Rory said with a smile.

"Uh huh," was all the woman said as she eyed Rory's boxer shorts and the large bulge his wallet made in the front.

It was an awkward few moments as the elevator slowly moved downward. The elevator doors opened to the central courtyard and Rory quickly led Candy out.

"Oh dear!" was the comment from the woman back inside the elevator when she saw the gun in the back of Rory's boxer shorts.

Rory pulled the handgun from the back of his shorts as they ran towards the front lobby of the hotel. They quickly reached a patio area with a line of potted plants on the left and a number of patio tables on the right. A few people sitting at the tables turned and began to titter at the sight of the man and woman running in their underwear.

A gunshot rang out. Crack!

A bullet clipped off one of the clay pots and a woman screamed.

Rory pulled Candy to cover behind a huge clay pot that held a small tree. Rory tried to peek out to see where the men were.

Crack!

The bullet chipped tiny pieces off the pot, sending fragments into Rory's cheek before he could duck. It was painful but he ignored it. They had to keep moving. Rory took Candy's hand and they ran low towards the front lobby.

Crack!

There was a sound of a bullet ricocheting off a metal chair beside them.

Candy screamed, slid to a stop on the terrazzo floor and squatted down, hands over her head.

Rory skidded to a stop in his bare feet and ran back to Candy's side. He saw the men running towards the pots and tables but he was afraid to return fire in case he hit someone innocent.

Then he had an idea. Rory held the gun in both hands and took careful aim at the middle of the huge clay tree pot and fired.

Crack!

The bullet buried itself safely inside the pot but it had served its purpose.

The men chasing them immediately ducked for cover.

Rory urged Candy to her feet and they began running again. Their bare feet slapped across the terrazzo floor.

Crack!

A ricochet sounded off the floor just beside them.

Candy screamed.

Rory pulled her behind another large pot. Leaning out quickly, Rory pulled the trigger.

His bullet buried itself into another heavy pot.

The men ducked for cover again.

Rory urged Candy to move and they were running again. They slanted right, running around another large pot.

Crack! Crack! Crack! Crack!

Bullets ricocheted off the furniture and the floor beside them.

Rory pulled Candy to the right towards a short hallway, putting several large pots behind them and the pursuing gunmen. Their bare feet slapped against the floor and echoed off the walls of the hallway. Bursting into the crowded lobby, Rory and candy slid to a stop.

There were shocked looks as Rory stood there in his gray boxer shorts and Candy in her yellow brassiere and panties. Rory held the gun under his left armpit.

Laughing and wolf whistles filled the air as the two threaded their way through the crowd towards the front doors. A woman screamed when she spotted the barrel of Rory's gun and the crowd panicked. People began scattering to all sides of the lobby.

Rory and Candy ducked out the glass front doors of the hotel. Rory's Jaguar XK R-S was parked around the side to the right. Rory looked back.

Several men burst into the lobby inside the hotel, raising their weapons.

Rory pulled Candy hard to the right.

Crack! Crack! Crack!

The glass front doors of the hotel shattered and blew out, sending sharp shards of glass flying after the fleeing couple.

Rory pulled Candy around the corner of the building.

Candy stumbled and fell, crying out.

Rory pulled her to her feet and they began running across the pavement.

Candy tried to look back and nearly stumbled again.

"Just keep running!" Rory yelled.

Candy complied, putting on a burst of speed.

Rory dug into the front of his shorts, searching for the car keys. Pulling them out, he aimed it at the Jaguar and unlocked the doors.

Candy ran hard around to the passenger's side and jumped in, pulling the door shut hard.

Rory jumped into the driver side. He placed the gun in his lap, pulled the door shut and started the vehicle. Putting the car in reverse, he floored the gas pedal. The tires squealed and smoked as the Jaguar shot backward. Rory hit the brakes, steered hard to the left. The Jaguar slid backwards in a sliding curve. Rory put the car into drive and stepped on it again. More squealing and smoke rose from the tires. Finally gaining traction, Rory steered hard left around a line of parked cars.

Crack! Crack! Crack! Crack! Crack!

The windshields, back windows and side windows of numerous cars were blown out as the shooters tried to get a bead on the fleeing Jaguar.

Candy screamed and put her hands over her head.

Crack! Crack! Crack!

The Jaguar roared across the parking lot towards the back entrance. Reaching the back roadway, Rory steered hard to the right and accelerated. The Jaguar's tires squealed as it shot away from the pursuing gunmen.

"Are you okay? You're not hit?" Rory asked as he glanced over at Candy.

Candy shook her head no as she crossed her arms over her chest. "I'm okay," she said in a small voice.

Rory banged the steering wheel with his right fist and cursed, "We left the thumb drive—"

"No, I picked it up just before we started running," Candy said. She turned a little and dug into her left brassiere cup, pulling out the tampon shaped USB drive.

"Good going," Rory said with a nod. He placed his 9mm handgun standing up in the cup holder beside him and looked into the rear-view mirror, "How in the world were they able to find us so fast? Doesn't make any sense."

Candy sat silently in the passenger seat.

After a moment, Rory looked over at Candy, "You didn't call out—?"

"I had to tell my sister about Yim," Candy said in defensive anger. "I *had* to."

Rory banged the steering wheel hard again and he nearly spun out. Getting it back under control, Rory floored the Jaguar and the engine growled as they sped into the night.

Chapter 21

THE JAGUAR WAS PASSING Francis-Stevenson School on the left when Rory applied the brakes. They skidded to a stop.

"What's wrong?" Candy asked with fear in her voice. She turned her seat to look at the road behind them.

Rory didn't answer as he put the Jaguar in reverse and the tires squealed. A quick left on the steering wheel and the Jaguar came to a sliding stop beside the left curb. Rory jumped out and ran to a yellow bin marked 'Clothes and Shoes'. He lifted open the lid and strained to slip his arm down into the opening. After some effort, he pulled out a black garbage bag. He ran back to the open car door, tossed the garbage bag over to Candy and got back in. He put the car in gear and the tires screeched as they pulled away from the curb.

"What's this?" Candy asked she looked down at the garbage bag in her lap.

"Hopefully something to cover us," Rory said as he followed the curving road around to the left. "That was a donation bin. See what's inside."

Candy began untying the black garbage bag.

Rory was passing a small park and a soccer field on the right. Both were empty of people. He slowed the Jaguar and turned right. Bumping across the sidewalk, he crossed a patch of grass and drove across the soccer field, where he nosed the car into some trees. He turned the headlights off but turned on the interior lights, "Hopefully, it's not all women's clothing."

"No, it's not," Candy said she pulled clothing from the bag. "But it is old." She had a few dresses in her hand, choosing one with a blue pattern that she placed on the console. She then pulled out a brown paisley shirt that she passed over to Rory. Then she pulled out a pair of brown corduroy, bell bottom pants that she passed over as well, "You'd be in style if we were in the 60s."

"You're right. I'll stick out like a sore thumb but it's better than just the underwear."

Candy looked into the bag, "That's it. No shoes."

"It's still better than nothing," Rory said as he pushed a button to move his seat back to get the pants on. He realized his wallet was still in his shorts and he discretely retrieved it, propping it in the second cup holder.

Candy slipped the blue dress over her head, "Normally I wouldn't wear this if I were 90."

"But you will when you're half-naked, right?" Rory said as he pulled the corduroy bell bottoms on.

"Only because someone is shooting at us," Candy said/ She lifted her butt off the seat and slid the dress down to cover herself. She then slipped the other two dresses back inside the garbage bag and tossed it over into the backseat.

Rory finished buttoning up the shirt and pushed it inside the corduroy jeans before he spoke, "You have to be more careful or we're going to get killed–"

"I *had* to tell my sister and I'm not apologizing for it," Candy insisted. She crossed her arms defiantly across her chest. "She *had* to know about Yim."

Rory bit his lip, trying hard not to throw her out of the car.

"This is *not* about us. This is about the President of the United States being spied on," Candy stated. "By the damn Chinese!"

After a moment of looking out the side window he turned to Candy, "So, what did she say when you told her?"

Candy had a hard set to her mouth, "She was shocked. I could tell. When I told her about Yim and exactly what he was doing, she didn't say anything for the longest time."

Rory pursed his lips as he looked out into the darkness, "So...what did she want you to do–"

"She wants me to try and meet with Lance Washburn again. But this time over at Theodore Roosevelt Island," she explained. "There's a footbridge across the Potomac on the western side I can take–"

"It's too dangerous–"

"I'm going," Candy said firmly. She flipped down the sun visor and checked her two-tone brown hair in the mirror. She flipped the visor back up, "My sister is talking to President Lane. While they work on the spying problem, Lance will be going with armed guards in a helicopter to the island. And if those Secret Service guys show up again they'll be arrested–"

"Did you tell her they were Secret Service?"

Candy shook her head no, "I just told her men were trying to kill me again and–"

"Did she ask how you got to Washington, DC?"

"No." Candy looked at Rory, determination on her face, "Now, can you take me over there? Or do I have to find a cab?"

"Where is a helicopter going to land over on that island–?"

"They know what they're doing," Candy said in a harsh, loud voice. She gestured angrily with her hands, "Stop with all the stupid questions. These are professionals."

Rory looked at her with his jaw set hard.

"You won't have to worry about taking care of me anymore," Candy said with a flip of her hair, "*My sister* will take care of me from now on."

After a few moments, Rory started the Jaguar and turned the headlights on. Flooring the gas pedal, Rory drove backwards quickly out of the trees, ripping up grass and dirt. He cranked the wheel hard to the left, ripping up a half moon in the grass of the soccer field. He stopped abruptly, the car sliding back briefly, then drove the pedal to the floor as the Jaguar ripped across the soccer field and bounced at an angle over the sidewalk and down the street.

Chapter 22

RORY SLOWED DOWN and exited the George Washington Memorial Parkway. The sharp right turn put them into the northern end of the parking lot leading to the Mount Vernon Trail. The parking lot was dark and empty.

"You can let me out here," Candy said.

"I can take you right down to the footbridge–"

"No," Candy insisted. "Just let me off here–"

"This thing doesn't make any sense–"

Candy opened her door as Rory was driving.

Rory hit the brakes hard and slid to a stop on the asphalt.

Candy started to get out her partially opened door, then hesitated. Instead of getting out, she leaned back across the console and gave Rory a kiss on his cheek. "Thank you for everything," she said. Then she turned in her seat and got out of the Jaguar, closing the door. Candy then began walking quickly towards the far end of the parking lot and the entrance to the footbridge.

The sun was just starting to peek over the horizon as Rory watched her walking away. He glanced to the left and looked at the darkness of the island across the river. He looked in the air over the island. He didn't see any helicopter. He didn't like this. But what could he do? He watched Candy walk away into the darkness. He could hear the sounds of cars whizzing by to the right on the highway. The only other sound was the purr of the Jaguar. Rory made a decision. He gunned the Jaguar and made a tight turn, heading back for the Parkway.

PIECES OF GRAVEL CRUNCHED underfoot as Candy Jossel walked along the parking lot, a sign pointing her towards the footbridge. A heavy, early morning mist hung over the river to her left, drifting out from the forested island on the other side of the Potomac. She turned when she heard the engine of Rory's Jaguar roar. But the headlights didn't head towards her as she secretly hoped. Instead, the headlights turned and the Jaguar accelerated away, heading back to the highway. The sound of the car faded away and the sudden silence made her feel very uneasy. She stood there for a moment, listening and looking around. Then she started walking towards the footbridge again. Passing a large tree at the far end of the parking lot, Candy began walking along a short, dirt trail. The smell of car exhaust from the nearby highway mixed with the scent of the earth and grass.

A few minutes later, Candy set foot on the up-slope of the footbridge. She stopped and nervously licked her lips. Traces of the low mist curled around her shoes as she listened intently. All she could hear was the noisy morning traffic going by on the Parkway behind her. She glanced back.

The tops of vehicles, zipping along the highway, appeared just beyond the low stone wall.

Candy looked across the river at the trees and the shoreline. There was no sign of any other human being. Everything was quiet. Taking a deep breath, Candy began walking up the footbridge over the Potomac.

The busy sounds of the traffic slowly receded behind her, replaced by the early morning twitter of birds and the soft sound of the water flowing below the footbridge.

If it wasn't for the circumstances, this would be a peaceful morning walk for Candy. Instead, her nerves were on edge. It wasn't long before she was at the apex of the curved footbridge. Still no one else in sight. She looked to the left, at the distant sound of a motorboat. It was somewhere upstream, hidden in the low mist. Candy watched warily in that direction as she walked. She looked downstream and something in the early morning light caught her eye along the shoreline to the right. She stopped.

Three men in suits were running through the trees along the riverbank.

Candy squinted, wondering.

The men were heading for the end of the footbridge behind her.

Her body started shaking. She turned and began walking quickly now, heading for Roosevelt Island across the footbridge. She stopped dead in her tracks when she saw movement up ahead.

Two men in suits were running towards the end of the footbridge on the far side of the Potomac.

Candy started to run towards them, her bare feet slapping on the bridge. Suddenly she realized neither one was Lance. Candy stopped and looked back.

The three men had reached the end of the footbridge and were running towards her. Lance wasn't in that group either.

Candy put her hands on her head as she looked back and forth between the men on either side, rapidly approaching her. She was trapped.

"Jump!"

The voice barely registered with Candy.

"Candy, jump," the voice yelled again.

It sounded somewhere below the footbridge. Candy hesitated, then stepped to the upstream side of the footbridge and looked over the edge of the railing. Below her, in the mist, was a figure with his hands cupped to his mouth.

"Jump!"

It was Rory. In a boat. Candy looked to both ends of the footbridge again. The men were drawing closer.

Candy cupped her hands to her mouth, "My sister probably sent them."

"Just jump before it's too late," Rory yelled again.

Candy looked to each side of the footbridge again and then back at Rory, shaking her head no. She stepped away from the railing and turned to her right. Her eyes went wide.

Leading the charge from the island side was the man in the black pinstriped suit.

Her hands went to her throat. Her breath became ragged.

"Candy," Rory yelled from below again.

Stepping over to the railing again, Candy looked down at the boat.

Rory waved for her to jump.

Candy's hands gripped the edge of the railing tightly, "It's...so far...."

"Hurry. You can do it." Rory waved his arms for her to jump.

Her hands shook as Candy took a deep breath and then threw a leg over the railing. Straddling the railing, she took another deep breath before she pulled the other leg over and stood on the narrow ledge on the other side. Her whole body shook as she slowly turned her body and looked down at the water. She held onto the railing tightly behind her. Candy looked to each end of the footbridge again.

The men were approaching fast.

Decision time.

"C'mon Candy, you can do it," Rory yelled again.

Candy looked back to the water, then closed her eyes, pinched her nose and jumped. Candy's blue dress shot into the air over her head like an inside-out umbrella. She sliced into the brackish water and disappeared. Coming up a moment later, she gasped for air, frantically treading water.

Rory leaned over, grabbed the back of her dress with his left hand and pulled her towards the side of the boat. Pinning her body against the side, he reached behind with his right hand and twisted the throttle on the outboard motor. The outboard rumbled and Rory steered the boat to place it under the footbridge as he dragged Candy through the water.

Angry shouts sounded from above.

A gunshot rang out. Crack!

A bullet splashed into the water.

Candy yelped and flinched. The black water boiled around her as she was dragged.

Once under the footbridge, Rory aimed the boat through the mist towards Roosevelt Island. He dragged Candy through the brackish water until he reached the first big concrete pylon.

Then Rory idled the outboard engine and used both hands to pull Candy into the boat.

Candy flopped on her face like a wet mackerel, the water draining from the wet cloth of her dress.

Crack! Crack!

Bullets splashed into the water a couple of feet away from the boat.

Candy yelped in fear and went into a fetal position, hands over her head.

Rory twisted the throttle and accelerated, staying beneath the footbridge.

Crack! Crack! Crack! Crack! Crack! Crack! Crack! Crack!

Bullets began peppering the water on both sides from above. Shot after shot rang out as the men tried to kill them from above.

Rory stayed under cover of the footbridge, ignoring the small explosions of bullets penetrating the water on either side as he concentrated on staying dead center.

Crack! Crack! Crack!

Once he was close to the island, Rory veered north into the mist and applied full power as he headed upstream.

Crack! Crack! Crack! Crack! Crack!

Bullets splashed in the water beside and behind the boat.

Rory zigzagged to spoil their aim as he and Candy made their escape, leaving the footbridge behind.

Chapter 23

RORY STEERED THE MOTORBOAT upstream through the early morning mist. The gunshots behind them had finally stopped. The only sound was the outboard motor pushing the river aside

Candy still lay on the bottom of the boat in a fetal position, with her hands covering her head.

"Are you okay?" Rory asked. He reached down in worry and touched her bare foot.

Candy turned over cautiously, pushing the wet strands of hair off her face, "Yeah, I think so."

Satisfied, Rory looked into the mist again, following the shoreline of the river as it bent to the east. He watched for the docks of the small marina where he had stolen the boat.

Shifting around on the floor of the boat, Candy sat up on her hip. Her wet dress clung to her body, "I guess - I guess I almost got us killed again. But I had to tell my sister...."

Rory started to say something, then held it back. He pressed his lips together to keep the words from spilling out as he shook his head.

Candy opened her mouth to say something but seemed to think better of it. She used both hands to push the wet hair away from her forehead. Pulling her knees up, she wrapped her arms tightly around them as she sat staring ahead into the mist.

Rory spotted the dock through the mist and angled the boat sharply towards it. He stopped beside the weather-beaten wood and cut off the outboard, "We need to hurry and get to my Jaguar. We have to assume they'll come looking for us. And there are only a few marinas for them to check out."

Candy nodded and got to her feet. Her wet feet slipped as she tried to leap onto the dock.

Rory caught her waist and steadied her.

Within moments, they were in the Jaguar and Rory was steering out of the parking lot. They shot through a round intersection and headed north. Within minutes they were into the early morning traffic on the Whitehurst Freeway. Rory sped several miles along the highway then accelerated and cut off a car as he took an exit at the last minute. Rory made a number of quick turns until he was sure they were safe...for now.

RORY CONTINUED TO DRIVE around city blocks, thinking in the silence of the car. Candy had said little since they had run from the boat to the Jaguar back at the Marina. She had retrieved a brown print dress from the garbage bag she had thrown in the back seat earlier and discarded the soaking wet one. That was it. Rory made a right turn and after a few moments he pulled to the curb and parked.

Candy didn't say anything for a moment until she realized where they were. She looked at Rory with some anxiety on her face, "We're in front of the Shops at National Place. It's only a couple of blocks away from the White House. You said you didn't want me to go there earlier because I might be recognized."

Rory nodded, "Hide in plain sight I always say. And we don't have much choice right now." Rory picked up his wallet from the cup holder where he had left it, "You to stay in the car while I get us a change of clothes. I've spent enough time in the 60s"

Candy thought about it for a moment and then shook her head, "No. I'll go with you." She flipped down the vanity mirror and worked to wipe away the running mascara from under her eyes,

"Not a good idea. Remember all those newspapers with your picture under the main headline?" Rory countered.

"I highly doubt anyone's going to recognize me like this," Candy said.

Rory shook his head no, "It's too dangerous."

"And if someone comes along out here while you're in there?" She shook her head, "No. I'd rather stay with you."

Rory raised an eyebrow, "Yet back at the bridge–"

But Candy wasn't listening; she was already getting out of the car.

Rory blew out a frustrated breath and then stepped out of the car himself.

"Have you got a credit card?" Candy asked as Rory stepped around the front of the car to join her on the sidewalk.

"They could be watching my account. Keep in mind they are Secret Service," Rory reminded her. "Better if we use cash. I should have enough."

Candy nodded in agreement and they headed for the main doors of the three-level, indoor shopping mall. Her underwear was still very damp and the dress clung to her in spots. Her hair was also wet and straight, attracting a lot of strange looks as they entered. Their bare feet also added to the stares. After visits to a couple of department stores, a few beauty salons and several pharmacies, Rory led Candy to a women's washroom on the third level and she went inside.

Rory leaned over the railing and watched the crowds far below, mulling over what had happened. Candy's dedication to her sister was uncontrollable and could easily get both of them killed. But what could he do? Would she listen to reason if he addressed it? He highly doubted it. Then he thought about the men chasing them. Back in Louisville, Candy said she saw the men talking to the police inside the crime tape at the murder scene. And the police had also been used to block off the front and back doors of the office building when they went inside after Candy. They obviously had deep influences back in Kentucky. Did they have the same influence here? He hadn't seen any evidence of the police being part of the chase back at the hotel. And they weren't at the exits when they ran. He wondered if that meant he could find a sympathetic ear within the authorities here. If he found enough evidence to support Candy's innocence, would they listen?

Rory's thoughts were interrupted when he heard heels clicking behind him. Rory turned around and saw a woman he really didn't recognize walking out of the washroom. Candy's hazel eyes were now a bright blue, thanks to contact lenses. Her multitone brown hair was now platinum blond and extended past her shoulders, thanks to hair dye and hair extensions. Round sunglasses, false eyelashes, and a dark spray-on tan completed the amazing transformation. She now wore a red blouse, tight blue jeans, and 5-inch high heel sandals. Candy now stood six feet tall, now only a couple of inches below that of Rory's height.

"So that's why you bought all that stuff," Rory said in amazement as Candy walked towards him.

"Yes. And I can tell you like a certain part of my disguise better than the rest, Mr. Steele."

Rory looked up from her heavily padded bra and smiled, "Just wanted to make sure everything looks natural."

"Uh huh."

"Well, I'm sure people won't recognize you now," assured Rory as he glanced back down at her chest.

Candy nodded, "And if all the cops are like you, they won't even notice my face."

Rory shrugged, "Women wouldn't wear things like that if you didn't want us to look. I just don't want to disappoint you."

"Uh huh."

"Let's go get something to eat."

AN HOUR LATER, RORY sat at a table inside a small pizzeria just outside the mall. An empty pizza box sat in front of him as he waited for Candy to come out of the washroom. He continually monitored the sidewalk outside, watching for any signs of trouble. As he sipped on his coke, his mind continually ran through everything that had happened to this point. The whole thing was very troublesome. Some things made sense. And some didn't. The men chasing them were definitely trying to kill Candy, even if they couldn't positively retrieve the backup. They were afraid she knew something or she had seen something. What could it be? The Chinese spying on the United States? That was a possibility. But the fact that Candy had to search through Yim's computer to discover it, meant there was more. It must have been something easy to see when she went in and made that back up at campaign headquarters back in Louisville, Kentucky. They had missed it somehow when Candy had looked though Yim's computer back at his house. Rory wondered if they should just go back there and steal the computer this time. His thoughts were interrupted when he saw something that changed everything.

CANDY STEPPED OUT OF the washroom, walked across the pizzeria and sat down across from Rory. She took a deep breath and ran her fingers through the blonde hair on her shoulder in a nervous gesture, "So...what do we do now?"

Rory didn't answer her. He simply stared off to the left.

Candy looked down at her lap for a moment. Then she looked up at Rory and spoke in a quiet voice, "I know you have reason to be angry with me, Rory. But you have to understand the situation. When my mother and my sisters died...."

Rory continued staring to his left without a word.

Candy said a few more words but stopped when she realized Rory wasn't listing to her. But it wasn't because he was angry. Something was bothering him. She followed his intense gaze. He was looking directly at the large television mounted high on the wall behind the service counter. Black letters inside a red ribbon of color ran across the bottom of the screen and announced 'Breaking News.' Candy finally tuned in to what the somber news anchor on the screen was saying.

"As we said in the last hour, this is the second major news story that has marred the Presidential win of Connor Harrison

Lane. The home of Lee Park Yim, in the Woodley Park area here in Washington DC, burned to the ground last night. Police sources tell CNN that a body, believed to be that of Yim, was found in an upstairs study by firefighters once they were finally able to enter the building. Yim was the IT Manager for Lane's political staff and was working at Lane's campaign headquarters down in Louisville, Kentucky. He, along with other permanent members of Lane's team, moved everything here to Washington, DC after Lane won the Presidency. Those same sources tell us that an overturned propane space heater in the study is believed to be the cause of the fire. One reason not known was why Yim would have been using a space heater in the house last night. It has been very warm in the area over the last few weeks...."

Candy bent over the table and whispered to Rory, "Did you see a space heater in the study? I didn't see one."

Rory shook his head solemnly no.

"Those men who kidnapped us must have killed Yim and destroyed all the evidence," Candy whispered in frustration.

"Maybe not," Rory replied as he watched the newscast.

Candy looked at Rory, "What do you mean?"

Rory chewed on his lip for a moment and then spoke in a low voice, "Killing Yim would make sense. Maybe the people Yim was working for are trying to cover their tracks. Or maybe they're sending a message to others in their organization, mess up and you die. But...destroying the computer would make no sense. At least not right away. All the back doors they have in place could still provide useful information. Setting up another first would–"

"But I'm sure my sister will have alerted everyone by now," Candy insisted, "and all the back doors will be cleaned up."

"True," Rory said as he stared at the television. "But it goes beyond that. We had to leave quickly. We didn't have a list of the people they were spying on to give your sister, did we?"

Candy shook her head no.

"I remember seeing dozens and dozens of icons. It could be one hundred Senators in the government...or it could be a combination of senators, state governors, ambassadors or any other number of political figures they were spying on. Right now, we have no idea of who or how many," Rory reasoned.

"And they can't interrogate Yim because he's dead," Candy said she followed his line of reasoning. "So there's no telling how long it will take *or* if everyone gets alerted–"

"It goes far beyond that," Rory said.

"What do you mean?"

"How did Yim set up the back doors, in all of those computers, in the first place?"

Candy gave it some thought, "Maybe he infected their computers with a remote access Trojan virus to set it up."

Rory nodded slightly in agreement, "Maybe. But that works best when you are casting a wide net to randomly infect a large number of computers. Maybe you send out 10 million e-mails and 10% of the people are foolish enough to open the attached zip file to get infected. But I highly doubt they would do it randomly in this case. They had specific targets in mind. And they're not all necessarily living in one place, like here in Washington. If you did use email, what happens if these specific targets never open up the zip file attached to the e-mails you send? What if they never download a file from the Internet or use a web application or fall for any other of the methods normally used to infect computers?" He looked directly at Candy and answered the questions himself, "Then you have to do it *directly*." When Candy nodded her head slightly in solemn agreement, he added another question, "Do you really think Yim traveled over all 52 states to infect the computers on his own?"

Candy's eyes went wide when she began to understand Rory's logic, "Do you think the Chinese had spies breaking into all those places?"

"It's a possibility but I highly doubt it," Rory said skeptically. "The risks are high that someone would get caught if they did it that way. It would make more sense to infiltrate computer companies or to own them outright. You said ZongChi Technologies Limited was a Chinese manufacturing and technology company?"

Candy nodded yes, "They deal in software and hardware."

"Then they could also supply software or hardware with built-in back doors to any company they owned, infiltrated or simply sold to," Rory reasoned. "We're talking about a massive conspiracy to infect computers across America, if not further."

Candy shook her head in bewilderment, "What are we going to do? How do we stop them?"

Chapter 24

RORY LED CANDY out of the pizzeria and back into the mall. The place was busy, with people moving, talking, eating and shopping. They were totally oblivious to what Rory and Candy had uncovered.

"What are we doing back in here?" Candy asked. "I thought we got everything we needed before? Shouldn't we be finding some way to stop ZongChi Technologies from spying on the United States?"

"I just need one more thing. Then we can start to fight back," Rory said. He browsed the mall listing at the entrance for what he needed. "There we go. It looks like it's....that way." Rory led a fidgety Candy along the mall avenue among the crowds until he found the mobile phone store. Ten minutes later he and Candy left the store with a couple of prepaid cell phones he had paid cash for. They walked back out the front entrance and headed eastward, where they crossed 14th Street NW and sat on a small bench in Franklin Park. Rory set one of the cell phones to speaker so Candy could hear the call. Then he dialed a phone number as Candy fidgeted beside him. Rory placed his hand on her bouncing left knee, "Patience, grasshopper."

Candy gave him an embarrassed smile but he only succeeded in stopping her knee from bouncing for about 12 seconds.

"Hello," answered a deep voice on the other end of the call.

"Uncle Murdock, it's Rory."

"Rory! We've been worried about you. We haven't heard from you for several days. Doc Spencer down in Louisville says you never showed up."

"I was there but got dragged into another case," Rory said. "I can't say much right now, the Secret Service might be listening in."

There was a slight pause on the other end. "What do you need?" It was more a statement than a question.

"I'm in Washington, DC. I need you to have Skye fly here and buy me a new car. Mine may be bugged. And I don't want to use my credit cards, in case they can trace me that way. There are other things that will need doing but I'll let her know that when I see her."

"I take it face to face communications are safer than digital in this matter?"

"Correct."

There was another brief pause. "Okay. She'll be taking off in 30 minutes. It's an hour and 15 minutes flight time on the Learjet. Contact her when you're ready."

"Thank you," Rory said. Then he added, "Uncle Murdock, can you ask Skye to keep a low profile when she gets here?"

"Of course. I'll make it a point to ask her that."

There was a brief moment of silence and then Rory and Candy heard Murdock MacLeod begin a low, deep laugh.

Candy looked at Rory, wondering what was going on.

A low, melodious voice sounded in the background on the other end of the line, "Is that my big brother asking me to keep a low profile again?"

Rory laughed as he hung up.

SKYE STEELE STEPPED off the Learjet 85 at Washington Dulles International Airport carrying a large, black duffel bag. At 6'-2" inches tall, with green, sparkling eyes, fiery red hair that flowed off her shoulders and an Amazon-like body, Skye was anything but low profile. The limousine driver, waiting beside his car, became flustered as this tall beauty approached in a sleek, cat-like walk. She stopped by the back door and raised an eyebrow.

"Oh right," muttered the limo driver as he fumbled to open the door for his client.

Skye smiled at her effect on the man. Her black leather jacket and pants whispered as she threw the large, black duffel bag onto the back seat, then got into the back of the limo.

The limo driver let his eyes drift down her body and he swallowed.

"The nearest Jaguar dealership please," Skye said in a low, melodious voice. She cocked her head after a moment.

"Oh...right...right," muttered the limo driver as he realized she was looking at him with an amused smile. "Uh, right away," he said as he closed the door and scooted into the driver's side. Skye ignored his frequent glances in the rearview mirror as they moved through the traffic.

An hour later, Skye had just finished her purchase of the Jaguar when her cell phone rang. She answered it as the sales manager, the new car salesman and four other men stood around the showroom checking her out from all sides.

"Hello?"

"Ciamar a tha sibh?" Rory asked on the other end of the call.

"Tha gu math, tapadh leibh," Skye said.

"A bheil an t-acras ort?" Rory asked her.

"Ceart gu leòr. Tha an t-acras orm," Skye said.

Rory spoke slowly and clearly, "Seachd..seachd. Trì...ochd."

Skye nodded, "Mar sin leibh an dràsda." She closed the cell phone and winked at the sales manager, "Tapadh leat." She turned and left the men behind in total confusion.

CANDY WAS TOTALLY CONFUSED as she stood beside Rory under a tree in Franklin Park. "What was all that? I didn't understand a word you said. Who were you talking to? *What* were you talking?"

Rory smiled, "I was using Scottish Gaelic in case anyone was listening. I gave the coordinates to where we will meet the person I was talking to."

Candy looked around her in alarm, "Do you really think...?"

Rory shrugged, "It *is* the Secret Service and I don't want to take any chances."

"Is that why we took the car several blocks away and walked back here?"

Rory nodded as he placed the cell phone on the ground, lifted a foot and smashed it under his heel. He picked up the remnants and deposited them in a trash bin, "Now, let's go across the street." He pointed to a restaurant and began walking.

"What are we going to do?" Candy asked she hustled to keep up with him.

"Have a coffee and wait," Rory said. He kept a watchful eye on individuals around them as they headed for the street.

"I don't understand why we aren't going after ZongChi Technologies," Candy said in frustration.

"We will," said Rory. They stepped off the grass and onto the sidewalk. Rory didn't see any suspicious vehicles parked nearby. But that didn't mean they could let their guard down. Doing that before had nearly cost them their lives. "Right now we have to wait for someone," Rory added as he took Candy's hand and started across the street.

"Who?"

"You'll see. Patience little grasshopper," Rory answered.

"I wish you would stop calling me that," Candy grumbled. "I don't even know what that means."

Rory laughed, "I guess I just watch too many old television programs."

RORY AND CANDY WERE finishing their Reuben sandwiches on the outside patio of the restaurant and lounge when a low engine growl caught their attention. An F-Type V8 S silver Jaguar convertible pulled to a quick stop in the parking space just outside the front entrance.

The driver got out and strode around the front of the sleek automobile. The attention of everyone on the patio became focused on the tall, shapely redhead, dressed in black leather, as she approached. She took off her sunglasses and put them in the top pocket of her leather jacket as she strode like a panther across the wide sidewalk.

Rory rose from his chair and stepped out to greet the beautiful woman. They kissed each other on the cheek and embraced for a moment. Then they turned to look at Candy who now rose from her chair. "Candy, this is my sister Skye."

Candy held out her hand and looked up into the sparkling green eyes of Skye Steele. She was mute and wide-eyed as Skye shook her hand.

"Why don't we sit down," Rory said. He called the waitress over as Candy and Skye sat by side-by-side across from Rory.

Skye ordered a western omelet, toast, and coffee. As the waitress left, she passed the car keys over to Rory, "What do you need me to do?"

Rory pulled a prepaid cell phone from the pocket of his jean jacket and passed it over to Skye, "I made some notes on here while we were waiting. It outlines basically what we've found and the situation that we're in right now."

Skye nodded and placed the cell phone in the side pocket of her leather jacket.

Rory glanced at the table of people next to them. They were engaged in their own conversation but Rory still leaned forward and spoke in a lower voice, "I need you to work on the ZongChi Technologies angle of this case. They've set up a computer network to spy on people across America—"

Candy's body tensed as she leaned forward, whispering urgently, "Shouldn't we be taking care of that ourselves. That's the most important thing—"

"More important than the fact you still have a murder charge hanging over your head?" Rory asked her.

Candy blinked and looked at Skye, "I...I didn't do it–"

Skye patted Candy's left forearm, "I know you didn't. If you had, you wouldn't be sitting here. My brother would have you in jail right now."

Candy didn't know what to say as she looked over at Rory.

"I understand your dedication to your sister, Candy," Rory said. "But those men are still trying to kill you. They haven't alerted the authorities that you're here in Washington DC, have they? There isn't a manhunt for you here. There is no newscast about it. They don't want *anybody* talking to you. They framed you for murder and we need to figure out why and prove your innocence. Right?"

After a moment, she relaxed a little and nodded.

"There are still a lot of things in this situation that don't make any sense. Believe me, we have a lot of things to do yet," Rory assured her. He turned his attention to Skye again, "ZongChi is headquartered in New York. I'm not sure what you can do, but we need to find some way to prove what they're doing."

Skye nodded, "I'll take the Learjet back home and take care of that. Uncle Murdock can give me the GPS coordinates for your car and I can take care of it before–"

Rory cautioned her, "I wouldn't go close to it. I'm sure they have the car bugged. They'll track you to the airport and maybe go after you before you can take off."

Skye pursed her lips, then nodded her head once in understanding. "But we could also use it as a decoy to give you some breathing room."

"I don't want you hurt..."

"And I don't want you hurt either," she said "But it's what we do, right? Protect people...and each other?"

Rory smiled and nodded. He looked to the curb, "So, what else did you bring me besides a cool car?"

"There is a black duffel bag in the trunk," Skye told him. You'll find a half-dozen prepaid credit cards in there, several small, prepaid, burner cell phones, and a Baby Eagle."

"A Baby Eagle? What in the world—" asked a confused Candy.

"It's a 9 mm handgun that my brother prefers," Skye said with a smile.

"Oh," said an embarrassed Candy, "I thought..."

Rory had to smile himself. Just then the waitress reappeared and set down a plate with the omelet, a small plate of toast, and a cup of coffee in front of Skye.

"This looks good," Skye said enthusiastically as she reached for some ketchup and poured a little beside the omelet.

"You enjoy yourself. We should get going. We have a lot to do," Rory said. He stood up and Candy and Skye did the same.

Skye shook Candy's hand as her brother was stepping around the table to her side, "I'm very glad to meet you. Don't worry, my brother will take good care of you."

"Thank you. He already has saved my life - more than once. Although he did have me running around in my underwear."

Skye's eyebrows went up, "So soon?"

"Don't start," Rory said as he stepped to his sister and hugged her, "Tha gaol agam ort."

"Tha gaol agam ort-fhèin," Skye replied.

"Let's get going, Ms. Jossel," said Rory. "We've got a lot to do." Candy nodded.

Rory led Candy away from Skye and headed for the Jaguar.

"Keep in mind it has a top speed of 186 miles per hour," shouted Skye. Then she smiled and said to herself, "Although I'm sure you would have found that out for yourself, big brother." She picked up a knife and fork and started into her omelet.

Chapter 25

RORY PRESSED DOWN on the accelerator and the V8 Supercharged engine purred as he pulled out into traffic, "This thing can go from 0 to 60 mph in 4.2 seconds if I remember correctly."

Candy protested as the acceleration pressed her back in her seat, "Please don't test your memory unless we absolutely have to. I'll puke everywhere."

"No problem," Rory said. "But my sister realized this is the type of car with the speed we would need if those guys come after us again."

"Uh huh," Candy answered skeptically. "This exact car is necessary."

"Well, at least this way we escape with class," Rory retorted.

"Okay, James Bond. If you say so. Now what?"

Rory became a little more serious as he turned right and accelerated again, "Actually, I never did ask you after that fiasco, where you went for a swim in the river. Do you still have the USB drive?"

Candy tapped her patted left breast with her right hand, "It got wet but the cap kept the water off the USB connector."

"That's not exactly where you're supposed to put a tampon you know."

"Very funny. Now please keep your eyes on the road."

"Then stop trying to distract me."

"It's not my fault men are easily distracted by big boobs," Candy remarked.

"And they are big," Rory said as he glanced over again.

"I'll let you sleep with them tonight," Candy said.

"Really?"

"Of course, I'll be in the other room while you do."

Rory had to laugh, "Touché." He turned the Jaguar left and accelerated. "We're going to have to figure out what's on that USB drive that's so important to them."

Candy had a confused look on her face for a moment. "But...we already know. The Chinese are spying on politicians–"

"There has to be more," Rory insisted. "Remember, you yourself said a backup is usually done to save important things like program data, documents or e-mails. Do you think you would have detected the back-doors by simply looking at the contents of the USB drive?"

Candy gave it some thought. Then she shook her head no. "It's possible...but I highly doubt it."

"Then there has to be something else," Rory concluded.

Candy nodded her head slowly, acknowledging the truth. There had to be something more on the USB drive.

Rory slowed the Jaguar, turned right and entered a curved parkway. It was the entrance to the elegant and historic Hay-Adams Hotel. The Italian Renaissance style building, constructed in 1928, was a popular destination for Hollywood celebrities, political elites, and anyone else wanting to experience a stay in luxury. But that wasn't Rory's purpose in bringing Candy here. Retrieving the black duffel bag from the trunk, he gave the keys to a young man and escorted Candy inside.

Candy's voice was a whispered, "Wow." She gawked at the amazing interior of the hotel. Sparkling chandeliers, carved plaster ceilings, rich wood-paneled walls, walnut wainscot and quality, upholstered furniture left a lasting impression on any visitor. "Why here?" she asked.

"Just thought it would be a good idea," Rory said as she stepped up to the reception desk. Using one of the prepaid credit cards Skye had given him, Rory set them up in a two-bedroom penthouse suite.

The elevator took them up to their room on the top floor. Candy's eyes shot wide open in amazement again as they stepped inside the room to see more intricately carved plaster ceilings, wood paneling, tailored upholstery and a beautiful ornamental fireplace. Rory set his duffel bag down as Candy took a look in one of the two bathrooms. "It's all marble and brass in here," she yelled out to Rory.

Rory pulled his weapon out of the duffel bag as Candy wandered over to the window where she threw open the curtains.

"It's the White House," she exclaimed as she looked out. "I can see the White House, Rory."

"I know," Rory said as he donned the shoulder holster for the weapon. "I thought it would be good if you could see where you will be once we get this thing solved. You and your sister–"

Rory was cut off as Candy rushed across the room and threw her arms around him, hugging him tightly, "Thank you, Rory, for helping me. I know I've put us in danger–"

"You're welcome. Now. why don't we go downstairs and have a good solid meal before we start to figure this out."

"Okay. I'll just use the washroom," Candy said.

Rory placed the Baby Eagle in the shoulder holster under his jean jacket. He had to be ready for anything. He knew those men would not quit looking for them. It was possible they could show up here at any time. It was also possible that Candy would do something to lead them here, to put them in danger again. He could never rule out that possibility, no matter what she said.

Rory took Candy down to the Lafayette Restaurant. It over-looked both the seven-acre Lafayette Square as well as the White House, which delighted Candy. Rory tried to keep the conversation light to get her relaxed. There was a lot more work and possibly danger ahead. Rory splurged to keep her spirits high. They dined on Maine Lobster Salad, pan-roasted sea bass and enjoyed a nice Pascal Jolivet Sancerre wine.

"DID YOU GET HER?" THE electronic voice asked from the other end of the cell phone call.

Torion Blacker sat behind the steering wheel of the black SUV and led out his breath, "No. She was on the footbridge and we had her trapped. She had nowhere to go. Until this Steele character showed up in a boat beneath the footbridge. She jumped in the Potomac...and they got away."

"You didn't think enough to have a boat of your own as insurance?" the electronic voice asked in anger. "You're not thinking."

Blacker bit his tongue and clenched his jaw, "You're right. Despite knowing Steele's background, I still underestimated him–"

The passenger door of the black SUV opened and a huge, muscular man with a blond crew cut slid inside and sat down. "I'm here," he stated in a low base voice.

"Good. Since you need a new partner Blacker, I've sent you the Dane," stated the electronic voice.

Blacker nodded a greeting in recognition and received one in return, "We've worked together before."

"The Dane will take care of Steele. You just need to find him and the little–"

"We know where he went–"

"Don't interrupt me again. Wait until I'm finished speaking, do you understand?" the voice said in a firm, icy tone.

"Got it." Blacker looked to his right and the Dane smiled.

There was a brief silence on the other end of the phone. "Now. Where did they go?"

"We tracked his Jaguar to Dulles Airport," Blacker explained. "It's still in the parking lot. We scoured the terminal but couldn't find him or the woman. We also couldn't find any indication he took ground transportation *back* into the city. But our sources did inform us Steele's company Learjet flew out of JFK to Dulles and then returned to New York not long ago."

There was a period of silence on the other end of the phone again. "It looks like Steele figures he will just surround her with the home team and keep her safe."

Blacker agreed, "That's what it looks like."

"Do you think she still has the backup?"

"Unless she lost it, when she jumped into the river, we have to presume she still has it."

"You're right. Get that backup this time. And kill Steele and the woman and whoever else gets in the way. Don't make me repeat myself."

Torion Blacker looked over at his new partner. The Dane always had a smile and a glint in his ice-blue eyes when killing was involved.

Chapter 26

BACK IN THE ROOM at the Hay-Adams hotel, after both Rory and Candy had a nice, hot shower, it was time to go to work. Rory had paid the concierge a handsome amount of money to get them a laptop. He placed it on the small work desk in the living room of the suite and pressed the start button. Then he went over and poured a couple of cups of coffee as Candy discreetly pulled the USB flash drive from her padded brassiere.

Candy sat in the chair in front of the laptop and plugged the flash drive into one of the side USB ports. She opened up the USB drive and began to sort through the contents.

Rory walked over holding two mugs of coffee and set one down to the right of the laptop for Candy. He dragged a chair over to Candy's left where he sat sipping from his own mug. He watched as folders and files zipped past on the screen as Candy scrolled through them. "Wow, there are a lot of files on that flash drive," he remarked.

"Uh huh, it's a 64-GB flash drive," Candy said.

"You're kidding. I didn't think they made them that big."

"They just started. And no wisecracks about the size of tampons I use."

"You do realize you just used tampon and crack in the same sentence?"

Candy snorted a short laugh, "You're such a big kid, Steele."

"A big lovable kid though, right?"

Candy nodded her head several times as she continued looking through the contents of the drive. "Off the top of my head, the most important things on here are the demographic data files I mentioned before." She made circles with the mouse pointer around three folders.

"You really think this is important stuff, don't you?"

Candy nodded her head vigorously, "Definitely. Remember how the opposition was using those celebrities when the campaign run first started? Those two movie stars...?"

"Vaguely," Rory admitted. "I'm a Canadian with dual citizenship but I don't pay a lot of attention to politics on either side of the border. Just enough to know we're usually getting screwed."

"Very funny, Steele," Candy said. "Although a little true," she added with a nod of her head. "Anyway, we were able to figure out which celebrities we could use on our side that would appeal to each specific segment of the base that we needed for votes. It's all about data mining. We had analysts and data crunchers figuring out which celebrities and fund raising dinners to match and where to hold them. We figured out how to best use everything from supermarket promotions to which senior homes to have Lane or his running mate visit. We had detailed information on swing state voters and how to reach them effectively...."

"I can tell you're very enthusiastic about it."

Candy nodded her head, her tone proud, "It was my sister's brain wave."

So all those analysts and data crunchers were at the campaign headquarters in Louisville?"

Candy shook her head no as she continued sifting through the files.

"No?" Rory's eyes narrowed, "Where were they working on all this data?"

Candy opened one of the demographic data folders as she gave the question some thought, "Actually... I'm not really sure...."

"You're not sure?"

Candy shook her head no as she glanced at Rory, "No, my sister took care of those things. We just talked about it a lot and looked over the data as we shaped the campaign as a team." She closed one folder and opened another. "It was an amazing opportunity. I'm just glad my sister let me help."

Rory tugged at his lower lip as he watched Candy work. Where were those analysts and data crunchers? And where was the data being crunched? Rory had an uneasy feeling about a possible answer. He would have to come back to that later. "Let's ignore those for now," Rory said. "What other things are there?"

Candy closed the folder, took a breath and let it out slowly while she gave his question some thought, "Well...there are political strategy files. The strategy team members would have brainstorming sessions and come up with ideas for Lane's consideration. But a lot of those files are based around the demographic data we just looked at. As I said, we could figure out ways to shape the campaign in minute details, even down to targeting specific neighborhoods where we could swing votes to our side."

Rory nodded his head in understanding, "Like finding out the neighborhood Eskimo doesn't like the yellow snow created by local drunks, so you promise to remove it, if he votes for you."

"Right. I'm not sure if you belong in a think-tank or a drunk-tank."

"Hey, I'm trying. What else?"

"Well...we have various sets of email files," Candy said as she clicked on one of the folders, revealing another set of folders. "These are separated into various categories such as strategy, fund raising, opposition strategy, opposition comments...."

"So Lane and his people would have ammunition to attack his opponents during media scrums or debates and speeches. That kind of thing?"

"Right," agreed Candy. "It's always good to know what your opponents are saying and how to counter them." She backed out of that folder and opened another, "This folder holds the name of the businesses and individuals who contribute to Lane's campaigns."

"You said contribute and campaigns... plural," Rory stated.

"Right," Candy confirmed. "As I understand it, most of these people have backed Lane since he started running for public office years ago. And they have continued to back him whenever he ran a campaign."

"Interesting. That sounds like a place to look closer," Rory said. "Was there ever any mention of improprieties regarding fund raising around Lane's presidential campaign?"

Candy gave it some thought and shook her head slowly no, "Nothing that I can remember hearing about."

"How about past campaigns?" Rory asked her.

Candy shook her head slowly no again. "I don't think there was ever anything like that. Lane has always run clean campaigns from what I know. And I know my sister would never get involved in anything like that," Candy stated emphatically.

"Okay, fair enough," Rory. said He gave it some thought for a moment and then said, "Well, we have to start looking closer some time to see what information or data those men want to stay hidden. Why don't we just start with these financial folders and see what pops up?"

Candy reluctantly agreed, "That's a tall order. There are so many files...that's going to take a long time...."

"You're right. But it's as good a place as any to start digging for an answer to why someone wants you killed. Just browse each file and look for something to jump out at you."

Candy nodded her head and started going through the files.

"I'll get us some more coffee. This could take all night," Rory said as he got up and stepped over to the coffee maker.

"Too bad. I guess that means you won't get a chance to sleep with my padded bra."

Rory turned around at the coffee pot, "Hey! You're just trying to get me to take over for you and work at a feverish pace to get it done fast."

"You saw right through me."

Rory poured coffee into each mug and then turned to look at Candy again, "Was that with you in....or out of the bra?"

HOURS LATER, RORY AND Candy had gone through the financial records and had moved on to a mountain of emails. Nothing had looked out of place beyond a few interesting tidbits. But there was nothing that would take down a President.

Chapter 27

THE EMPIRE STATE BUILDING, New York City

SKYE STEELE STOOD on a tiny outdoor ledge of the Empire State building, 103 stories above the brightly lit street below. Few people ever got higher than the 102nd-floor observation deck. Standing with her toes peeking over the edge, Skye felt the adrenaline rush through her body. Time to go to work. Time to fly. She slowly opened her arms and allowed the wind to buffet against the arm material of her wingsuit for a moment. Then she closed them. Skye slowly tipped forward and anticipated the event that was about to unfold, flying over Midtown Manhattan like a flying squirrel over a forest floor. Her feet left the ledge and she plummeted straight down, heading for the intersection of Fifth Avenue and West 34th. The wind whistled past her ears as she started counting backwards, using the forces of gravity to accelerate to the required airspeed. 5-4-3-2-1. Opening her arms and spreading her legs, the suit began to convert the airspeed into lift. She began to fly!

Banking her body slightly left, Skye began a slow spiral around the Empire State building, working her way slowly outward over the neighboring skyscrapers. At 1 AM in the morning, the buildings were lit up and the view that stretched to the horizon was breathtaking. Working her way up through the Empire State building and avoiding all the security guards had been a challenge. The exhilaration of flying over the Big Apple was the reward. Skye briefly allowed herself the opportunity to experience it. She felt the wind rushing past her body and she tasted the adrenaline coursing through her veins. A once-in-a-lifetime experience. She enjoyed it for a moment, then set her mind to her task. As she continued to spiral outward, Skye began to look over the various landmarks she had memorized from pictures. She moved outward over several blocks and saw the red dragon logo that marked the old, 40 story Renaissance-style building that housed ZongChi Technologies. She angled her wingsuit to take her to the right of the building and then began a slow spiral inward to take her to the roof. She had to time this perfectly. Having to add a parachute to go with the bag holding her climbing gear and rope would have made her too heavy. She watched intently for antennas, guide wires and anything else that could end her life in an instant. She was now moving ten feet above the roof and only several feet away from the building. She banked her body quickly left to take her over the roof, waited for a few seconds and then did a tight spiral to break her speed. Her wingsuit stalled 6 feet above the roof and Skye dropped. She flexed her knees and dropped into a crouch on the roof. Her right foot landed on something in the darkness under foot and pain shot up from her ankle as it twisted. Skye grit her teeth as she hobbled a few steps, fearful she wouldn't be able to continue. But the pain went away after a few moments and she began taking off the bag holding her climbing gear and rope. Then she removed the wingsuit and rolled it up tightly. Now dressed only in her black body suit, Skye carried everything over to the edge of the 40 story and peered over. There was a narrow ledge two stories below that was her target. She donned her chest harness and set to work. Anchoring a rope on the roof, she then threaded it through her ATC rappel device and tied an autoblock knot. She was ready. Stepping backward onto the edge of the roof, Skye took a deep, calming breath and then began to rappel down the side of the building. Within moments, she eased herself onto the 18-inch wide decorative ledge.

Peering through the glass into the darkened room, Skye Steele could see a steel desk, an oak credenza, and a few bookcases. She was outside someone's office. This was going well. She reached behind her and slipped a 2 foot long, medical suction cup bar harnessed on her back, around to the front. She placed the bar against the glass and pushed forward, activating the suction cups on each end. She then pulled out a glass cutter, coated with diamond chips, from a small carry bag at her waist. Skye had figured entry through the door on the roof would have triggered an alarm. She was gambling they wouldn't expect someone to break in through a fixed window. She bent down carefully as far as she could and placed the cutter about a foot above the sill, then scored the glass smoothly and evenly. She traced a square just big enough for her to slip through. Slipping the glass cutter back into the carry bag, she then tapped several times on the bar, breaking the glass along the score line in a perfect rectangle. Holding the bar and pushing the glass forward, she slipped through the opening and placed the glass gently on the floor. She slipped off the repelling gear and left it on the floor as well.

Skye Steele took out a small penlight and cast the narrow beam of light around the room along the baseboard. She found a wall socket that would work perfectly. Holding the penlight in her teeth, she knelt in front of it and pulled out a small plug-in antenna from the carry bag at her waist. Pushing it into the wall socket, Skye watched as a small, red LED light on the plug-in lit up. It started flashing and then turned a solid green. Next, she searched the walls around the room until she found the wall thermostat for temperature control. Moving over to it, she held the pen light in her teeth again while she pulled the square cover off, accessing the wires underneath. As she suspected, everything was tied into the Internet. She pulled out another small device and used clips to attach it to the wires. It blinked green for a few seconds and then turned to solid green. She pushed the device gently back to nestle in the wires and replaced the thermostat cover.

THE HIGHLANDER BUILDING, Manhattan, New York

Murdock MacLeod sat patiently in the offices of Highlander Investigative Services Inc, waiting for indication from the computer screen that Skye had placed the antenna. Murdock hadn't worked in the field for years, leaving that for the next generation in the form of his nephew and niece, Rory Mack Steele and Skye. But that didn't mean he didn't enjoy the thrills a case entailed. But at 82 years old, it entailed vicariously enjoying that feeling from long-distance, like tonight. Beside him sat another niece, Avis, the company's resident computer expert and researcher. She wasn't quite as patient, with her leg bouncing in anticipation of getting on with her job.

Avis shot forward in her chair when a red dot on the screen turned to a flashing green and then to a solid green. She began typing rapidly on the keyboard in front of her. "She's done it," she said enthusiastically.

Murdock pumped his fist.

"We're tied into their electrical and Internet system," Avis informed him.

"The antenna Wi-Fi signal looks strong," Murdock said with a nod.

"It is," Avis confirmed. "The electrical system is giving it a nice boost. Once I get things started, we won't need the one in the wall socket."

Murdock nodded and rose from his chair, "I'll get us each a tall mug from the new Keurig coffeemaker while we wait."

"Make mine one of those Doughnut Shop ones."

"Okay, I'm going to try the Breakfast Blend," Murdock said as he hustled away to the small office lunchroom.

ZONGCHI TECHNOLOGIES

Skye reached for a black, square wastebasket beside an oak desk and placed it in front of the plug-in antenna. It would look like she was trying to hide it. But someone stepping into the office would see it. Once they discovered the plug-in antenna, the odds were they wouldn't look for any other devices. Ignoring the unopened laptop on the desk, Skye walked over to the door and peeked out into the hallway. Everything was still and quiet. Slipping out into the hallway, Skye headed for a stairway at the end of the hall. Her feet didn't make a sound as she watched for lights under each doorway that she passed. Slipping out into the stairwell, she closed the door quietly behind her and peered over the railing. There wasn't a single sound below. Looking up, everything was quiet as well. She began climbing the stairs to the 40th floor. Reaching the top landing, she opened the door and discreetly checked the hallway. So far, so good. Moving quietly but quickly down the hallway, she passed a set of elevator doors on her left. Another 30 feet and she found the office of the CEO of ZongChi Technologies. There was no light under the door. She slowly turned the doorknob, opened the door and slipped inside, closing the door quietly behind her. She moved swiftly across the large room to the wide oak desk that sat in front of the huge window, looking out onto the skyline of New York City. Skye tapped the keyboard in front of the large computer screen and it sprang to life. Just as she had hoped. No one would expect someone to come all the way up to the 40th floor to access a computer and bypass all the computers and servers on the numerous floors below. Skye sat in the CEO's large, plush office chair. Opening a desk door on the right side she found the computer tower. She slipped a USB flash drive out of her carry pack and held it in her left hand. Ignoring the two USB ports on the front of the tower, using her right, she reached to the back side instead and felt for a USB port. Finding an empty one, she transferred the USB flash drive to her right hand and plugged it into the open USB port at the back. This way, no one would notice it unless they pulled the tower out. Access on this computer used by the CEO would allow Avis to bypass all the necessary passwords to gain full access to the system. Once she was in, it wouldn't matter if someone found the drive. She closed the door, stood up and pushed the office chair back in place.

THE HIGHLANDER BUILDING

"Were in!" Avis yelled.

Murdock came hustling back, carrying two steaming mugs of coffee, "No password needed?"

"Nope," Avis said as she typed furiously on the keyboard. "We're through with access into the complete system. Like we thought, no one expected an intruder to come through this route."

"Any evidence we've been detected?" asked Murdock is he set her mug down to her right on the cherry wood desk.

Avis was silent as she typed away. She finally shook her head, "No. Nothing. If anyone is watching, it just looks like an insider is working on the system. And it looks like I have...access to all the passwords. I'll make a record of every single one. Now...if they find the USB drive and remove it, we still have access through the thermostat."

Murdock pumped his fist again, "That's my girl, Skye!"

Avis smiled and stopped typing, "Do you want me to inject and start the program?"

Murdock took a slow sip of coffee as he stood there, rubbed his white beard and did some thinking. "No. Let's take advantage of the situation. Inject the program, but let's start downloading before we proceed further. We have several hours before people start going into work over there. If you get any indication we've been detected, then don't wait for my signal. Strike. Okay?"

Avis lifted her hand and came down with one finger on the 'enter' key, "Okay." She rubbed her hands together enthusiastically, "Now, let's find out what these bozos have for us."

ZONGCHI TECHNOLOGIES

Skye Steele left the CEO's desk behind and moved to the door. Opening the door just a crack, she listened. Still no sounds. She slipped back out into the hallway, closing the door quietly behind her and headed back for the stairwell.

A bell dinged and the elevator opened.

Two men stepped out and now stood between Skye and the stairwell. In the front was an oriental man in a business suit. He was about 5'7" but stocky. His lapel badge identified him as the head of security for the building. The man just behind him was about an inch below Skye's 6'-2" height and dressed in a black pinstriped suit. He had an authoritative air about him. Before anyone moved, a third man walked slowly around to stand beside the two men. This one was about 6 foot 8, with a blond crew cut, a cold smile and a tight, black T-shirt that revealed rock hard, sculptured muscles.

Chapter 28

WASHINGTON, DC

RORY AND CANDY left the Presidential suite in a low mood. They had been unable to find anything else of any consequence that would explain why someone would want to kill to secure the backup files on the USB drive. There was no evidence of any financial improprieties or personal indiscretions on the part of the new President-elect of the United States. There wasn't even the slightest hint of a scandal in any of the political team surrounding the President in any of the e-mails.

"Why don't we get a drink first before we head over to the restaurant," Rory offered.

"I need one," was all a depressed Candy could say.

The bar was called Off the Record and it was filled by caricatures of Washington's political elite from the present and into the distant past. They sat at a small table in the corner, away from the crowd. Candy asked for a Margarita while Rory settled for a neat shot glass of single malt Scotch. They sat nursing their drinks, neither one saying a single word. Rory was worried. Despite the revelations about the Chinese and their computer spy ring, He still didn't have a satisfying answer as to why someone wanted to kill Candy. Or how he could get her out of this. And he couldn't understand how the Secret Service was involved in framing this young lady. But there was another matter that bothered him a great deal. Would Candy pick up the phone and call her sister, exposing where they were, putting them in danger again? Rory gently broached the subject, "Candy...you've been pretty dedicated to your sister and–"

"And it almost gotten us killed, I know," Candy interjected angrily.

Rory nodded, holding back his own anger now, "I was just wondering why. She seems pretty special to you...."

Candy nodded. She unclenched her jaw and seemed to drift off in thought for a moment. "My sister was there for me when I needed help...and I didn't deserve it...."

"I doubt that's true–"

"No! I was a real screw-up. And she was there despite...." She seemed to want to say something but held it back. Then she shook her head slowly and sadly, "And my sister lost so much...."

Rory prodded after a moment."What do you mean?"

Candice whirled her drink in a tight circle, clinking the ice against the side of the glass, "My father was Warren Howard Jossel. He ran a small import and export business. In the 1980s, several U.S. Governors led a trade mission to China. My father had grown up with one of the politicians and was asked to go. It turned out to be his lucky break. He made some great contacts over there and his business became very successful. After that, I remember a number of politicians coming around to the house. I even remember some US government official showing up at his office for some reason. Anyway, Keira was the oldest and she was so proud of my father. She was always trying to skip school to spend time with him at work. She said she was going to take over from him like a son would. There were only four girls in the family, no boys. Dad loved it and paid for her to go to college and then to get an MBA, so she could run things when she was ready. He even said he was going to name the business 'Jossel and Daughters.'"

"Sounds like a nice family story," Rory said.

Candy nodded her head in agreement, "Unfortunately, things went sideways. Mom and the two middle girls...I'm the youngest...were killed in a car accident when we were going to the county fair. My dad and I survived."

"I'm sorry," Rory said. "How did it happen?"

Candy stared at her drink for a moment, obviously thinking back to the tragedy. "It was...it was a drunk driver who was responsible...."

Rory could tell there was something eating at her. It was the way she answered and how she hesitated before offering the brief explanation. "Was the drunk driver charged?" he asked, wondering if that was where the problem lay.

Candy seemed to be lost in thought briefly. Then she swirled her drink again like she was trying to swirl away her thoughts, "The other driver was killed too."

The other driver too? Rory thought that comment seemed out of place, concerning the tragic circumstances that took so much of her family. He would've expected some anger but....

"Anyway," Candy continued, after another moment of reflection, "my father was devastated... and the business... fell apart. That devastated my sister, know what I mean? Losing our mother and her two sisters... and then losing the business she had dreamed about for so long and worked so hard to take over with my father... and suddenly...there was no business."

Rory nodded in understanding.

Candy started talking faster, the words spilling out of her now, "With everything that happened, my father went downhill fast and... when my father passed away... I went screwy myself. I stopped going to school...drugs, alcohol, partying...I was a mess. My sister was there for me. She took me in for a year, got me straightened out. I finished my last year of high school and then Keira paid my tuition when I went away to college. She was there for me." Her drink was swirling faster and a little splashed onto the table.

Rory reached out and placed his hand on hers, "But you can't blame yourself."

The drink stopped swirling and Candy clenched her jaw hard.

Rory felt she was still holding something back, but he didn't press. There was no doubt she would continue to put her sister ahead of her own personal safety. That could prove fatal, but what could he do?

They sat there in silence for a few more minutes, nursing their drinks until Candy finally spoke up, "I'm sorry, Rory. I don't mean to get so angry...."

Rory nodded sympathetically, "I know. When it comes to family, it's sometimes hard to keep our feelings hidden. I can re-member–"

"That's it," Candice said emphatically.

"That's what?" Rory looked across the table and saw Candy's eyes were wide open in surprise.

"That's why we can't find the information," she said as she put her drink down on the table. "As you would say, it's hidden...in plain sight."

Chapter 29

ZONGCHI TECHNOLOGIES, New York

"**WELL, WELL, WELL,**" Torion Blacker said. He took a step forward to stand beside the 6-foot-8 man with the blond crew cut. "Unless I miss my guess, you are Miss Skye Steele. You're definitely not the one I expected to see. But I guess you never look a gift horse in the mouth, isn't that what they say?"

Skye cocked her head, "You call me a horse again and you'll lose your teeth."

Blacker raised an eyebrow. His eyes coolly appraised the shapely body in the black cat-suit. Then he looked directly into Skye's green eyes and jerked a thumb to his right, "Why don't you to try and go through The Dane here first."

The monster of a man took a step forward and smiled coldly.

Skye raised an eyebrow, "The Dane? You mean like a Great Dane? Is he your pet?"

The Dane's fists clenched and the smile left his face.

Tapping her thighs lightly with her hands over and over just above her knees, Skye called out in a high-pitched voice, "Come on boy, come on. Why don't you come here, roll over and I'll scratch your tummy?"

The Dane stepped forward, reaching out and trying to grab her by the neck. But she was too quick and stepped back. He threw a punch and she countered. He threw another punch and she countered that one as well. The Dane narrowed his eyes. He went into a combat stance and advanced again, raining various martial arts blows on his opponent. She countered all of them expertly.

Skye winked at her opponent when he stopped to consider his next move. She watched as the man in the black pinstriped suit took a few steps up behind her massive opponent. The stocky head of security took up the position just to his right.

"Let's get this over with. We have to find Steele and the woman," Blacker said.

The Dane nodded and swept his left foot out.

Nimbly stepping back, Skye watched for his next move.

The Dane swept out his right foot.

Skye jumped forward instead of backward.

The Dane froze in surprise.

Skye kicked out The Dane's plant leg

The big man collapsed to the floor with a thud and a grunt as the air was knocked from his lungs.

Spinning to her left, Skye brought her left boot around high, landing it on the head of security's shoulder, knocking him against the wall. She spun to her right and moved low, sweeping the legs out from under the man in the pinstriped suit.

Blacker collapsed to the floor, landing hard and cursing.

Skye took off running for the stairs. She heard one of the men yelled instructions behind her. He was going to check the offices to see what she was up to while the other two pursued her. That would lower the odds in her favor if they managed to catch up.

Feet started pounding down the hallway in pursuit of her.

Skye reached the exit and moved swiftly into the 40th-floor landing. Instead of running down the stairs themselves, Skye jumped up onto the metal railing instead. Standing sideways, she expertly slid down the smooth top of the railing, making the turns down to the 39th-floor landing like an expert skateboarder. She continued sliding downward on the railing, finally jumping off when she reached the 38th-floor landing.

The door banged open on the 40th-floor. Footsteps began pounding down the stairs.

They were definitely in pursuit but Skye's skateboarding trick had increased her lead on them. Skye bounded into the hallway and made a run for the room where she had cut the hole in the glass. As she ran, she estimated her head start and calculated there still wouldn't have enough time to get her gear on before they would be on her. As she reached the correct door, she reached into her carry bag and pulled out the cutter. She tossed it hard, letting it slid farther down the hallway. Then she ducked into the room, leaving the door slightly ajar. She was gambling only one would check the room, lowering the odds in her favor again.

The Dane and the head of security scrambled into the hallway from the stairwell and began running. The head of security noticed the partially open door on the right. All doors were normally closed when staff left. But he also saw the glass cutter lying on the floor further down the hallway. He put his hand out to stop The Dane. He moved closer, whispering, "It looks like she went that way. But I'll check this room out, just in case. You keep going and I'll catch up."

The Dane nodded and headed off at a run.

The head of security pulled a handgun. Facing the partially open door, he prepared himself. He brought up his foot, kicking the door in enough to slam it back against the wall, in case anybody was hiding back there. Then he burst into the room. His attention was caught by the large opening in the window and the bundle of equipment on the floor just below it.

Skye sprang into action from behind the desk. She jumped on top of it, took one step and the used the far edge to launch herself forward into a dropkick attacking maneuver. She slammed the head of security in the chest with both feet as he turned.

The head of security yelped in pain. His weapon fired into the ceiling as he was knocked backwards, banging the back of his head hard against the floor.

Skye expected him to be out cold but he sprang to his feet and attacked. Skye spun to the left, out of the way. She had to get this over fast. The gunshot would definitely bring others in here.

The head of security moved to his left and turned to face her.

Skye took a step and threw another dropkick at the Oriental's chest. It knocked him backwards and he went through the hole in the window. Skye heard his screaming all the way to the pavement below, where it stopped abruptly.

Skye ran for the window, picked up the climbing harness and began to put it on. She had to move fast, before the gunshot brought the other men. But before she could get the harness on, The Dane burst into the room.

The Dane looked right at Skye Steele and grinned, "Round two."

Skye tossed the harness to the side and went into a combat stance just as The Dane did.

The Dane moved closer in his crouch. He looked at her breasts, "Nice set."

Skye ignored the dig. He was moving differently this time, obviously ready for the skills he now knew she had. They moved in a martial arts dance around the room that was lit only by the soft light from the hallway through the open door. The Dane attacked and Skye countered skillfully. He changed his stance slightly and attacked again in a different method. Skye countered every move but she could tell he was testing the variety of her skills. They danced and parried around the room. As they passed the oak desk on her right, Skye saw The Dane make a movement towards it. Then he moved in a feint to her left. Skye didn't fall for the move. The Dane brought his right leg up in a roundhouse kick but she was already moving out of the way to the right. She stepped on something and stumbled backwards. She suddenly re-alized he had taken something from the desk and threw it on the floor. Before she could react, he was on her. She tried to spin away from him but The Dane gripped her wrist and stepped around behind her, placing a hand between her shoulder blades.

The Dane pushed Skye hard forward and her stomach slammed into the back of the oak desk, knocking the wind from her. Before she could recover, The Dane slammed her face down on the desk over the laptop with his left hand. Holding Skye in place, now bent over the desk, The Dane reached down to her hip and grasped the material of her black bodysuit with his hand. His muscles flexed as he ripped away a section of material, from her waist to her upper thigh across her backside, exposing her black, silk panties completely. "Why don't we get to know each other before I throw you out the window," he growled. Then he placed his fingers into the waistband of her panties and yanked them down, exposing her naked bottom. He kicked her left foot out, then her right foot to spread her legs apart. He grinned maliciously as he pushed his zipper down.

Skye concentrated on his body position, looking for a way out instead of what he was going to do to her in a moment. A thought came to her quiet mind and she struggled to get the laptop out from under her chest. Finally getting it to slide upward on the desk, she pushed it past her face. Skye extended her arms, paused to make sure of her aim, then tossed it hard back over her head.

The laptop smashed into the top of The Dane's nose and he howled in pain. Blood gushed and he brought both hands up to his face.

Skye rolled over onto her back on the desk, lifted her legs and kicked out at The Dane. He was massive and she only managed to push him back one step. But it was enough. Skye shot forward onto her feet and kicked The Dane square between his legs.

The massive man brought his hands away from his bloody face and clutched at his now painful genitals.

"I'm the one who decides who puts what and where, when it comes to my body!" Skye Steele told him in anger. She reached over and picked up a heavy oak chair, bringing it down over her head and onto The Dane's back as he was bent over.

The wood exploded everywhere as The Dane collapsed to his knees with a groan.

Skye brought her foot up into his Adam's apple. There was a satisfying crunch.

The Dane tipped over onto his face, gagging.

Skye stood looking down at him for a moment, then headed for the window. But she suddenly found herself banging into the floor with her left shoulder. The Dane had spun around on the floor, sweeping her feet out from under her with his massive right arm.

"I'm going to stick it in every hole you've got," he spat in a hoarse, strained whisper. He staggered to his feet, his face bloody.

Skye flipped her feet back over her head and rolled to her feet just as The Dane came at her. She countered several blows from him, backing up slowly as he advanced.

The Dane growled as he rained heavy, angry blows on his opponent. He began moving back and forth in front of her, trying to find the right angle of attack as he varied the direction of his blows, backing up his opponent.

Skye gave ground, gauging the distance to the hole she had cut in the glass window until it was time. She lifted her right hand and beckoned him forward with her fingers, "Come on pussy, is that all you've got?"

The Dane's face was bloody and angry as he yelled and lunged for his victim.

Skye deftly stepped to the side and tripped The Dane as he went by.

The Dane's eyes shot wide open in surprise as he realized what was about to happen. His neck came down on the one foot section of sharp glass left above the sill. It was a reverse guillotine. The Dane's massive body hit the floor with a thud while his head fell to the street 40 stories below.

Chapter 30

WASHINGTON, DC

RORY COULD BARELY KEEP UP with Candy as she rushed back up to their suite. She stopped at their door, fumbling for her key card. Rory calmly reached around and slipped his own key card into the lock. The light barely turned green before Candy was pushing through the doorway into the suite. She ran for the laptop and Rory could see her pulling the USB drive from her padded bra. Candy opened the laptop and started it up, fidgeting anxiously until it was ready to go.

"What exactly are we doing?" Rory asked as he sat beside her.

"Changing the file attributes," Candy said.

"What does that mean?" Rory asked. He watched her maneuver the mouse across the screen.

"When you first buy a computer, a number of files and folders are hidden by default," Candy explained as she began clicking the mouse button. "Important system files and important folders are hidden automatically to keep people from deleting files by accident. Unless you know what you're doing, there's really no reason to ever need to see these hidden files."

"Okay, so how does that help us?"

"You can turn the ability to hide files and folders off and on by changing the attributes on them," Candy said. She maneuvered the mouse pointer to My Computer>Tools and chose the folder options. She clicked on the view tab and then the advanced settings. Clicking the radio button for 'Show hidden files and folders', she then clicked 'Okay' at the bottom. Plugging the USB drive into the port, Candy opened up the files again. Then she began scrolling through the files and folders, looking for anything new that stood out.

"Stop. Go back," Rory said as he pointed at the screen.

Candy scrolled back.

"Too far...there," Rory said as he pointed at a folder labeled 'Guan Di'. "Isn't that...?"

Candy put a hand to her mouth in surprise, "That's the word he used for his password."

"The Chinese God of War or something like that, wasn't it?"

Candy nodded as she double clicked on the folder. A form popped up asking for a password. "What should I put in?"

Rory scratched his head, "How about Guan Di again?"

Candy nodded in agreement and typed it in. There was a beep and the form came up again. "It didn't work. And it says we only have three more tries."

"Really?"

Candy nodded. She keyed in 'Yim' as a password. The computer beeped again. "Crap," she grimaced. "We only have two more tries."

"Isn't there some kind of password cracker you can get?" Rory asked her.

Candy shook her head, "That won't work. Password crackers use brute force. Those programs run through millions of combinations until it finds the right one."

"And we only have two more chances."

"Right," Candy said.

"What happens once we go through those two more attempts?"

"Either it locks us out for a set period of time. Or...."

"Or what?"

"Or it's set to wipe everything out as a security precaution," Candy said.

Rory stared at the screen. "The answers we're looking for must be inside that file. The question is, how do we get inside?"

"Yim probably used a simple password like before," Candy reasoned. "The question is, how do we figure out what it is? We can't access his computer to see if he made a record of it because it's gone. In fact, his whole house is gone–"

"But not his office."

"Do you think we might find it there?"

"It's worth a look," Rory concluded.

ZONGCHI TECHNOLOGIES, New York

Skye Steele had to move quickly. If the man in the black pin-striped suit showed up, she could be in trouble. He looked more like the type to use a gun. And use it well. Picking up the rope, she deftly threaded it through the ATC. After yanking the rope a couple of times to make sure it was still securely fastened on the roof, she stepped over the headless body and onto the ledge.

The breeze against her naked buttocks reminded Skye her black panties were still down where the jerked had pushed them. No time to do anything about that now. She gripped the rope tightly and began to move upwards, hand over hand. She was careful to keep herself away from the sharp edges of the hole she had cut in the glass. Once she cleared the upper edge of the hole in the window, Skye used her feet against the building to give her more leverage as she climbed. The climb was tough but years of physical training kept her moving up the side of the building with speed.

Ten feet from the top a gunshot rang out. Crack!

Skye felt a searing pain across her naked left buttock. She lost her grip with her right hand and banged face first against the building as her feet went out from under her. Her left bicep screamed in agony as she fought to pull all her body weight up with one hand. She fought to get traction with her feet and was able to move sideways along the wall.

Crack!

The bullet dug into the bricks and Skye felt sharp shrapnel explode against her neck. Her feet lost their grip again and Skye twirled with one hand on the rope, 39 stories above the street.

A deep voice shouted from below, "I found your Wi-Fi plug-in, girly. You're beautiful but not too bright. You failed. And once we complete the sweep of all the computer systems, we'll find where you tried to gain access."

Skye desperately fought to find the brick wall with her feet as she caught a glimpse of the man in the pinstriped suit looking up at her from the window below. He was aiming upwards. The fact he was in an awkward, twisted position as he tried to zero in on her body no doubt was her saving grace. Her feet found the wall.

She gripped the rope with two hands and propelled her body to the right and upward.

Crack!

Skye pressed her foot hard against the wall and moved back left and upwards.

Crack!

She pulled hard and pushed with her feet and was up over the roof parapet.

Crack!

A bullet ricocheted off the edge off the roof.

Skye rolled over and checked her left buttock. It was just a bloody graze but she had to grit her teeth against the pain. She couldn't let it slow her down though. The man in the pinstriped suit would no doubt head for the roof. And he probably wouldn't be alone.

Skye stripped the climbing gear off and threw it aside. Grabbing the rolled wingsuit, she sprinted along the roof, ignoring the pain in her left butt cheek. She had to get away from the rooftop door and behind it to give her additional time. Reaching the far end of the building, Skye unrolled the flight suit and started pulling it on. Pain seared through her left buttock as she slipped the material over the bloody wound. She heard the sound of the roof door banging open on the far side behind her.

Footsteps and voices headed out across the roof.

Skye pulled the suit up over her torso.

"There she is!"

No time left. Skye took two giant steps and leaped.

Gunshots ripped open the night air. Crack! Crack! Crack! Crack! Crack!

Bullets whined over Skye's head as she fell over the edge. She plummeted straight down towards the street, calmly pulling the front zipper up and closing the suit against the buffeting wind. Bringing her arms back in a streamlined position, she gauged her speed. This was nerve-racking because the street this time was a whole lot closer than the drop from the top of the Empire State building. Waiting until the last minute, Skye lifted her arms. But the downdraft between the building wouldn't let her fly! Skye fought with all her strength to fly but the street was coming closer. Skye relaxed her body, gained more speed, then lifted her arms and turned hard with all her might - and started to fly.

A driver was startled by the figure zooming just over the hood of his car and he ducked. The car veered onto the sidewalk and slammed to a stop sideways against a brick building. The driver slowly opened his eyes and peeked up through the windshield, "What the...?"

Skye used her speed to stay above the nearly empty streets, high enough to avoid the odd car and truck, startling the drivers. She managed to fly three city blocks before her speed began to drop. The landing was a little rough, her forward momentum throwing her off her feet as she touched down. Performing a tuck and roll to get herself back on her feet, Skye was on the move. Her Humvee was still several blocks away and she started to run.

A green and red taxi turned the corner just ahead and drove in her direction.

Skye flagged it down.

The taxi driver tried to go around the weirdo in the street but she refused to get out of the way. The taxi finally stopped.

Skye grimaced, her butt wound screaming as she sat in the back seat. She gave the driver the street corner where she needed to go.

But the taxi driver just staring at her over the seat.

"Costume party," was all Skye said.

"Uh huh. And watcha 'spose to be?"

"A flying squirrel," Skye said. "I need you to get going, please. I'm in a hurry."

"Don't flying squirrels have to do with nuts and stuff?"

"I think so," Skye said as she clenched her jaw.

The taxi driver nodded to himself, "That would make sense."

Skye leaned forward, "If you don't get moving, I'll rip yours off."

His eyebrows shot up and then the taxi driver complied quickly.

Within ten minutes Skye was paying the fare with money from the Humvee. As the taxi left, she climbed back into the big vehicle, sitting gingerly as she started the engine. Then she pressed the phone button on the steering wheel to access her cell phone through the Bluetooth connection. She issued the voice command to dial the office.

"Highlander Investigative Services," answered the deep voice, *"you're on speakerphone."*

"Uncle Murdock, you need to get out of there quickly," Skye said with urgency in her voice.

"What's wrong Skye?" Murdock MacLeod asked her.

"Three men discovered me in the building. Two are dead, the third is still alive. They knew who I was," Skye explained. There was silence on the other end of the line and she could hear her uncle walking quickly across the office floor.

"Avis," MacLeod called out. "Avis," he called again.

"Yes?" answered Avis in the background.

"It's Skye. She says the operation has been compromised. Have we been detected?"

There was a brief pause, "No. It doesn't look like it right now. Why?"

"I'm positive you're going to have company very soon," Skye said. "Can you get out of there and continue later?"

"Give me a minute," MacLeod said in answer.

Skye gripped the steering wheel of her Humvee tightly, her anxiety high over the welfare of her family members. She could hear them talking and she wanted them to drop everything and get out of there immediately. But she knew they wouldn't if it meant abandoning the effort to prove someone's innocence.

MacLeod came back on the phone, "No, it's not possible right now, Skye. I've been searching for specific information while Avis is in the middle of a massive download of information that she can't interrupt. We've already filled several of our 3-TB external hard drives with pertinent information. I've found some info to help but it's not enough. We have to keep siphoning every piece of data we can from their system in case we get knocked out before we can prove our client's innocence."

"I understand. But I'm positive our friends are going to be visiting you with some very bad intentions," Skye said, her concern mounting.

MacLeod was silent for a moment, obviously thinking the situation through. "Can we forget about those files Avis?" he asked.

"Those are compressed video and recorded conference chats. We can't afford to pass them up until we know what they are," Avis replied.

"You're right," MacLeod agreed.

Skye cursed silently as she listened to them. She banged her fist against the steering wheel. She had to do something to protect them as long as she could.

Chapter 31

TORION BLACKER SAT IN HIS SUV. He was watching the forensics team working inside the yellow crime scene tape in front of the ZongChi Technologies building. He had started a search for any evidence to show the computer system had been compromised by the Steele woman, but he had to abort it and was fortunate to get out of the building just before the police had arrived. His cell phone rang. It was tied into the vehicle's Bluetooth through the radio and he tapped a button on the steering wheel, "Yea?"

The metallic voice came through, sounding anxious for news, "What happened?"

"It was the Steele woman who showed up at ZongChi Technologies," Blacker answered.

"And...?" the metallic voice asked impatiently.

"The Dane lost his head...."

"I know all about his penchant for cruelty. I really don't care how badly The Dane went off on her."

"No. I mean, he *really* lost his head. She cut it off." Blacker loved this part. He should have been left alone to choose a partner and handle the matter. And he loved letting a superior squirm when their plans failed. He smiled just a bit, "I'm watching the police pull his head out of the front seat of a car, while a forensic team works on his body 40 stories above it. Then - there's the body of the security chief lying on the pavement beside the car."

There was a long silence on the other end of the call. "Was there anyone there with her?"

"No."

"No?"

"It doesn't look like it."

"Just the one woman?"

"That's right. Steele and the woman didn't show up anywhere here."

The voice cursed softly, "Which means they must still be in Washington. What was the Steele woman doing there?"

"I found a Wi-Fi plug-in she placed in one of the offices–"

"She got into the computer system?"

"It's possible," Blacker said. "But I'm not sure how far she got before we found her. The police took over the entire building before I could get a complete sweep finished. But I can tell you the Chinese inside are frantic. And it doesn't look like it has anything to do with the bodies...or the head. Their interest is solely on their computers. But I can't tell if it's because of the breach or because the police are right there, taking control of the building as a crime scene. They could stumble onto everything in their investigation."

There was a lot of cursing on the other end of the call.

"I can fly back–"

"No," interrupted the metallic voice. "Not right now. I need you to find out what happened there first."

"I'll stay under the radar as much as possible–"

"I don't care about that," barked the metallic voice. *"If she was using a Wi-Fi plug-in, there's a good chance someone outside the building was using it to gain access."*

Blacker nodded his head in thought, "The Steele's have an office here in New York...."

"Then do whatever you need to do. Right now! Find out what they know or who they talked to. Eliminate anyone and everyone associated with the breach. We need to end this before anything else is compromised. I'll arrange for all the resources you need."

"I understand–"

There was a lot of angry swearing on the other end before the call ended.

Chapter 32

SKYE STEELE PEELED OFF THE WINGSUIT, ignoring the pain as she pushed it down over her bloodied buttock. Removing the rest of her clothes, she finally pulled her black panties back up, grimacing as the thin material slipped up over the gunshot wound. Then she climbed into her leather pants and a denim blouse. She opened the center console and pulled out her custom-made, double shoulder harness. Slipping it on, she then pulled on her black leather jacket. Pulling two Glock 19s from the locked glove compartment and four extra 19 round magazines, Skye Steele was ready. Starting the 6.5 L V8 Turbo diesel, she cranked the steering wheel hard left and floored the accelerator. The tires squealed under the weight of the 5900-pound vehicle and the tires smoked as she did a power u-turn in front of several oncoming cars. She ignored the honking horns as she accelerated for the office.

ARLINGTON, VIRGINIA

Jun "Danni" Kang of the People's Liberation Army of China had been alerted to the breach at ZongChi Technologies. On his cell phone was a picture of the target responsible for the breach,

Skye Steele. She had escaped and he would have to hunt her down in New York if others failed again. However, there were pictures of two other targets of more immediate importance. Rory Mack Steele and Candace Ella Jossel. Both were said to be across the Potomac River and staying somewhere in the Washington, DC area. He was to head across and be ready to act at a moment's notice, once their hiding place was determined. Danni contemplated the pictures of all three. Jossel was a soft target. She would be no problem. The other two were more than that. Danni knew competence and danger when he saw it. He smiled. This would be fun. But he wasn't stupid. He recalled a military tactic from Sun-Tzu's military treatise, On The Art of War: 'Though an obstinate fight may be made by a small force, in the end it must be captured by the larger force'. He immediately sent out signals to gather the other ten assassins in his cell.

WASHINGTON, DC

Rory drove at a brisk clip through traffic to Yim's main floor office on 12th Street NW. Leaving the Jaguar in a small parking lot down the street, they walked the half block to a tan and brown building. The front entrance door was still open and they went inside. A directory listing showed them where Yim's office was located. They walked across the lobby and down the hallway to the left. The first office door on the left was TechCom IT Consulting, Yim's company name.

Candy tried the doorknob but it was locked, "How do we get in?"

"Keep an eye out," Rory said as he took out what looked like a small jackknife.

"What's that?"

"Lock picking tools," Rory said as he took a thin, L-shaped wire from the back of the jackknife. He also opened up one of the blades, then crouched in front of the door, going to work on the lock.

"So that's how you got into Yim's house. Cool," Candy said. "I'm your lookout...or your moll...."

"I'm not a mobster," Rory said in amusement. The door clicked.

"Whatever," Candy said as she slipped through the door when Rory pushed it open.

"There's probably enough light from the street–" But it was too late. Candy had already flipped the light switch and the office was lit up. Rory closed the door and rushed across the room to close the blinds across all the windows to the street outside. When he turned around, Candy was already in front of a computer at a desk. He shook his head. She didn't seem to have any idea that you didn't alert people when you broke in. He let out a short, sharp breath of exasperation and began looking around the office. It was large space, with a number of filing cabinets and bookcases. There were two other desks with computers on them.

"This computer is running but...there doesn't seem to be anything on it," Candy said.

"How about one of these other ones?" Rory asked as he stepped over to one of the desks. He tapped the space bar on the keyboard and the computer monitor sprang to life, "This one is on as well."

Getting up from her chair, Candy walked over to another desk. "So is this one," she said after a moment. She sat down in the chair and looked over the contents of the computer. "But I don't see anything at all on this one either. No data, no word files, nothing."

Rory looked over at her, "Nothing?"

She shook her head," No." Then she said, "Well...there is a software to program and reprogram flash memory but...that's it. Other than that, it's totally empty."

Rory reached for the mouse on the desk in front of him and clicked on the computer's hard drive and files. He wrinkled his brow and sat down to check again. He shook his head, "You're right. I don't see anything on this one either."

Cocking her head, Candy looked at Rory, "Why wouldn't he have anything on these computers if this was his office?"

Sitting back in the chair, Rory looked around the office, thinking. Then he snapped his fingers, "This is just a fake office. If he was working for the Chinese, helping them to spy on the US, then he didn't need clients."

Candy looked around the office for a few moments as well, then looked over at Rory, "Then why did he spend so much time in here that day we ended up going over to his house?"

Rory slowly shook his head. She was right. Why would he? Rory pulled open the top drawer on the right side of the desk. He closed it and opened the one below it. He slid it closed, "Nothing." Stepping over to another desk, he checked the drawers. Finding nothing, he looked around and then walked over to a larger desk, sliding open a drawer. He stood there, looking down.

"What's in there?" Candy asked. When he just continued staring, she got up and walked over to look inside herself. The drawer was filled with half-inch thick white boxes that were 8 inches long. Each one had a label with a name printed across it. Candy reached inside and pulled out one out. She opened the end flap of the box and slid something out part way. "It's a PC card," she said.

Rory took up one of the boxes and looked inside himself, "He must be building computers here."

"And I know what for," Candy said.

Rory looked up at her.

Candy ran her finger across the name on the side of the box, "Fullmer. He's a senator from Arkansas." She pointed inside to each one, "Coppinger. He's from Utah. Schmidt, Rhode Island...."

Rory closed the drawer and sat down in the chair, opening the next drawer down. There were more white boxes with names on them. He reached in and pulled one out, opening the box.

"That's a video card," she said. She reached down and pulled another one out. "Another video card," she said as she opened the end flap.

Rory got up and walked over to one of the filing cabinets. He pulled it open. "There are more in here in folders," he said. He walked his hands through several of the folders, "Each folder with a part also has a work order attached to it. It looks like they're from...three different computer companies. Maybe more."

"Rory?"

He glanced back at her.

Candy walked across to him. She had a PC card in her hand and she indicated the name imprinted just above the circuits. "Copyright ZongChi Technologies," she said.

Rory nodded his head, "So he spent time his time in here building computers. Using ZongChi parts."

"Or programming the parts," Candy said. "Keep in mind what I saw on that first computer. Software to program flash memory. He could program or erase and reprogram a computer's BIOS chip or alter some of the new storage devices for computers using flash drives instead of the standard hard drives." She glanced around the room, "He may have a few programs to do some other things like that."

Rory nodded, "That confirms what we suspected. ZongChi Technologies is spying on the United States. Maybe even her allies. From this office here in DC, a stone's throw from Congress, Yim was perfectly positioned to infiltrate any target's computer system."

"And since they can't get direct contracts with the government, they're working through third-party computer companies," Candy said.

"It's more likely ZongChi owns those companies. It's not unusual for companies to hide ownership of other companies through dummy corporations," Rory told her. "I would imagine they have other Yims around the country doing the same thing, wherever they need it."

Candy headed for the door, looking back at him, urgency written across her face, "We have to go. We have to let people know, we have to let my sister know, right now."

"Hold on, Candy."

She whirled around, But—"

"Keep in mind we already have my sister Skye looking into ZongChi Technologies," he reminded her.

Candy opened her mouth to protest.

Rory held a hand up, "*This* will give added weight to our suspicions, Candy. But the problem is - this only confirms what we already know." He paused for a moment and then asked her pointedly, "*Why* did we come here in the first place?"

Candy's shoulder's slumped, "To find a password for the backup." She looked around the room, "But...if there is a record of it...how do we find it?"

"You're the computer whizz, you tell me."

Looking around the room again, Candy finally shook her head softly, "I have absolutely no idea."

Rory clicked his tongue, thinking. "I guess we just keep looking for the needle in the haystack. I'll start looking through each of the filing cabinets and see if something pops up. Go back through each of these computer systems and double check for files where he could have recorded his passwords. Even geeks have to have some kind of hard copy."

Candy wrinkled her brow, "But there aren't any files, remember?"

"We have to check for *hidden* files as well. Remember?"

Her face reddened and she headed for the nearest computer, "Right, I forgot about that."

Rory felt weary at the constant arguing. Her dedication to her sister was clouding her every thought. It nearly got them killed - and he knew it still could.

Chapter 33

AN HOUR LATER, not finding anything on the computers, Candy had joined Rory in looking through the filing cabinets. But another hour of digging turned up nothing of any consequence. They turned to the bookcases and began going through each book on the shelves, flipping through the pages at first. Then they realized the password could simply be written on one of the pages. It was painstaking work, having to look at each and every page. But still, nothing turned up. Rory finished going through his last book. As Candy continued on her side of the room, Rory's attention went to the Chinese figurines around the room. He picked one up and a thought formed in his mind. He walked over to a large genealogy chart on one wall. The Yim name was on top and the chart worked downward and back through dozens of generations in China. One line was of particular interest to Rory. "Candy, what was that Chinese name Yim used for his password?"

Candy stopped what she was doing and looked over at Rory, "Guan-Di. Why? We already tried that, remember?"

Rory nodded as he did some deep thinking. "Is one of those computers hooked up to the Internet, to access Google?"

Candy went over to the first computer she had looked at and sat down. "Yes," she said after a moment. "Why? What do you want me to look up?"

"Look up our character Guan-Di, will you? Tell me what it says."

Candy did a Google search, "Okay. It says 'Guan-Di or Guan-Yu was a general serving under the warlord Liu Bei–"

Rory turned, "Guan-Di or Guan-Yu? We tried the first, how about the second?"

Candy shook her head no.

"You want to plug the USB drive in and try it?"

Looking skeptical, Candy said, "Keep in mind we only have two tries left."

"True," Rory said. "But unless we try it..."

Candy nodded in agreement after a moment. She pulled the USB drive from her bra and pushed it into the front USB port. She brought up the password protected folder and typed in Guan-Yu. The computer beeped and she groaned, "That didn't work. We only have one try left."

Rory grimaced. He rubbed his chin for a moment and then said, "Go back to the google search and read me the rest on our friend Guan-Di. Does it say where he was from or where he was living?"

Candy called the web page back up and began reading. After a few minutes of mumbling, she read out loud, "He is often reverently called Guan Gong, which means Lord Guan, or Guan Di, which means Emperor Guan. His hometown, Yuncheng, has named an airport after him." She looked up at Rory, "Is that significant?"

Rory nodded as he looked at the genealogy chart, "Yim's father and forefathers were living in Yuncheng, Shanxi province in the People's Republic of China."

"Really!" Candy whispered. "That's probably why his family was so interested in this Guan-Di guy."

"Even more than it," Rory said.

"What do you mean?" Candy asked him.

"Yim and his family believe they are descended from his dynasty," Rory said.

"They can trace their family back that far?" asked an astounded Candy.

"Somewhat," Rory said. "He and his father have been involved in tracing their family history through DNA. They are supposed to be part of a Haplogroup or ancestral group that goes back thousands of years in that part of China. It also looks like he claims to have DNA evidence that leads directly back to this Emperor Guan, through both his paternal and his maternal ancestry, just 2000 years ago."

"*Just* 2000 years ago? How many people can do that?"

"I have no idea," Rory admitted as he stroked his chin in thought.

"Okay," Candy said slowly. "But exactly how does this information, interesting as it is, help us?"

"Well, unless I miss my guess, his password is probably one of these numbers next to Emperor Guan's name."

Candy's eyebrows raised, "A number on a genealogy chart! That's a huge leap. And a lot of guesswork."

"True," Rory admitted.

Candy got up and wandered over to the genealogy chart to stand beside Rory, "You said *one* of these numbers. How would we know which number to type in?"

Rory crossed his arms and just stood there, thinking for a moment before he answered, "Okay. Here's my thinking. He has a Mitochondrial DNA number recorded, which comes through the maternal line. He also has a Y-DNA number that comes through the paternal line."

"Okay," Candy said as she followed along. "So...you think it's one of those two?"

"Considering it's been estimated that 200 million baby girls are killed in China each year because they're unacceptable - I say he used the one through the male line." He looked directly at Candy to see if she agreed.

Candy cursed under her breath, "We only have one try left, Steele."

"True...Jossel."

Candy walked over to the desk and sat down behind the computer again. She sat still for a moment, thinking. "Okay, I've got nothing. Give me that number. Let's try it," she finally said.

Rory spelled it out slowly, "N-LLY22Z."

Candy entered the number, then lifted her hand to press "Enter' on the keyboard.

Chapter 34

THE HIGHLANDER BUILDING, Manhattan, New York

SIXTEEN MEN in four black SUVs followed Torion Blacker around the corner to the front of the ten-story, black marble building that held the offices of Highlander Investigative Services. Blacker pulled to a stop in front of the entrance. Two of the trailing vehicles pulled in behind him. The third pulled to the left and parked across the street. The fourth SUV turned left to park behind the third.

A loud roar pierced the night and a black Humvee rammed into the fourth SUV in mid-turn, T-boning the vehicle and smashing the left side in. The black SUV was pushed ten feet down the road, the tires smoking and shredding, before it first flipped. It flipped a second time as the Humvee slammed into it again and pushed it hard for another six feet. Then the black Humvee screeched to a stop. The SUV continued tumbling down the street before it finally came to rest on its roof.

Temporally stunned by what had happened, four men finally reacted and jumped from the third black SUV, drawing their handguns.

But Skye Steele was already out of the black Humvee, a Glock 19 in each hand. She went on the attack immediately, firing her weapons as she strode towards the black SUV on the right. She recognized each man was wearing body armor, so she aimed high.

The first man on the sidewalk side of the SUV went down from a head-shot. The second man on the left side of the street took a bullet in the neck. The man ahead of him took one bullet in the eye and one in the forehead. The second man on the right got his gun up and fired twice.

Skye continued walking and firing, maintaining her calm.

The men on the left were starting to exit their vehicles.

The second man continued trading fire with Skye until he took a bullet in the mouth and two more in the neck His body crumpled to the street.

With her targets on the right eliminated, Skye coolly pivoted, aiming for the two vehicles on the left. She squeezed both triggers and opened fire.

Ducking from the sudden spray of bullets, Blacker, and the others took cover behind their vehicles. Glass shattered, headlights imploded and the bullets made Swiss cheese of the hood, fenders and body panels.

Releasing both of the empty magazines at the same time, Skye turned and sprinted to her left.

Blacker and his men were slow to react. By the time they started returning fire, their target was out of the street and running across the sidewalk.

Bullets chipped pieces off the building facade and Skye felt marble shrapnel rain on her leather jacket. She turned the corner of the building and ran down the alleyway towards a private side entrance. Punching in a code, Skye unlocked the door and slipped into the building. She shot out the surveillance camera above the door, then bounded up the stairs to the second floor.

BLACKER CURSED AS HE rose from behind his vehicle. Half his force was already wiped out by that bitch. Eight men quickly moved from their own cover towards Blacker.

A tall, muscular black man with a French accent spoke up. This was Jean-Marc Huneault, leader of the group sent to assist Blacker, "Still a go?"

A security guard inside the building, appeared at the glass front doors, his weapon drawn. He looked out at the men on the sidewalk.

Blacker held his credentials up with his left hand, hiding the weapon behind his thigh and slowly approached the entrance doors. He spoke in a loud voice, gesturing down the street, "We had an accident. We need to use your phone."

The guard wasn't sure what to do at first. The request seemed strange, considering government agents should have cell phones. But seeing the overturned SUV down the street, he reached up and unlocked the door. It was his last act. Blacker lifted the weapon in his right hand and fired a single shot through the glass into the man's forehead. As the security guard's body slowly collapsed to the floor, Blacker turned and spoke loud, finally addressing Huneault's question, "Yes, still a go."

Huneault nodded and ran for the front entrance. The other seven followed behind him, weapons drawn.

Blacker held the door open for them, "We need to act fast, the police will be on the way. We kill her...and anyone else we find inside. No survivors."

Nodding his understanding, Huneault entered the building and ordered one of his men to pull the security guard's body out of view from the street.

Blacker locked the glass front doors and then headed for the large security desk in the center of the lobby where the security guard sat. Each of the mercenaries he was using had earpieces and microphones on their body vests. He would coordinate the assault through the video cameras at the security desk. Blacker sat down and stopped the system from recording more video through each surveillance camera throughout the building. Next, he erased every digital recording to ensure there was no evidence of him or the team.

SKYE REACHED THE SECOND-floor landing and took out the camera high above the exit door with a single shot. She pulled open the door and ran down the second-floor hallway. Running hard across the marble floors, she finally reached the bank of four elevators. She stabbed the call button to bring an elevator car to the second floor. It was an agonizing wait. The bell dinged and the doors began opening on the first elevator. She slipped inside and hit the "emergency stop' button, holding it in place. She shot out the surveillance camera high in the right corner. She did the same with the second elevator and the third.

THREE RED LIGHTS FLASHING on the security board caught Blacker's attention. "The Steele woman has stopped three of the four elevators cars on the second floor. Stop the last one before she gets it," he called loudly.

One of the men jumped to the elevator button and jabbed at it. The elevator dinged and doors opened on the right. "Got it," he yelled back.

Blacker turned his attention back to the board. He cursed as he realized she had also taken out a number of the surveillance cameras. "She's also taken out the surveillance cameras in those three elevator cars. And she has taken out a camera for a side entrance and on the second-floor landing on the stairs to our left."

"We could take the elevator directly to their offices on the top floor," one of the men said.

Blacker gave it some thought. "She could shoot through the doors as you go past," he reasoned.

A tall, redheaded mercenary with an Irish accent stepped forward. This was Jack O'Toole, Huneault's second in command, "And anyone on the top floor could concentrate their firepower on the single elevator car." "He gave Blacker a cold smile, "We need to take out this Steele woman before we move up."

Blacker nodded, "You're right."

SKYE STABBED THE ELEVATOR call button over and over but the last elevator car wasn't responding. She cursed, realizing they must have kept it down on the first floor. Skye moved quickly to the left, heading for the nearest set of stairs. When the other cars didn't respond, they would know where she was. They would know she was on the second floor and she was gambling they would come to get her first, instead of going all the way to the

50th floor. She pulled her weapons as she shouldered the stairway exit door open. She stepped into the landing.

Running footsteps echoed upwards from the stairs below.

Skye leaned over the railing and waited.

The pounding footsteps came closer. Then they stopped. It was quiet.

Skye stayed patient and in position.

Two men, weapons aimed, jumped into view on the stairs below. They had expected to catch her off guard. They didn't.

Skye calmly fired, catching the man on the left in the top of the head and shoulders with the fusillade of bullets.

The man on the right pulled back and her bullets ricocheted off the stairs and walls. She brought her aim up a little higher - estimating the angle of ricochet - and fired. She heard a cry of pain as she emptied her magazines. Releasing the empty magazines, they fell to the dead body lying on the stairway below as she reloading quickly. Then she shot out the surveillance camera and exited the stairwell. Back into the hallway, she took careful aim at the surveillance camera at the far end of the hallway on this side of the building. One shot took it out and she began running back towards the elevators.

One of the men was just stepping out of the elevator doors.

Skye aimed on the run and fired. At least six bullets tore through his skull.

The body fell backward against another man trying to emerge from the elevator. The second man opened fire but the dead body threw his aim off as he toppled backward, unable to cope with the weight of the dead man.

Skye kept firing as she ran, bullets gouging into and ricocheting off the wall.

The elevator doors started closing but the body was in the way. The second man worked frantically to pull the dead weight inside to allow the doors to shut completely.

One of the other two men in the elevator stepped to the side and aimed through the opening, trying to get an angle on Skye.

Skye fired once with each gun and the man banged back against the elevator wall, sliding to the floor. She reached the edge of the elevator and fired between the open doors, aiming for the moving body parts inside.

The man struggling with the body emitted a cry of pain as a bullet clipped his forearm. But with the help of the fourth man, he managed to pull the body. Then he raised his weapon, firing through the closing gap, just hoping to keep the attacker off enough to let the doors shut.

Skye felt a bullet graze the right, upper arm of her leather jacket. Her weapons were clicking on empty as the elevator doors closed. She dropped the empty magazines and reloaded with her last two. Looking up at the floor indicator, Skye saw the elevator had returned to the main floor.

Chapter 35

WASHINGTON, DC

CANDY'S HAND DESCENDED and punched the 'Enter' button. The computer beeped again. Candy looked up at Rory briefly in hope and then looked at the monitor. Both her hands shot straight up in the air. "We're in," Candy shouted in triumph.

Rory realized he had been holding his breath. He let it out in a relieved sigh and shook his head, "Don't scare me like that again."

"Wow," Candy exclaimed as she looked at the screen.

Rory walked over to the computer to look at what was inside the previously password-protected folder. What he saw were two long lines of folders, side-by-side down the screen. "That's a pile of hidden information. That must be what they're trying to hide," Rory said.

Candy nodded, "Where do we start?"

"Start at the top and we'll work our way down," Rory told her as he pulled a chair over to sit down.

Their attention on the computer screen was broken when the door to the office swung open and bounced back hard against the wall with a bang. Something flew through the air and bounced several times across the office floor.

"Duck!" Rory yelled. He grabbed the front lip edge of the desk and lifted with all his strength, flipping the desk forward. The computer and everything that was on top of the desk crashed to the floor.

Candy was barely off her chair.

Rory placed his hand on her shoulder and rammed her to the floor. He fell on top of her just as an explosion filled the room. The noise was deafening and the desk was moved back against their heads.

Automatic weapon fire came next. Bullets ripped into the desktop.

Candy screamed.

Rory pulled his Baby Eagle. Leaning to the right, he aimed the gun around the edge of the desk, through the hazy smoke and towards the door. He fired twice.

The automatic weapon firing ceased.

Rory looked up and over the desk and fired two more shots through the open door into the hallway. Ducking down again, he looked around through the hazy smoke, trying to find a better defensive position. He realized the explosion had knocked out the window glass to the street. Rory grabbed Candy's elbow and urged her to get up, "Run. Go through the window. Hurry."

Candy looked up over the desk, confusion on her face.

"Just go," Rory urged her as he fired twice more through the open doorway. "It's our only chance."

Candy looked like she was about to cry but she scrambled to her feet and ran across the room.

Rory was up and moving sideways behind her, shooting a couple more times through the open doorway, pinning the attackers down.

A hand appeared around the edge of the open doorway, holding an automatic weapon. Bullets sprayed the desk area where they had been, ripping the top of the desk apart.

Candy screamed again as she jumped onto the window-sill.

Rory took two big steps and was up beside her. "Move," he yelled. Both of them jumped at the same time onto the sidewalk covered with shattered glass.

Candy stumbled forward onto her hands and knees.

Rory turned and fired two more shots back through the open window to keep the attackers at bay.

Candy yelped in pain.

Rory turned to see her getting up from the glass filled sidewalk. There was no time to check her out, "Sorry, we have to move, Candy." He grabbed her by the elbow and steered her down the sidewalk, away from the blown-out windows. A few doors down, Rory realized they were still sitting ducks dueto the streetlights. He guided Candy left between two parked cars.

Automatic weapon fire opened up again from behind them. Bullets ripped and tore into the vehicles. Windshields and side windows were blown to pieces, shattered glass flying everywhere.

Candy squatted, screaming as she put her hands protectively over her head.

Rory fired two shots back at a dark figure leaning out the blown-out window.

The figure ducked back inside.

Rory urged Candy to get up and they began running again, using the line of cars parked along the side of the street as protection. They finally reached a spot across from the small parking lot where they had left the car. Rory looked back over the top of the parked vehicles and saw several dark figures running from the area of Yim's office. But they weren't running down the street towards them, they were heading across the street to a vehicle. Rory took the opportunity to guide Candy out from the safety of the parked vehicles and across the sidewalk into the parking lot. They jumped into the silver Jaguar convertible without opening the doors. Rory started the vehicle and the tires screeched as he backed out of the parking spot. Flooring the accelerator, the V8 Supercharged engine roared and the tires squealed as they shot across the parking lot. The silver Jaguar smashed through the yellow gate arm of the parking lot and bounced into the street. Rory turned hard right and accelerated. In his rearview mirror, he could see a black SUV heading their way fast. Rory shot through a red light, barely squeezing between cars coming from both directions. He looked over at Candy, "Are you okay?"

Candy nodded as she held her left hand with her right. Her left hand was bleeding and there was blood on her cheek.

"Were you hit?"

Candy shook her head no. Her voice was quavering as she answered, "I...I just cut myself on the glass..."

"What about your cheek?" Rory asked her as he glanced in the rearview mirror. The black SUV behind them ran the red light as well.

Candy used her right hand to check her left cheek. She wiped away blood and looked at it, "No. It's okay. It's from my hand."

Rory nodded, "Good, good." He slammed the brakes on, putting the Jaguar into a sliding turn at the corner.

Candy leaned sideways, desperately holding onto the edge of her seat.

"Put your seatbelt on," Rory yelled at her.

Candy reached back for the belt but missed it as the Jaguar skidded right around another corner, the SUV still in hot pursuit. She was thrown back and forth as the Jaguar fishtailed.

Rory got it back under control.

Candy finally snagged the seat belt and buckled up.

Rory rammed the gas pedal to the floor.

Candy screamed as she was forced back in her seat by the rapid acceleration.

Rory glanced into the rearview mirror and saw the black SUV turning the corner behind them as well. It was further back now but still on the chase. Rory accelerated past several vehicles, the wind whipping over the silver convertible as he took chances to put distance between them and the attackers.

Candy screamed a couple of times at close calls as the Jaguar moved in and out of traffic, including the opposite lane.

Rory saw an on-ramp coming up and he cut across the front of a large transport.

Candy screamed again at the near miss.

At the top of the on-ramp, Rory accelerated hard, cutting off more traffic. The 550 hp engine under the hood growled and the speedometer hit 180 mph, leaving the black SUV far behind.

Chapter 36

THE HIGHLANDER BUILDING, Manhattan, New York
BLACKER'S HEAD TURNED QUICKLY as the doors to the stairway opened. O'Toole and another man stepped out. O'Toole shook his head and made a cutting action across his throat. Four had gone up to take her out. That meant two more were down. Blacker clenched a fist and cursed. His attention was caught by the elevator doors opening. Huneault and another man emerged, propping up a severely wounded man between the two of them as they exited. Blacker could see a body lying on the floor inside the elevator. He cursed again. This was not going well.

Huneault and his partner set the wounded man on the floor, propping his back against the security desk. "She was waiting for us outside the elevator on the second-floor," Huneault explained as he stood up.

"And she was at the top of the stairs, waiting for us on the second-floor landing," O'Toole added. "I doubt she can have much ammo left."

Cursing, Huneault shook his head as he looked at O'Toole, "No. And she can't be in two places at once."

Blacker's jaw clenched as he nodded in agreement. She couldn't hold them off forever.

O'Toole looked from Blacker to Huneault, "So how do you want to work this?"

Giving it a moment's thought, Huneault said, "Take Wallace and go back up those stairs. Monovo and I will go across to the other set of stairs. We put her in a pinch, making it nearly impossible to cover both sides."

Blacker nodded his agreement with the assault plan, "I'll let both of you know if she uses the elevators."

The Irishman nodded to Huneault, "Tell us when you're in position and we'll make the assault at the same time."

Huneault nodded. He and his partner headed off at a run for the far end of the building. The Irishman took his partner back into the stairwell.

When the four mercenaries were out of sight, Blacker calmly pulled his FN Five-seveN semi-automatic pistol from its holster, turned and fired a bullet into the brain of the wounded man before he could react. Blacker reholstered the pistol and returned to the video cameras. He banged his fist on the desk when he realized the Steele woman had taken out the other stair camera as well as both ends of the hallway. He was totally blind and couldn't coordinate either of these teams. All he could do was listen to the assault through his ear piece. He wished he could kill this Steele woman personally. Within moments, the 'go' signal was given and both teams were going up the stairs.

BOTH SETS OF MERCENARIES were cautious as they moved up the stairs to the second floor. Each team of two worked in tandem, one man covering above as the other climbed to the next turn in the stairs. Both teams arrived at the second-floor landing unimpeded. There had been no shots. There were no sounds to indicate someone was using the stairs to climb higher. And Blacker had given no signal that any of the elevators had moved. Conclusion: she was still on the second floor.

The Frenchman spoke in a low voice into his microphone, "Enter the hallway on three."

The acknowledgment from the Irishman came right back. They were ready.

Huneault counted down, "3-2-1-Go."

Both teams entered the hallway, weapons at the ready, on both ends of the building. They slowly worked towards each other. They checked all doors on either side of the hallway as they moved along. Every door was locked. The two teams of mercenaries were closing the distance to each other now. Their anticipation heightened.

Huneault whispered into his microphone, "The elevators."

The redheaded Irishman nodded. He smiled. It made sense. It was the only place the woman could be hiding. Using hand signals, the two teams slowly focused their attention on the three elevator doors that were still open. Once they were both in position, they sprang forward from each side, checking the two outside elevators. No one. Each team had a man check the roof of the elevator car. No one hiding.

O'Toole indicated the final, middle open elevator. Huneault nodded his agreement. She had to be there. They readied themselves. Then both teams sprang forward, converging on the last open elevator. No one. All four men looked at each other in confusion.

SKYE HAD ACCESSED A maintenance ceiling panel by climbing on top of the chrome waste receptacle just across from the bank of elevators and hiding. Now she silently pulled the ceiling panel op and set it aside. Pulling her weapons, Skye tipped over headfirst into the opening, holding herself in place with her knees. Now upside down and behind the men, Skye opened fire with both Glocks. The four men turned and began firing back. But they weren't expecting their target to be hanging upside down from the hallway ceiling and their bullets went into the walls. Most of Skye's thirty-eight remaining bullets buried themselves in the head, face, neck or shoulders of the mercenaries, ripping them apart. The bodies hit the floor as Skye's empty clicks echoed down the hallway. Skye pulled herself back up into the ceiling, holstered her weapons and jumped down to the floor. She dragged all four dead bodies into the center elevator and sent it back down to the main floor.

BLACKER HAD HEARD THE distant gunfire but now everything was quiet. "Huneault?" he said into his microphone. No answer. "O'Toole?" He heard a 'ding' over at the bank of elevators and the doors on one of the elevators slowly opened. He could see dead, bloody bodies inside. He cursed. The woman had taken out all sixteen men. His head turned as a wailing siren sounded outside.

A car screeched to a stop in front of the building. It was a police cruiser. Two young NYPD officers were out of the car immediately. Drawing their weapons, they moved to check the dead bodies on the far side of the street.

Blacker knew they would be the first of many officers descending on the scene very shortly. He pulled a handkerchief from a pocket and calmly began wiping down the security board as he kept one eye on the officers outside.

In a few moments, the two officers moved back to the three dark vehicles parked just outside the front entrance. One of them spotted the bullet hole through the glass doors and alerted his partner. The other nodded and both officers cautiously began moving towards the front entrance of the building.

Blacker pocketed the handkerchief, then pulled his Secret Service shield and hung it from the top pocket of his suit jacket. He put his hands in the air and walked towards the front glass doors. "Secret Service," he yelled as he reached the glass doors. "I'm going to open it, okay?" he said as he pointed cautiously to the door.

One of the officers nodded.

Blacker reached down, unlocked the doors and pushed one door, "Glad you officers are here." As they came inside, he took a step back and pointed to the body slumped over by the security desk, "I've got one wounded prisoner."

The first officer walked by Blacker, "He looks more than wounded."

"No, he just needs a paramedic, There are some dead perps in the elevator, though. My partner is on the second floor chasing another."

The second officer walked past Blacker as well, "Why is the Secret Service here? And what in the world happened?"

Blacker pulled his weapon silently. "Nothing you need to know about." He placed a bullet in the back of each officer's head.

The two police officers fell dead, killed instantly.

Holstered his weapon, Blacker wiped the door handle with the handkerchief, then moved through the front door to his vehicle. Getting in, Blacker did a U-turn in the street and parked a few buildings down on the right-hand side. He shut off the engine.

Within moments several more NYPD cruisers shot past his position, heading for the scene of the shooting.

In his rearview mirror, Blacker saw lights flashing beyond the overturned SUV at the other end of the street.

In moments, more cruisers converged on the scene from that direction.

Things were going sideways quickly. He had a call to make. Blacker started his vehicle and hit the call button for his cell phone on the steering wheel. Some people were not going to be too happy.

Chapter 37

WASHINGTON, DC

RORY PULLED OFF THE FREEWAY and drove to a 24-hr pharmacy, where he bought a first aid kit. In the parking lot, he cleaned Candy's face, checking to make sure it was only blood. Fortunately, there was no cut.

"What happened back there? What blew up?" Candy asked in a shaky whisper as Rory gently picked up her hand to work on it.

"That, my dear, was a grenade," Rory said as he wiped away blood from the palm of her hand.

"A grenade!"

Rory nodded, "They've upped the ante, that's for sure." He found a nasty cut and cleaned it with antiseptic.

"The Secret Service is throwing grenades at us now!" Candy exclaimed.

"I don't think it was the Secret Service," Rory said as he pulled out a package of bandages from the first aid kit.

"Who else could it be?"

"I'm not sure," Rory admitted. "Probably the Chinese."

"Do you really think that's possible?"

"Keep in mind, Yim was working for the Chinese. And keep in mind, my sister is looking into ZongChi Technologies. Between us here in DC and her in New York, we're probably poking the bear," Rory said as he began to bandage her hand.

"That's the Russians," Candy said. "The bear is the Russians."

"Okay, poking the panda."

Candy raised her eyebrows, "That sounds kinky."

"True," Rory said with a smile. "Anyway, I'm sure those Secret Service guys who kidnapped us, they were probably the ones who burned Yim's house down and took the computer. But there wasn't anything on the news report at the time of the fire or after that indicated anything had happened to Yim's office. It made me think we would be safe to go there. I wasn't thinking about the Chinese and I let my guard down."

"Do you think they were waiting for us to go there?" Candy asked.

"Maybe. But we were in there too long before they attacked," Rory reasoned. "More than likely, they went there to move everything out and stumbled on us."

"Okay. So, let's say it was the Chinese trying to kill us. Why use a grenade? That would probably mean destroying everything in there."

"Our presence there would mean everything inside was probably compromised anyway. They had no idea what we had looked at or what we knew."

"Okay, that makes sense," Candy said. She flexed her bandaged hand, "So, what do we do now?"

"Probably best if we go back to the hotel," Rory said as he put everything back into the first aid kit. "The Chinese won't give up. And the attack shows they're deadly serious about killing us and protecting their spy network. They will pull out all the stops to hunt us down now."

Candy's face reflected the fear she was feeling in her heart at that moment.

Rory started the Jaguar, "It's becoming more and more important for us to find out what's on that flash drive–" He suddenly looked over at Candy. "The flash drive!"

Candy patted her left breast, "I pulled it out of the computer port when you yelled."

Rory looked relieved, "Thank goodness for your big boobs."

"Hey! It was my hand that did it, not my big boobs," Candy protested.

AN HOUR LATER, RORY cruised the block around the elegant Hay-Adams hotel several times, watching for any suspicious vehicles or characters on the sidewalk around the hotel.

In the passenger seat, Candy's her eyes nervously glanced around, watching every person they passed.

Rory decided everything looked okay. He cranked the Jaguar right and finally entered the front driveway. He gave the hotel valet his keys and guided Candy back inside the hotel. He remained alert all the way up to their room. Everything looked quiet, but he knew that could change in a heartbeat. Once they were inside the room, Rory relaxed just a bit and they ordered up room service.

Candy went to the laptop and got it running. "Do you still remember the password?" she asked him she plugged in the USB drive.

Rory walked over to the desk and pulled out a crumpled piece of paper from his pocket, "I took the liberty of tearing away the part of Yim's genealogy chart that had the number on it. I didn't think he would be needing it any time soon." He uncrumpled the paper and handed it to Candy.

"Good thinking," Candy said as she took the torn piece of paper in hand. "You're more than just a pretty face."

"I like to think of myself as brains and beauty all in one package."

"Modest too," Candy said as she typed in the number. She hit enter and the folder was unlocked again. Rory sat beside her and they began looking through the dozens of folders inside.

HOURS LATER, RORY STOOD at the window, looking out at the White House in the distance as he contemplated what Candy was finding - or not finding - in the hidden files.

"I'm sure we're going to find something, Rory," Candy said.

"I know," Rory said as he mulled over everything that had happened. "There has to be something there. The question is - will we find it before they find us?"

"Don't talk like that," Candy protested. Then she glanced over at him, "We should be safe here, right?"

Rory didn't say anything in reply as he stood there, hands behind his back, looking out of the White House.

Candy swallowed and went back to work on the files.

Rory's cell phone made a small buzzing sound. He pulled it from his pocket and saw he had a text message from his office.

"Most of the emails in this one folder are the names of donors to Lane's campaigns over the years," said Candy. "There are folders going back...ten years."

"That would go back to the time just before he ran for governor?" Rory asked her. He began reading the text message on his cell phone.

"Uh huh," Candy answered. She continued looking through the information on the screen, "That's when he started running for political office."

"What was he doing before that?" Rory asked her, but his mind was only half on their conversation. The information in the message wasn't anything he had expected. It had to do with the death of Warren Howel Jossel - Candy's father - but he wasn't sure how it fit into the efforts to prove her innocence.

Candy sat back and was in deep thought for a moment. "I'm not sure what he did before running for political office. He was in some type of business...but I don't remember much else...."

"Why was he so popular as governor?" Rory asked her as he tapped his cell phone against his chin, thinking. "I remember hearing that he had a high approval rating among the voters."

Candy nodded enthusiastically, "He was loved by everyone. When he was first elected, he got several businesses to move to Kentucky and created a lot of jobs."

"That's an amazing coup for any politician. Where did these businesses move from?"

"I'm not really sure," Candy said. "I think they came from different locations. But then he got three automotive assembly plants to open up in Kentucky, as well as a raft of auto parts supply companies, to feed the plant."

"Really? That's an even bigger coup for a politician. Where did these automotive plants move from? Detroit?"

"Oh, they didn't move in. They were actually built by the–"

Rory turned to look over at Candy. She was staring straight ahead like she was in shock.

"What's wrong?"

"I...I just remembered who Lane talked into building those automotive plants," Candy said in a low voice.

"Who?"

She looked over into Rory's silver-blue eyes. "The Chinese."

Rory couldn't help but raise an eyebrow, "Really?" He looked down at the text message again about Warren Jossel. It was based on information found in a ZongChi Technologies file. He frowned to himself, "They keep showing up in this case."

"It could just be a coincidence," Candy said dismissively after a few moments. She crossed her arms over her chest, obviously not wanting to believe anything bad about Lane. Or anyone around him. But her face had a worried look on it.

"Maybe," Rory said. But he was not totally convinced it was just a simple coincidence. After another moment of thought, he asked her, "Is there anything in those files about it?"

Candy let out a sharp, "No." She seemed to resist the thought and then she let out an irritated sigh, putting her hand on the computer mouse, "At least nothing I've come across. I'll keep on looking. Maybe I'll see something about it. But I'm sure it's just...."

Rory could tell Candy was a little shaken at the revelation. He turned back to look out the window. He decided to keep the information in the text message to himself for now. He doubted Candy would handle it well. And truthfully, he didn't know *how* it fitted in. Or *if* it did. There were a lot of pieces of the puzzle just floating around now, defying assembly. But, at the same time, an outline was beginning to form in his mind.

Chapter 38

THE HIGHLANDER BUILDING, Manhattan, New York
TORION BLACKER SAT IN HIS VEHICLE, watching
the forensics teams work the crime scene on the other side of the
yellow tape. All the bodies were still in place in the street and
inside the building. He imagined it would be hours before they
were moved to the city morgue. But that part was of no consequence. He was watching for the Steele woman. He liked to be
proactive and not wait, but he had no choice here. He didn't have
any contacts here on scene that he could use, so he had no way of
knowing what was happening on the inside. And since her name
hadn't popped up on his police scanner, he had to surmise she
had simply disappeared into her office once the police had arrived and secured the building. She was a real pro. She had probably used untraceable weapons. And since he had made sure none
of what happened was recorded, the police would have no way
of knowing she was involved in wiping out his team. Too bad.
He had hoped she would be taken to a precinct nearby to make
a statement. That would have given him another shot at her. He
just had to stay patient and wait. He had put in calls for help and
people were now watching around the block, in case she used another exit. If she came out, he would know it.

His cell phone rang. He hit the answer button on the steering wheel, "Yes?"

"Any sign of the Steele woman?" the harsh, metallic voice asked.

"No," was all Blacker said.

There was silence on the other end of the line for a moment. "Are the police talking to her? Or anyone else in their office?"

"I don't think so," Blacker said. "I've been listening to the police scanner and there is absolutely no mention about her involvement in the shootout at all."

"That's good," the metallic voice said. *"I'll pull some strings with NYPD. I'll find out exactly what they know."*

"That's a good idea. I think–" A sound high above the street interrupted Blacker's conversation

"What's wrong?" the harsh voice asked immediately.

Blacker didn't reply. He was listening intently. The sound was from a helicopter. The news helicopters had been shooting reports for all the media outlets all night. But they were much higher than this one seemed to be. "Hold on," Blacker said and he was out of his vehicle fast, looking up from the sidewalk. A black helicopter was leaving the roof of the Highlander building. He caught the Highlander company logo on the side of the helicopter as it turned and then disappeared over the building. He got back into the vehicle, cursing at what was happening.

"What's wrong?"

"An intel screw-up, that's what," Blacker yelled.

"What you mean?"

"Those mercenaries you had on payroll screwed up," Blacker said harshly. "They didn't check for all avenues of escape from the building. They didn't check to see if there was a helicopter pad on top of their building. And there is! Someone just flew off in a helicopter belonging to Steele's company."

There was a lot of cursing on the other end of the line.

"Yeah, tell me about it," Blacker said. He banged the steering wheel with a fist. "Now we have no idea if the Steele woman or other staff members are inside or not."

"I'll make some calls and start a search. There is an online service the provides flight tracking for both commercial and private flights. We'll find their flight plan and—"

"Provided they filed a flight plan," Blacker said harshly. "I wouldn't. Considering our attack on the building, they may have just flown out without—"

"Then I'll call in favors and get someone to track them on radar. I'll have the military scramble a jet if I have to," the metallic voice yelled.

"Just as long as you find them. And I want a helicopter and a plane ready for me to pursue them where ever they go—"

"Fine!" The call ended abruptly.

Blacker sat there. He pounded his fist on the steering wheel again and again. What a screw-up. Had the woman left on the chopper or was it someone else? And why? And where? He had no choice but to sit and wait. And that just made him angrier. He would follow that Steele woman to the ends of the earth and strangle her with his own bare hands.

THE HIGHLANDER COMPANY helicopter descended to a roof helipad two blocks away from the Highlander building.

Skye Steele slipped out of the helicopter to the roof.

The helicopter took off, taking Uncle Murdock and Avis on to their destination.

Moving low across the roof to the door, Skye descended one floor to the elevators. She had unfinished business.

According to the report on the police scanner, two officers were found face down inside the front door, shot in the back of the head. There could be several explanations but only one made sense. Those two officers were responding to the report of gun fire and trusted someone enough to let him or her get behind them at the front door. Skye imagined that someone they trusted was also responsible for the attack on the Highlander building, trying to kill her family.

The elevator reached the ground floor and Skye moved quickly out the front entrance and jogged one block over. Skye entered the rear entrance of a medical building and moved through to the front lobby. Slipping out the front door, she turned right and stopped beside a large planter that offered her cover.

The crime scene was being worked to her left in front of the Highlander building. She could see the two SUVs that had been parked in front of the building were still there. The dark sedan that had been parked in front of them was not there. Someone had definitely left the building alive.

Skye closed her eyes and imagined how the battle outside had taken place. She focused on the man in the black pinstriped suit who had exited from that sedan. She had the impression he was a government agent of some type. Opening her eyes, Skye scanned up and down the street.

There! The dark sedan was parked on this side of the street, facing the other way.

Skye stayed close to the buildings and moved up the street.

There was definitely a single figure in the driver seat. A man. From the angle of his head, he appeared to be looking into his rearview mirror, watching the crime scene.

Skye pulled her cell phone from her pocket, keeping her head down as she approached the sedan. Activating the cell phone spy software Avis had installed, Skye quickly found a cell phone signal coming from the sedan. The cell phone had high-security features and she wouldn't be able to access the phone calls, e-mail messages or texts. She had already anticipated that. She accessed what she really wanted, the global-positioning-system chip. Cloning that signal into her own cell phone, Skye turned around and headed back into the shadows of the building. She made a call.

Avis answered, "Did it work?" The beating sound of the helicopter blades echoed in the background.

"Looks like it," Skye said. "Now I want you to file that flight plan for our Learjet into Washington."

There was silence a few moments, then Avis said, "Done. Uncle Murdock says the helicopter will return to that helipad for you within twenty minutes."

"Thanks." Skye ended the call and now waited, watching the cloned signal. Would the man in the pinstriped suit be told about the flight plan? She only had to wait five minutes. He was receiving a call.

A moment later, the dark sedan quickly pulled out of the parking spot and raced away.

She definitely had the right person. And he *was* either government or someone with inside government contacts, someone at the highest levels, who was able to monitor and access the online flight plan form. She wanted to confront mister pinstripe, as she had done with his men, but that would have to wait. But as long as he kept his phone, she could find him at a moment's notice. And she would know if he came near Rory and Candy...or her family here again.

See you in Washington, bozo, she thought as she set off at a jog.

Chapter 39

WASHINGTON, DC

THE SUN WAS JUST COMING UP when Rory had room service deliver a nice breakfast while Candy took a shower. They had stayed up most of the night with little sleep, sifting through all of the new files they had found. Using the Internet, they had checked out the lists of campaign contributors. It had taken a long time but nothing stood out, no red flags were raised. They had found files detailing each of their monetary contributions, but nothing seemed to be illegal there either. Rory nibbled at a plate of sunny-side-up eggs and turkey bacon.

Candy came padding out of the bathroom, running a brush through her long, platinum blond hair, "Short hair was a lot easier, let me tell you."

Rory didn't say anything as she sat down at the small table and started to eat her own breakfast. He contemplating calling his office but there was always the fear that someone was listening, somehow, somewhere. He watched Candy rush through her applewood smoked bacon, country style potatoes and cheese omelet, eager to get back to the laptop and the files. He didn't blame her. Having someone trying to kill you is bad, but not being able to do anything about it was worse. She was looking for some way to fight back.

Finishing only three-quarters of her breakfast, Candy picked up her mug of coffee and headed over to the laptop, "I'm going to get started again, okay?"

Rory watched as she opened up the files again and started to work again. "Sounds good," he said. "Give me a couple more minutes and I'll be over to help." He carried his own mug of coffee over to the window instead and looked out at the White House in the distance. His mind continued to churn over the same questions. Why was someone trying to kill Candace Jossel? Was it just about the Chinese spying? That *was* a good reason to want her dead but the whole episode started because she had made that backup. He was convinced they were trying to cover up something more. But what? Was it something she saw? Was it something she knew but didn't realize it? Even more important, who was behind it all? Rory looked at the wall clock. He had received that text message from his office last night but nothing beyond that. And he still hadn't heard anything from Skye herself since she had flown back to New York. Had something happened to her when she started looking into the ZongChi Technologies angle? The grenade attack in a civilian setting here in Washington, DC meant the people behind this were willing to do anything to protect their secrets. He was getting worried.

"Maybe you should get another computer," Candy said.

Rory turned to look at her, "Why?"

"I found a number of individual folders for Super PACs and it's going to take a long time to go through all of these," Candy told him. "With a second computer, maybe you could take care of that while I continue sifting through other files. Would do you think?"

Rory nodded. He walked towards the telephone to call the concierge when he stopped in his tracks. He did some thinking. Then he looked at her, "Did you say found a number of folders for Super PACs?"

Candy looked over at him, "Yeah. Why?"

Rory slowly walked over to the desk. He took a sip of coffee as he looked at the folders on the screen.

"What are you thinking?" Candy asked him.

"Just a hunch. Take a quick look on the Internet. Tell me how Super PACs are supposed to work."

Candy gave him a questioning look for a moment, then called up a web browser and began to check out Super PACs on the Internet. She read through a few things as Rory stood over her, drinking his coffee, "Okay," she said. "It says Super PACs are a supercharged breed of political action committees. That's what the PAC stands for, political action committee. It's used by individuals or organizations to raise and spend money to elect or defeat candidates for public office."

"Okay," Rory said slowly, "but what's the connection between the political candidates and the Super PAC?"

Candy ran her fingers through the lines of text on the computer screen. She sat up straight, "It says they're not supposed to coordinate their efforts with the candidate's campaign." She looked up at Rory.

Rory looked down at her, "If that's the case, why would Lane have their information in the computer at his campaign headquarters?"

Candy just stared up at him for a moment.

"How much are they allowed to raise? Who controls it? What else does your search say?" Rory asked her. When Candy didn't react, Rory gave a nod to the computer screen. He knew she didn't want to look further, that it could bump up against her rigid beliefs in the goodness of certain people, but they had to.

After another few seconds, Candy turned back to the screen and began to browse through the material. She sat back but didn't say anything. Instead, Candy went back to the Google search page and ran another search with the parameters 'super pac' and 'fund raising'. She browsed through some of the material, then she did another search with added parameters.

Rory drank his coffee, calmly watching as she read the material. He could see everything she was reading and not much was different despite the variety of search parameters she used. When she did another search and began to look through more material, Rory walked over and poured himself more coffee. He slowly walked back over to Candy, "Doesn't look good, does it?"

Candy didn't say anything for a moment. She called up a few more articles and browsed through them. Candy was very aware Rory was right there behind her, reading the same things and she now spoke in a low, angry voice, "I'm sure my sister didn't know anything about this,"

"I didn't say she did," Rory said. "Super PACs are used to raise unlimited funds to either help or attack a political candidate. It's a way to get around spending limitations on most individuals and organizations, isn't it?"

Candy nodded her head slowly a few times.

"Do you have any idea how much money Lane's rival spent on his campaign?" Rory asked her.

Candy hesitated for a moment and then began doing another search, "It says Simon Wayne Pellars and the Super PACs on his side raised and spent nearly $1.1 billion."

"That's with a B?" Rory whistled.

"And Connor Harrison Lane and the Super PACs on his side raised and spent... $2.3 billion."

"That's twice as much," Rory said.

Candy didn't look up but asked him in a quiet voice, "Do you think that's how Lane won? By cheating?"

Rory thought about it for a moment and then said, "Maybe. But there has to be more to it. He's in for four years. It would raise a scandal, that's for sure. But could it get him impeached? That would be a tough fight."

Candy nodded. She didn't seem to want to say much else.

"Open up each folder for the Super PACs," Rory instructed her. "Are any dollar figures associated with each one?"

Candy moved her hand to start and then sat back, "But...we already know Lane and the Super PACs spent $2.3 billion. We already did that search."

Rory just waited a moment and then said, "Are you afraid of what else we might find if we look?

Letting out a small breath of frustration, Candy began opening up each folder and scanning their contents "There are dollar figures showing," she said finally. "And the dollar figures are pretty high. Just a minute, there's a folder at the end entitled Super PACs a-z." She opened it up and there was a financial spreadsheet with the same title. Candy double clicked it and opened it up. She gave a gasp as she looked at the bottom line.

"$12.7 billion," was all that Rory said.

Chapter 40

SKYE STEELE WATCHED THE SUN coming up through the side window of the Gulfstream G650 business jet. She was tired after the long night and the steady purr of the Rolls-Royce BR725 engines was putting her to sleep. She contemplated contacting Rory and letting him know what had transpired at the office. No doubt there would be a news report–

The voice of Ron McMillan, the pilot, came over the speaker, "Miss Steele, we have a problem."

Skye pressed the internal communications button on the armrest, "What is it, Ron?"

"I've just been informed by the air traffic control tower at Washington National Airport that we won't be able to land there."

Immediately on alert, Skye asked, "Why not?"

"Apparently a bomb threat was phoned in. They're diverting all traffic until further notice–"

"How about Dulles International Airport–?"

"I asked them the same thing. They've received a bomb threat for Dulles as well," McMillan said. "They're suggesting we divert to Baltimore-Washington International Airport."

Skye gave the news some thought. "Did they give any reason for sending us specifically to Baltimore-Washington International Airport?"

McMillan didn't answer right away. Then he said, "No. It's the next closest airport for commercial aircraft. That's the only reason I can think of."

Looking out the window, Skye gave it some more thought.

After a moment, McMillan asked, "Do you want me to head to Baltimore-Washington?"

Skye pulled out her cell phone and hit speed dial, "Hold on for one moment, Ron."

Avis answered on the first ring, "Yes?"

"It's Skye–"

"You just left. Is everything all right?"

"Ron just received word there was a bomb threat at Washington National Airport."

"That's where you're supposed to land–"

"They also had one for Dulles Airport," Skye added.

Avis paused for a heartbeat, "That sounds like someone doesn't want you in Washington right now, doesn't it?"

"That's what I thought. Ron says we're being diverted to Baltimore-Washington International."

"That would put you an hour-and-a-half away at most from Washington," Avis said. "Not much of a delay if that was their purpose."

Skye gave it a moment's thought, "Do you still have a lock on our friend's cell phone?"

"I think so," Avis said. "Let me check on where he is."

Skye waited patiently for an answer.

"*This is interesting,*" *Avis said after a few moments,* "*the signal is just south of Baltimore....*"

"In the vicinity of the airport, I would guess," Skye said.

"*Sounds like it could be a setup–*"

"Miss Skye?" It was the pilot over the speaker system. He sounded alarmed.

"Yes, Ron?"

"I'm picking up chatter between air traffic control in Washington and several pilots," McMillan said with urgency. "Along with the bomb threats on the ground, there was also a report of a stolen aircraft that could be used in a terrorist attack. An air force jet is being sent to intercept a Gulfstream G650 business jet."

Skye sat up quickly, "Are they targeting us specifically?"

"I have no way of knowing for sure," McMillan answered. "I'm sure there could be other Gulfstream G650 business jets in the area of Washington DC. But...."

"Any idea how long we have?" Skye asked him quickly.

"No," McMillan said. "If they had to scramble a jet from the ground, maybe eight or nine minutes. But if they're already airborne...they travel two and a half times faster than we can move...so not much more than a few minutes."

"*You have to get out of there Skye!*" *Avis said over the phone.* "*The incident at the Highlander Building shows these people are capable of anything.*"

Skye knew she was right. No matter how far-fetched it sounded, they could be in serious trouble very quickly. "How fast can you get us down, Ron?"

McMillan was silent for a moment before he answered. "We can't land at Washington National Airport or Dulles without getting clearance. We could try to land anyway but - if we encounter the jet, they'd probably shoot us down on approach, figuring it was a terrorist attack. Baltimore-Washington International is the closest–"

"That's a setup, Clarke," Skye said, "that's what they want."

McMillan cursed softly, "The other airports here are too small to handle the G650." He was silent for a few seconds. "Our best bet is to head south to Richmond International Airport," he said finally.

"But that gives the Air Force jet more time to track and find us, of course," Skye reasoned.

"You're right," McMillan said glumly.

Skye tried to figure out what else they could do.

"I can call the Air Force and give them your call sign," Avis suggested.

"You can try. But I'm not sure you'll get through to the right people in time–"

"Miss Skye?"

"Yes, Ron?"

"I have an idea."

"What is it?"

"I could turn off the automatic dependent surveillance-broadcast equipment they use for the flight radar system to track the aircraft," McMillan said quickly. "Mr. MacLeod had the foresight to have the technicians rig up a switch to do that, because of the sensitive nature of some of the cases we handle. The problem is...." His voice trailed off.

"Is what Ron? We don't have much time."

"If I do turn it off...they could assume we're trying to avoid detection. Which we would be, of course. But - that would give the Air Force jet a very good reason to consider us hostile and...."

"Do it," Skye instructed him without hesitation. "But take a heading in the opposite direction *before* you to turn it off. Let's send them on a wild goose chase."

"Okay. I'll take a heading directly for the Pentagon first, then turn off the equipment and go low," McMillan said. The Gulfstream G650 banked quickly to the left.

Avis spoke up, a tinge of disbelief in her voice, "We must be creating a lot of havoc and getting too close for comfort for someone. I can see them diverting you away from Washington. But trying to get an Air Force jet to shoot you down over US airspace? That is cold-blooded murder."

"That it is," Skye agreed. She clenched her jaw. She couldn't wait to meet up with that bozo in the car and whoever was behind this whole thing.

There was silence and then Avis asked, "I think I heard Ron say you're heading for Richmond International Airport, then?"

"Right."

"Okay," Avis said. "I'll call ahead and get you transportation."

"Try and get a Blackbird or a Hayabusa."

"You sure?"

Skye hammered a fist onto the armrest and cursed, "Yes. Pay double or triple and get it delivered if you have too. Having to land in Richmond, Virginia puts me farther away from helping Rory."

Avis didn't say anything.

"I'm sorry. I'm not mad at you."

"I know."

"I'm going to turn the cell phone off in case they can track us that way as well," Skye said. "Keep an eye on our friend for me."

"Will do. Call me when you land," Avis said. She hung up.

Skye turned her cell phone off and sat back.

"Okay, here we go," McMillan said a few seconds later.

The Gulfstream G650 banked hard to the right. The sound of the Rolls-Royce BR725 engines rose in pitch as they headed for Richmond, Virginia at Mach 0.925.

Chapter 41

IT WAS CANDY'S TURN to stand at the window, looking out at the White House. The rich smell of coffee and sandwiches carried through the room but only Rory had been able to eat what room service had delivered. Candy just drank coffee. And right now, her hands were slightly shaking as she lifted the coffee mug to her lips.

Rory was making himself another coffee. He didn't say anything but there were some questions left hanging in the air. The possibility of her sister's involvement in a campaign that was raising money illegally was a stunner to Candy. But not so much to Rory. He was used to seeing the worst side of people when it came to getting what they wanted. But the attempts to kill Candy and the attack at Yim's office told him there were deeper secrets on the thumb drive. But what? And would it do them any good to find them?

Without turning, Candy asked him in a quiet voice, "So what do we do now?"

Rory didn't say anything as he walked up behind her to look out the window. He took a few sips of his coffee before he spoke. "Do you think you could do a little more digging into those files?"

Candy took a breath and let it out very slowly before answering, "Do we really need to?"

Rory thought about it for a moment. "Lane's campaign and Super PAC organizations spent $2.3 billion to get him elected President of the United States. That means there is $10.4 billion missing or unaccounted for. *That* is a lot of money. Lane has achieved his goal of being the President, so he's not jetting off to the billionaire's lifestyle right now. And I'm sure he wasn't hurting for cash before, although sometimes enough is never enough for some of these people. And your sister is definitely not off living the billionaire lifestyle either—"

Candy turned, the coffee in her mug splashing over the side, "My sister would *never* do that. Do you hear me? *Never*."

Rory looked at her calmly, "I never said she did. But somebody has that money. Don't you want to know where it went to? Somebody was responsible for raising all that money, for spending it and for it being hidden somewhere—"

"Not my sister. I know her. That is something *she* would never do," Candy insisted. Her coffee splashed over the side of the mug again because of her agitated gestures. She looked at the mug in anger like it was a traitor. She moved back over to the laptop, set her coffee down with a bang and began to look through the files again. Her voice was angry and determined, " I'll prove it to you. There *has* to be some indication of who did what and where the money is." She stopped, glanced in Rory's direction and lifted a finger, "And it won't be my sister." She went back to work on the files.

Rory calmly walked over behind her, sipping his coffee and looking over her shoulder as she opened up each and every file.

"You don't have to watch me," she said angrily. "I won't hide any evidence I find, despite what you think."

Rory didn't say anything. This definitely wasn't easy for her. He walked away and sat in one of the larger easy chairs, sipping coffee as he let her work.

Time passed.

Two hours later, Rory was getting them both a coffee refill when he heard a gasp come from Candy. He set the coffee mugs down and moved back over to her quickly, "Are you okay?"

Candy didn't say a word. Her hands were clamped over her mouth. She had obviously seen something that had shocked her.

Rory squatted down beside Candy, "What's wrong?" He turned the laptop just slightly to look at the screen, "What are you looking at?"

"Those files are...financial records," Candy said finally.

"For where the money went?"

"No. For where over $8 billion of the $10.4 billion *came from*," said Candy in a weak voice.

Rory looked at the screen. He cocked his head. He grabbed the mouse and closed the spreadsheet he was looking at and opened another. "Am I reading this correctly?" He opened and closed a few more, "These look like records of bank drafts to various donors and Super PACs–"

"They are," Candy said. "And you can look at as many as you want. They have all been funneled one way or another from the same source."

Rory looked up at Candy. He couldn't help but feel surprised himself.

Candy nodded, "They all came from the People's Republic of China."

Rory stood up, "That means–"

"China used our own stupidity against us," Candy said. "We don't want to limit freedom of speech and because of that, we allowed them the perfect opportunity to walk in and take over. They are using the Super PAC system for their own ends. The People's Republic of China was the major force behind Lane's run for the Presidency. They can now shape American domestic and foreign policy to suit their own...."

Rory nodded, "Connor Harrison Lane isn't just the President of the United States. They put their own candidate into power. He is the Chinese President of the United States!"

Chapter 42

RICHMOND INTERNATIONAL Airport

IT TOOK TWO HOURS after landing before Skye was able to get her transportation and she was livid. It now sat on the tarmac, next to a pickup truck and two husky men.

The men backed away as the woman in black leather strode across the tarmac. She was clearly half a foot taller than them. The one with the beard held out a pair of knee pads/sliders, "We kinda got lost, ma'am. This is what the lady ordered–"

"Don't call me, ma'am," Skye said. She snatched the knee pads/sliders from him, bent over and put them on. She stood up and held her hand out.

Oh, yeah." The bearded man took the other item from under his arm and held it out.

Skye took the Spidi Airtech armor jacket and slipped it on.

The other man with the buzz cut passed one hand over his hair as he held out a Scorpion EXO AT950 helmet.

She snatched the helmet from him and strode to the Suzuki Hayabusa GSX1300R motorcycle, "Is the gas tank full?

The bearded man nodded, "Yes, ma'am - uh - yes, sir - uh - I made sure of that like we were told."

"And the other items we ordered?"

The man with the buzz cut glanced at his buddy, "Uh, yeah, Freddy had me get the stuff from down the street. We don't stock that stuff. It's in the saddle bag on the right."

Skye straddled the Hayabusa and pulled on the helmet. Starting the engine without another word, Skye ripped across the tarmac to the back exit. She followed the route she had chosen before leaving the plane and she headed for the Interstate. The Hayabusa slipped through the wind like a Peregrine Falcon. And 9.86 seconds after entering I-95 North, Skye had the four-cylinder, short-stroke, DOHC mill engine running hard and she hit 194 mph.

Chapter 43

RORY STOOD BY THE WINDOW, looking out over the White House again. The view of the iconic building, coupled with their conversation about the Chinese, caused Rory's mind to go to the text message he had received from his office earlier. Rory pulled his cell phone out and reread the message.

"How bad do you think things could get?" Candy asked him. She was still looking through the files contained on the USB drive.

"What do you mean?"

"About the Chinese and what they've done...."

Rory tapped the cell phone against his chin, thinking, "There's no telling what the Chinese could do by controlling the man who is the President of the United States."

"They could shape our foreign policy...our domestic policies...everything...," Candy said.

"Actually, they could do more damage than that," Rory said. He put his cell phone back in his pocket and looked out at the White House again, "The government owns or operate major ports, commercial airports, toll road, bridges, buildings...they could sell a lot of the country's infrastructure to the Chinese government–"

But that would *have* to go through Congress or committees on sales to foreign entities," Candy said firmly. "Someone would scrutinize it or oppose it."

Rory nodded his head in agreement, "True. But keep in mind there is still $10.4 billion lying around like a slush fund. Do they use that to back other candidates for the Senate? Those Senators would be on their side in a vote down the road. Do they use it to influence sitting Senators in some way? Do you know how many people they could bribe with that kind of money?"

"Do you think that's possible?"

"Anything is possible, Candy. Especially considering what they've already done to this point," he said. "Over the centuries, nations have been willing to do many things to destroy their enemies. China considers the United States the enemy and they're willing to do anything to weaken this country–"

"We *can't* let the Chinese do that," Candy said emphatically.

Rory nodded but his mind was only half on their conversation. Stopping the Chinese was one thing. Protecting Candy and proving her innocence was his higher priority right now. And how would she take the information in the text message he had received? He could hear Candy typing away on the keyboard now and he knew loyalty to her sister was still driving her, "I can understand your concern. I'm sure they have a complete plan in place and will–"

"I don't care *what* plan they have in place," Candy said firmly. "My sister will put a stop to it."

Rory shook his head. He wasn't so sure, "That presumes she knows–" Rory felt a chill go through him. He turned and looked at Candy sitting in front of the laptop, "You didn't...?"

Turning, Candy gave Rory a defiant look, "I couldn't let my sister sit in the middle of that situation without knowing–"

Rory took a step towards Candy, his heart starting to race, "What did you do Candy? *What* did you do?"

"I accessed my account online and sent her an email," Candy stated firmly.

Rory clenched his fists, "But don't you realize–"

Candy banged the table with her fist, making the laptop jump, "I can't just abandon my sister after everything she's done for me. I won't. Do you hear me? I won't!"

He knew they were in trouble. Rory reached for his jean jacket as he pointed to the laptop, "Grab the USB drive and let's go."

Remaining defiant, Candy raised her head, "No. *My* sister will take care of everything."

The material on his jacket snapped as Rory put it on, "You do remember the last two times you did this? Your calls were intercepted and we almost got killed."

"But I sent an email–"

"Seriously? You've just uncovered a conspiracy with backdoors into computers and siphoning data and information and you don't think these guys can intercept a simple email and track it back to us?"

Candy opened her mouth and closed it.

Rory reached for the USB drive.

Snatched the USB drive from the port, Candy's fist closed around it, "Fine. But I'm not sorry–"

Rory looked her in the eyes, "You might be yet. Let's go." He turned and hustled across to the door as he pulled the Eagle from his shoulder holster.

Hesitating a moment, Candy followed him, slipping the USB drive into her padded bra.

Checking the peephole, Rory determined no one was outside in the hall. Opening the door carefully, he checked up and down the hallway. It was empty. Moving quickly, he led Candy down the hallway. She stayed close behind him but when they reached the bank of elevators, Candy turned left and hit the down button. Rory stopped, stepped back and took her firmly by the elbow, guiding her further down the hall.

"What are we doing?" Candy asked him.

"Doing everything we can to stay alive. And that means not being trapped in an elevator," Rory told her firmly. He pulled her into the stairwell.

"Seriously? But it's 10 floors."

"Good. We'll stay fit while we're trying to stay alive." Rory took a cautious look over the railing. With no signs of anyone on the stairs below them, they began the downward trek.

DANNI KANG HAD RECEIVED word two of his targets were staying at the Hay-Adams hotel. He stood at the front entrance with three men, looking at his watch. He was giving another three men time to cover the left entrance and one more trio to cover the back. Then they would enter from all sides. There was no escape open to the targets. He counted down: 5-4-3-2-1. Time to move. Kang led his men through the front entrance. Each man in his cell was primed and ready to take out their targets. Subtlety and silence would be used if possible. But with so much on the line, they were ready to inflict casualties on by-standers as well.

REACHING THE UPPER level of the hotel's main floor, Rory holstered his weapon and led Candy out of the stairwell. There were a lot of people milling about today, which made it easier to hide in plain sight. At least he hoped it would. A few minutes later, as they descended a small staircase to the lower level of the main floor, Rory spotted a group of men at the far end. Years of military training and working in his chosen profession against thieves and murderers had sharpened his instincts. The fact they were Chinese didn't hurt either.

One of the men pointed directly at them and said something. Three other men turned to look in their direction. They knew he had spotted them. One of the men pulled out a fully automatic Heckler & Koch MP7 machine pistol.

Rory knew they were in trouble. He pushed Candy hard behind one of the fancy square columns just as the man opened fire.

Bullets chewed away the fancy wood and brass on the other side of the column as screams filled the air around them.

One of those screaming was Candy.

Rory saw the bloody, bullet-riddled bodies of two innocent men and a woman fall to the floor beside them, dead. He pulled his Eagle as another Heckler & Koch MP7 weapon began firing from a different angle.

Bullets ripped away more wood and brass on the column.

Rory waited for a lull, then leaned out quickly, taking a shot.

One of the men jerked backward and fell to the floor. The other men leaped for cover.

Rory's second shot buried itself in the wall over the head of one of the men. He took advantage of the situation and grabbed Candy's arm.

She resisted, frozen in place out of fear.

He couldn't blame her. But they had to get moving while they had the chance. Rory pulled hard, getting her up and running woodenly back up the small staircase.

More automatic weapon fire erupted and bullets tore up the stairs just behind them as.

A man, crouched on their right, tried to run behind Rory and Candy as they passed. But he only provided a shield as bullets ripped into his body and he fell face down.

After twenty feet of running along the upper level, Rory skidded to a halt, pulling Candy back behind his body.

Three men were running from the back of the hotel. They spotted Rory and Candy and pulled out machine pistols.

From the corner of his left eye, Rory spotted movement.

Three more men were running from that direction.

Rory turned, yanked open the door to the stairwell and pushed Candy through.

Candy yelped as she landed face down on the floor.

Diving through the doorway, Rory landed hard on top of Candy.

Bullets ripped through the stairwell door as it closed behind them.

Candy screamed, covering her head with her hands as wood splinters showered down over her and Rory.

Rory realized the only way now was up. They were trapped!

Chapter 44

PULLING CANDY UP FROM THE FLOOR, Rory realized they only had one chance. He knew all the windows on the bottom floor had iron bars that prevented burglars from entering. But right now, they also kept Rory and Candy from getting out. They had to go up. Holstering his Baby Eagle, he led Candy up the stairs past the 2nd and up to the 3rd floor.

DANNI KANG INSTRUCTED four of his men to head for the elevator. They were to head to the top floor, run to the stairwell and swiftly work their way down to trap the targets. They wouldn't have much time before the police and probably a SWAT team arrived on the scene. Kang nodded to the rest of his men and they prepared to enter the main floor stairwell after Steele and the woman.

ON THE 3RD FLOOR, RORY moved as quickly as Candy could run to the west side of the building. When they reached the large window he was looking for, he realized it was sealed shut. He pulled his Baby Eagle and Rory began hammering away at the glass and the window frame with the butt of his weapon.

A very scared Candy uttered her first words since the gunfire had started downstairs."Are - are we going to jump?"

"No. There's a short archway over the alley between the two buildings. All we have to do is climb out and down a couple of feet and run across to the next building."

"Are you sure? I'm sure I can."

"You have a better plan?"

Wringing her hands, Candy turned this way and that - and then began pounding at the glass with her fists. She began to go into full panic mode, "It's not breaking. We have to do something."

Rory put an arm out and pushed her back. Then he stepped back, lifted the Baby Eagle and fired twice.

The bullets tore holes through the glass, sending spidery cracks in all directions.

He flipped the Baby Eagle back around again and resumed pounding on the window.

Candy leaped forward, pounding with her fists again.

The glass finally shattered and most of it fell away.

Rory cleared away the broken shards from the bottom sill of the window frame with the handgun.

Once he was done, Candy leaned through the broken window and was immediately relieved when she saw the archway across to the other building, "Oh. Okay. I can do that."

"Okay, hop up on the sill. " Rory took a quick down the hallway behind them as he cautioned her, "Be careful of the broken glass."

Candy lifted a leg to the sill, carefully gripped the side of the window casing with her right hand and pulled herself up. Then she took a breath to ready herself and took the two-foot jump down onto the concrete roof of the archway between the Hays-Adams hotel and the next building.

Rory climbed out the window and jumped down beside her. Then he turned on his heels, raising the weapon as he told her, "Go and get the window open and get inside."

Candy ran quickly across the narrow archway to the window of the neighboring building, She tried to open it, but it wouldn't budge. "It's locked," she yelled as she continued to try.

Rory cursed and moved backward to join her. Once beside her, he began hammering away at the glass with the butt of his weapon. After several sharp blows, it broke and Rory began cleaning away broken glass.

"Hurry! Hurry!" yelled Candy as she looked back.

Getting the glass shards cleared on the bottom of the frame, Rory held out his hand, "Okay. Go, go, go."

Candy didn't hesitate, she grabbed his hand and scrambled over the sill and through to the other side. She turned around and took several steps back, "Hurry up."

As Rory climbed onto the window ledge, he heard 'hey' from behind him. He spun around on his heels on the windowsill.

One of the Chinese men was in the broken window of the other building. He spotted Rory's weapon and started to bring his machine pistol up.

Rory put a bullet between his eyes.

As the dead gunman fell back onto the floor, another man with a machine pistol came running down the hallway. When he spotted Roy, he brought his weapon up.

Rory spun back around and leaped into the room, pushing Candy to the right, then dove for the floor to his left.

Bullets ripped through the open window and tore into the walls on the other side of the room.

Candy covered her head with her hands.

There was a lull, then another quick burst of fire.

When the firing stopped again, Rory knew the gunman would be coming across for them. He crawled to Candy. She was startled when he touched her. "We have to go. Crawl to the doorway. Hurry."

They were half-way there when more bullets ripped into the walls of the room. Candy flopped flat on her stomach and put her hands over her head, screaming.

Rory flattened as well but he kept his eyes up, waited for a lull in the gunfire. He watched the bullets tear up posters on the walls and realized they were in the US Chamber of Commerce building. The gunfire stopped and he lifted his head slowly, looking to see how far the gunman had gotten. He cursed.

There were two of them now. One of them was starting across the archway, moving low as the other covered him.

He firing two shots.

The man on the archway dropped to his stomach. The other ducked to the side of the window for cover.

Rory reached down and tugged at Candy's elbow, "Run low. Go, go, go."

Her foot slipped on the first attempt, but Candy got up and ran low for the doorway.

Firing another shot back at the men to cover her, Rory turned and ran low for the doorway himself.

Candy was on her hands and knees, leaning against the hall-way on the far side. "Which way?" she asked frantically.

Rory pointed to the left, "Run that way and around the cor-ner. We should be able to get downstairs and out the front door. I'll be right behind you in a minute."

Scrambling to her feet again, Candy took off at a low run.

Rory stood up beside the open door and looked to see where the pursuers were - he swore. Both of the men were now advancing across the archway - and there were more of them in the hall-way beyond the far window.

KANG HAD ARRIVED AT the broken window with six of his men and saw what was happening. He instructed the six men to hide their weapons and head back down to the front door of the hotel. They were to move swiftly down the sidewalk to the next building and cut off the exits over there. He then climbed through the window and joined the other two men out the arch-way in pursuit.

KNOWING HE HAD TO SLOW them down to give Candy time to get as far away as she could, Rory fired another shot through the broken window on the far side of the room. His cell phone rang. He was going to ignore it but the ring tone told him it was Avis. He fired another shot as he pulled the cell phone from his pocket, "Sorry Avis, but I'm kind of busy right now."

"I just wanted to let you know Skye was diverted to Richmond International Airport. It's going to take some time to get there. She was tracking one of the men involved in the attack on our building–

Rory cursed under his breath - and he had to fire another shot to keep the men pinned down. He decided he couldn't wait much longer, positive some of the attackers would be working around to the front of this building.

Avis heard the shot, "Oh-oh. Anything I can do?"

"Yeah, pray." He closed the call, pocketed the cell phone and ran after Candy.

Chapter 45

COVERED BY HIS MEN, Kang reached the end of the arch-way, moved to one side and sprayed into the room with his MP7. One of his men took the other side of the window frame, doing the same, creating a devastating crossfire into the room.

Kang signaled for the man to stop. There was no more return fire. Kang ordered the others to cover him and he jumped onto the window sill and darted into the room.

Police sirens were sounding now, descending on the hotel's location.

Hearing them, Kang's face hardened, now more determined than ever to hunt down the targets down before the police could intervene. He moved to the far doorway, covering the others to come inside. Once set, the three of them expertly moved into the hallway in hot pursuit.

COVERING THE DISTANCE in long strides, Rory quickly caught up with Candy and they now ran side by side down a long hallway, looking for a way down to the front door. There were people cowering against the walls, trying to figure out where and why there was gunfire. A woman spotted Rory's gun in his hand

and she screamed - that set off other screams. Rory cursed. He couldn't blame them. But the screaming would let the gunmen chasing them know exactly where he and Candy were–

Candy slid to a stop beside the elevators and punched a down button.

Rory turned and pulled on her arm, "That's too risky. Keep going and we'll find the stairs."

It was Candy's turn to curse. She was breathing heavy and her face screwed up as she took off at a slower run with him. It took several more minutes before they found those stairs. They were both slowing down as they ducked into the stairwell–

Gunfire erupted behind them - bullets ripped through the door as it closed, sending a shower of sharp splinters exploding in the air around them.

There were screams and shouts of pain from bystanders outside in the hallway.

Rory and Candy took the stairs two at a time, heading for the main floor. As they reached the bottom, Rory heard the stairwell door, two floors up, slam against the wall.

Footsteps began running down the stairs towards them.

Rory stopped, peeked upwards and fired a shot straight up.

The footsteps stopped immediately.

Rory hustled Candy out into the main floor of the building. They ran left down another long hallway, looking for the front doors. They found them but also found more trouble.

Four Chinese gunmen, armed with machine pistols, were bounding up the stairs outside.

Shoving Candy against the wall out of the line of fire, Rory knelt in a combat stance, providing a smaller target. He put a bullet through the glass door into the chest of the first man. In one smooth motion, he aimed and took down the second man.

The other two gunmen darted to the sides, firing their weapons through the front door as they moved out of his line of fire.

Diving to the right, Rory slid along the floor as bullets ripped over his head into the wall. Looking up, he yelled and motioned for Candy to keep going, "Go, go, go."

She hesitated briefly - then turned and began running.

Rory scrambled to his feet and began running low and sideways, watching for more of the Chinese gunmen to appear.

The group that had followed them through the window upstairs burst into the hall from the stairway - they looked for their targets - one of the men pointed and yelled, "There."

A circular information counter sat in the middle of the hallway and Candy skirted around it, looking back and trying to keep it between her and the men as she continued her frantic run.

Using it for cover, Rory dropped and spun around, coming up on one knee. Looking around the edge of the counter, he squeezed off three shots, taking down one of the men.

The gunmen at the far end of the hallway scattered for cover, firing blindly towards him.

Rory pulled back. Bullets ripped into the reception counter behind him. When the firing stopped he rolled to his right, fired a shot and scrambled to his feet, running again. He didn't see Candy anywhere now. Instead, he saw an exit door closing on the left just ahead of him. Driving his legs harder. Rory reached the door and pushed on it just before it closed shut. He ran through the exit and down three steps to the sidewalk outside - and stopped dead in his tracks. He now saw Candy. She was facing him and had a look of horror on her face. Behind her was the man in the black pinstriped suit - and the gun in his hand was pressed to Candy's temple.

The man in the pinstriped suit spoke calmly, "I suggest you put your gun down, Mr. Steele or the woman dies."

Rory looked for a way out of this. But there wasn't any. Behind him, the remaining six Chinese burst through the doorway, their MP7s immediately aimed at Rory. He had no choice. He dropped his weapon to the sidewalk and put his hands on his head.

The Chinese gunmen immediately move forward, taking charge of Rory, while also staring at the man in the black pinstriped suit.

The sounds of sirens continued to fill the air. The police were nearly on the scene of the gunfight.

The man in the pinstriped suit pulled out a cell phone with his free hand, "Kang. You had orders to eliminate them. They've been changed. We're being ordered to take them prisoner." He tossed the cell phone across to Kang.

Kang caught the phone but just started for a moment. Then he put the phone it to his ear and listening. He didn't seem too pleased but he nodded his head and ended the call. "He is correct. Get the vehicles."

Two of the men took off at a run.

As they all stood there, Blacker looked Rory directly in the eyes. His left hand moved up to Candy's padded left breast, slid intimately across it and squeezed her right one.

Candy closed her eyes.

Blacker then slipped his hand inside Candy's blouse and then her padded brassiere, slowly moving his hand over her naked breast inside. He grinned.

Rory saw Candy's face turned red in humiliation.

Then Blacker slowly pulled his hand out. He was holding the tampon shaped USB drive

Chapter 46

THE CHINESE GUNMEN pushed Rory and Candy through the side door into a large warehouse. It smelled of old wood and cardboard, had high ceilings and six large, floor-to-roof wooden pillars. On the far side of the warehouse were stacks of cartons and a number of pieces of packaging machinery. White boxes similar to those they found in the search at the office of Lee Park Yim were sitting on a conveyor. Which meant this was part of their spy operation - not that it mattered right now.

Blacker followed in behind them, "Take them away from the doors."

The Chinese gunmen moved Rory and Candy across the floor to the middle of the large, open space

"You won't get away with this," Candy snapped. "My sister works for the President of the United States and she'll hunt you down if you do anything to us."

The six Chinese gunmen looked at each other. One of the men shook his head and grinned, saying something in Chinese.

Kang laughed and then ordered three of the men to guard outside. He then pulled a handgun and aimed directly at Candy's head, "Who have you talked to about what you know?"

Candy now shook with fear. She held her hands up near her face, palms out as if she could ward off the bullet if he fired, "N-no one–"

"Now that's a lie," Blacker said. "We know Skye Steele met with you and Mr. Steele. So you *have* talked to someone. I would advise you not to lie again, Ms. Jossel. Mr. Kang here would love nothing better than to put a bullet in your brain."

Kang smiled.

Candy's body shook harder.

"Leave her alone," Rory said.

Kang shifted his aim to Rory's head, "Or what?"

Rory held his tongue.

Kang smiled coldly, "You care for her?" He reached out and placed his hand on Candy's breast.

"Please don't," Candy pleaded as the man squeezed.

Rory clenched his fists. He knew the man was trying to bait him into something foolish. And he couldn't afford to do that right now. The longer he could wait, the more likely they would have a chance to get out of this. But it wasn't easy.

"Wait until you see what else we do to her...unless you tell us who you two talked to," Kang said.

Rory looked Kang in the eyes, "You're a bastard and a coward. You know that?"

One of the other Chinese assassins stepped behind Rory. He turned sideways and drove a foot into the back of Rory's knee.

Rory's leg buckled and he fell to his knees. His attempt to goad Kang in return hadn't worked either.

Candy let out a cry.

Looking at Candy, Kang asked, "Do you want us to hurt him more? Or will you tell us what we want to know?"

"No. Please don't," Candy whispered in fear. "And I'm telling you the truth–"

Kang snarled as he took a step forward and aimed at Rory's face, "Then I'll ask you again, Ms. Jossel. Who did you talk to?"

"No one else, I swear to you," Candy cried as she raised her hands to her mouth.

Kang swung the gun around and pressed it hard against Candy's forehead, "Liar!"

"Don't–" Rory's words were cut off as the assassin behind him drove his foot into his back this time.

Candy yelped.

Kang pressed the gun harder into her forehead, forcing Candy to take a step back, "We know everything. We just want to hear it from you. You'll feel so much better when you tell us the truth."

"I am telling you the truth. Please don't hurt him," Candy pleaded in a voice filled with pain and fear.

Glaring at her for a moment, Kang pulled the gun away from her forehead. He turned and walked to Rory, who was still bent over on his knees from the blow. Kang pressed the gun against the top of Rory's black hair, "Tell - me - who - you - talked to."

Candy broke down in tears. "No one," she sobbed as she wrung her hands together. "No one...."

Kang glanced around at Candy and then he looked back down at Rory, his eyes glowing with the desire to kill someone.

"We have to keep them alive, Kang," Blacker reminded him.

But Kang didn't budge a muscle - his eyes remained fixed on the head under his gun and he pushed the barrel forcefully.

Wincing, Rory was sure it was all over. He waited for the bullet to come crashing through his skull.

"Those *were* our instructions," Blacker said firmly.

Kang sneered. Then he pulled the gun away from Rory's head and took a step backwards. "For now," he said ominously.

Blacker nodded. He gestured and watched as the Chinese assassin behind Rory pulled him to his feet.

Candy ran forward and threw her arms around Rory. "I'm so sorry. I'm so sorry for the email...."

"I know," Rory whispered. He put his arms around her in comfort.

Blacker mocked them "All very touching, Steele. But Kang *will* eventually get his way. And then, I head after your sister."

Rory turned his head and stared Blacker in the eyes, "In that case, good luck, you'll need all the help you can get."

Blacker's half-smile left his face and he sneered, "When I find her–"

"Did you get the backup drive, Blacker?"

Everyone turned and watched a figure stride through an open door. Rory noted it was a woman, about 6 feet tall, her short brown hair cut in a trim business style. She walked with a firm athletic stride, totally in charge of everything around her.

Candy blinked in total surprise and she wiped tears from her eyes, "Keira? What are you doing here?"

The woman ignored the question. "The drive?" she asked again in a demanding voice as she strode forward.

"Keira, what's happening?" Candy asked again as she stepped out of Rory's protective embrace.

The woman continued to ignore the question.

Blacker stepped past Candy and Rory towards the woman - who now held her hand out. She nodded once as he gave her the Tampon shaped USB drive. Then she raised an eyebrow, looking at the item in her hands.

Candy's hands went to her face in shock, "Oh, my god. No!"

Rory realized he was looking at Keira Blaze Jossel, Candy's big sister and the campaign manager of Connor Harrison Lane, the President-elect of the United States. And apparently one of the people - if not the main person - behind the men trying to kill Candy and Rory.

Chapter 47

CANDY JOSSEL TURNED and looked at Rory as she spoke in a strangled whisper, "It's my sister. She...."

Rory nodded as he gently put his arms around her again.

Candy's eyes revealed her sense of betrayal. Her heart was broken. Her voice was quiet and wounded, "All this time...every time I called...."

Rory just hugged her a little tighter. There wasn't much he could say. Words couldn't ease the pain she felt right now. He looked into the eyes of Keira Jossel. There was no pain there. Just anger.

Keira Jossel didn't flinch. She just looked at Blacker, "What did you find out? Do we know who they talked to?"

"We were just working on," Blacker said.

Kang spoke up, his eyes revealing a desire to inflict pain, "Just leave them with *me* a little longer. I'll find out."

Keira Jossel looked at him for a moment and then said, "All right, Kang. You get your wish." She lifted her fist, holding the USB flash drive up, "I have what I need. Just–"

"Did you get it, babe?" Everyone turned to see a tall, distinguished looking man step into the room and head across the floor towards them.

Rory narrowed his eyes. The man looked familiar. Suddenly, he realized he was looking at Connor Harrison Lane, the new President-elect of the United States.

Keira turned with fire in her eyes, "What are *you* doing here?"

Lane swept his arms out wide as he walked like he was performing on a stage, "I wanted to make sure everything was okay. Took me a while to get away from those Secret Service guys." Lane stopped beside Keira, a politician's smile on his face shaking his head as he looked at the others, "Those guys don't seem to listen to me, even if I *am* the President of these here United States of America."

"I told you I would take care of everything," Keira snapped at him. "Just like I've *always* taken care of everything from the start."

Lane held his hands up in mock surrender, "I know, I know. But I also needed to tell you personally that someone unleashed a computer virus into the computer system at ZongChi Technologies. It wiped out everything there and is working its way back into China." He frowned, "I have to tell you, the Chinese are really freaking out."

Keira turned her head slowly and looked directly at Rory. Her voice dripped venom, "You and your family will pay for interfering."

Candy pulled herself from Rory. Her voice was filled with anguish and hurt as she looked from Lane to her sister. "Keira, what have you done?"

Her lip curled as Keira spoke harshly to her sister, "What *needed* to be done."

"I... I don't understand... How could you do this?" Candy's voice was trembling, "How could you betray your own country–"

Now veins popped out on Keira's neck, "Betrayed my country? The way they betrayed our father!"

Candy's face was a mass of confusion, "What...what are you talking about?"

Keira took a forceful step forward, "The United States of America took away our father's business. They destroyed him. They destroyed our family. I'm righting a wrong–"

"No, Keira, that isn't what happened–"

"I *know* what happened!" Keira yelled. "I was working for Ambassador Pollard at the time. He told me what had happened. He told me how the government was moving *our* business to someone else. They had no right. I used the contacts I had made through Ambassador Pollard to eventually negotiate with the Chinese. I made a deal to get the business back for our family. Our own government didn't care about our father. Once Mom and Dana and Marion were killed in that car accident, it was all he had. They took it away from him. They destroyed our father. It's no wonder he died from a heart attack. *Their* betrayal killed him–"

"Oh. God, it's my fault. It's all my fault," Candy cried. She turned away, bent over and vomited.

The two Chinese men jumped back as puke splashed on their shoes.

Rory went to her aid, putting his hands on her back and shoulder, "Are you okay?"

"Get away from her," commanded one of the Chinese men. He pointed his MP7 machine pistol directly at Rory's head. "Now!"

Rory put his hands up and backed away slowly.

Candy threw up once more and wiped the back of her hand across her lips, "Oh, god, Keira, I'm so sorry. I'm so sorry...."

Keira stood there, looking at her sister, confusion crossing her face, "Sorry for what? What are you talking about?"

Candy straightened up slowly and turned around as she wiped a little more vomit from her chin, "It's my fault. I should have told you–"

"Told me *what*?" Keira yelled. "What are you talking about, you little fool. You've nearly wrecked everything I've worked so hard for–"

Candy took a step towards her sister, "Do you remember when dad was injured when he was working on our house?"

"Of course," Keira replied in annoyance, "what does that have to do with any of this?"

"Dad...was in tremendous pain," Candy explained. "He began drinking to ease that pain. He...he became an alcoholic–"

"How dare you!" Keira yelled. "How dare you class our father in with someone like the drunk driver who killed our mother and our two sisters–"

"Dad was driving. *He* was the drunk driver," Candy yelled back.

Keira shook her head firmly, "No. Everyone said mom was driving. And I was able to get a copy of the accident report. The other driver was drunk–"

"They covered it up," Candy interjected with force. "The police chief grew up with dad. Do you remember that? The other driver had no family. He had no relatives to harm. They put in the report that the other man was driving to protect dad."

"No!" Keira objected.

"Yes! I was there. I survived the accident. Remember? Not you. Me!" Candy yelled. "Dad was devastated. He had killed his wife and two daughters. He made me promise *never* to say anything to you–"

"You're lying," Keira said with some heat in her voice.

Candy shook her head firmly. "No. I'm telling you the truth *now*. That I was lying to you all those years. That's why we're in this mess. If I had only told you–"

"But the business–"

"It *wasn't* taken, it was *given*," Candy said firmly. "While dad was recovering, while he was trying to get sober, his damn government friends began to use the business to spy on the Chinese. It was a perfect cover for them. They had their spies traveling back and forth under the guise of doing business. When Dad found out, he didn't want anything to do with it. He didn't want you to know. He knew what the business meant to you, but he didn't want you involved with what they were doing. He was so proud of you. You were trying to do things the right way and he didn't know how to tell you. He made me promise *never* to say anything to you." Candy took a step forward and said in a quiet voice, "When he died from that heart attack, I went off the rails. I had so many secrets and I couldn't tell you...."

Keira Blaze Jossel stood there with a stunned look on her face.

Chapter 48

RORY WAS SURPRISED at the revelations himself. But it all started to make sense. All the pieces of the puzzle were fitting together. But all of this new information didn't help with one other important aspect. Once Keira Jossel and President-elect Lane left the warehouse, Rory and Candy were as good as dead. Kang was just itching to complete his original mission. To kill them.

Rory's muscles tensed as he looked for a way out. He couldn't wait much longer.

Blacker smiled as their eyes met. He knew what Rory was thinking and he pulled his handgun, the wolfish grin lingering on his lips. The message to Rory was simple, go ahead and try something. Please.

Now Rory concentrated on relaxing his body and sending a message to Blacker -'Okay, I'm done' - but his brain continued to look for a way out. The two sisters continued bickering - Lane stood back and watched them - Kang and the others did the same - only Blacker watched him. The problem was insurmountable - Rory needed to take a gun from someone to have any chance- but there was too much distance between him and Blacker or any of the men—

Rory detected movement in his peripheral vision - someone was high overhead on the other side of the open space. Discreetly glancing in that direction, he could just see a person moving on the other end of an old catwalk that was twenty feet above the floor. It was Skye! He was surprised to see her. She had obviously tracked one of the men here but Avis said she had been diverted - she was wearing an armor jacket and racing knee pads - he could only imagine how many cops chased her - and couldn't keep up - with some motorcycle she had used. Skye lifted a hand once - she knew he could see her. - then she gestured ahead.

Rory knew instinctively what she wanted to do. He had to find some way to create a diversion, something that would give her a chance to move to a spot almost overhead. If she made it without being detected, it could possibly give them a chance in a fight - although he had no idea how she could get from twenty feet overhead to the floor - he left that up to her -because a text message he had received back at the Hay-Adams hotel popped into his mind. That could do it. Rory looked at Keira and he spoke up in a loud voice, "There's something else your sister hasn't mentioned. Some extremely damning information we found when we infiltrated the computer systems at ZongChi Technologies."

Keira and everyone else turned their attention to Rory. Her eyes hard, Keira said, "We're not interested in what you have to say."

That gave Skye her chance. She began to move low, swiftly and silently making her way across the catwalk.

Rory spoke in a loud voice, hopefully covering any light footsteps as Skye moved towards them, "Maybe your sister will be interested." He looked at Candy, "The Chinese *knew* about the spy network the American government set up through your father's business. They found out through an American contact."

Keira gave a glance to Danni Kang.

Candy looked at Rory, a questioning look etched her face.

Rory's eyes bored into Keira's, "And the Chinese knew who *you* were from the beginning, They played you."

Keira narrowed her eyes, fists clenching, nostrils flaring, her voice a hot whisper, "That's preposterous. Don't think you can–"

"Your father didn't die of a heart attack." Rory paused for effect - to let that sink in.

Her lip curled now, "What are you talking about? My father–"

"Was *assassinated* by the Chinese - for what they assumed was his part in setting up the spy network."

It took a second to register. Then Keira's head snapped around and she looked directly at Kang.

Kang's cold expression confirmed the truth.

In an instant, Keira Jossel attacked Kang, screaming and tearing at his eyes with her fingernails. Candy back away abruptly, stunned by Keira's ferocious attack - a heartbeat later - she understood who this Kang was.

There was no more time for stealth. Skye ran hard, placed a hand on the railing and vaulted over. She came down sideways - the knee pads striking one Chinese gunman on the shoulders. He dropped to the floor with a scream of pain, his MP7 machine pistol hitting the floor and bouncing a few feet away. Her hard armor jacket struck the other one in the back of the head. This one fell hard to the concrete floor, splitting his head open and falling unconscious. His MP7 machine pistol clattered to the floor. The first man shook the cobwebs from his head and scrambled to his feet, one hand on a shoulder, grimacing. He spotted his weapon and went for it–

Skye came up on her feet as well and stepped in front, blocking his path to the machine pistol.

The Chinese gunman grit his teeth against the pain in his shoulder- pretending to give up - then whirled around on his feet, bringing a savage leg kick around at Skye.

She ducked and rolled, coming to her feet several feet away. But Candy had reacted by running over - intending to get the machine pistol from the floor and assassinate Kang - and when she started bending over - the gunman's kick hit her on the top of the head. She yelped and crashed to the floor.

Startled by his strike for a moment, the Chinese gunmen turned his attention back to Skye - taking up a fighting stance.

RORY MADE HIS MOVE, chopping down on the arm of Blacker, knocking the weapon from his grasp.

Blacker grunted with pain but countered by taking Rory's feet out from under him with a sweep of his left foot.

Taken off his feet, Rory landed hard on the concrete floor, grunting from the blow to his back that knocked the air from his lungs.

Blacker raised his foot and brought it down towards Rory's head.

Rolling away, Rory came up on his feet in a defensive crouch, trying to suck in oxygen, his lungs hurting.

Blacker compressed his extended fingers tightly and attacked with spear-hand thrusts, aiming for Rory's throat and eyes.

Countering every move expertly, Rory moved back with each thrust as he bought a few precious seconds to recover.

Blacker feinted a left blow to the chest - knowing his opponent's problem - and then thrust his right hand at Rory's throat - expecting to take him off-guard.

But Rory was expecting something like that - he stepped to the side - and used Blacker's momentum to flip him onto his back.

THE CHINESE GUNMAN attacked - Skye deflecting every blow from her opponent - studying his technique.

Them he took a step back - switched from his forward fighting stance to a rear foot stance - and attacked Skye again.

Skye countered smoothly, deflecting every blow again - watching and waiting for what she needed him to do.

The Chinese gunman faked a move to the left and then lunged with a blow aimed at her throat.

Skye deftly moved to the side and flipped him over - bringing her body weight down - she smashed the gunman's head down against the concrete. His lights went out.

KANG ROARED WITH PAIN as Keira's nails gouged deep scratches down his eyelids. He brought his right arm around and smashed her hard across the head.

Keira Jossel staggered from the blow.

Bringing his MP7 machine pistol up - bloody scratches around his eyes - Kang's lips curled - and he pulled the trigger.

The bullets ripped through Keira Jossel's body and penetrated President Lane's back as he was running away behind her

Before the two bodies even fell to the concrete floor, Kang spun around, aiming his weapon towards Skye.

Leaving Blacker lying on the floor, Rory shot forward, tackling Kang around the waist, driving him back

Kang's weapon fired upwards into the roof before he dropped it, trying to break his fall.

Rory landed on top of Kang and they grappled.

SHAKING THE FOG FROM his head, Blacker rose to his feet and headed for Rory and Kang.

Skye stepped in front of him.

His hands went up as Blacker lurched to a stop.

Bringing her right hand up slowly, Skye beckoning Blacker forward.

Blacker's smile was filled with malice. Cracking his neck from side-to-side to loosen up - to intimidate - and get ready - Blacker then took a Kenpo stance - paused - and employed a series of hard linear strikes and kicks.

Her face impassive, Skye countered every thrust - observing the technique.

Pausing again, Blacker switched to karate chops, aiming for her jugular, her throat, her collarbone.

Skye calmly deflected every blow.

Blacker tried front kicks, side kicks, knee strikes and roundhouse kicks.

But Skye was never where she was supposed to be - she was always one step ahead.

Stopping his attack, Blacker's chest was heaving from both the exertion and the anger. Wiping a hand across his mouth, Blacker pulled his lips back, baring his teeth, "Get ready, bitch. I'm going to rip off your clothes, spread your legs and–"

Spinning around, Skye delivered a powerful and angry roundhouse kick to Blacker's head.

Blacker's head jerked hard from the blow and his legs screwed out from under him, sending him crashing hard to the concrete floor.

Skye looked down at him, "You've got a real potty mouth, pal."

Grunting, Blacker rolled around to his hands and knees and bent over, holding a hand to his head and grimacing in pain.

Skye stepped forward and dropped down with an elbow to his back.

The air flew from his lungs and Blacker fell face down, his arms flailing out to the sides, striking Kang's dropped MP7 machine pistol. It went sliding across the floor.

RORY USED HIS FEET to flip Kang over his head. He heard the body land hard on the concrete behind him.

The sliding machine pistol hit Kang's body and stopped dead.

Spinning around, Rory got to his feet in a defensive stance - but he was too late.

Kang was grinning as he rose with the weapon in his hand, aimed directly at Rory's head. Skye was too far away. They both knew, once Rory was dead, she would be next.

The roar of an MP7 machine pistol filled the warehouse.

Jun 'Danni' Kang's head disappeared in a mass of gore. The nearly headless body slowly collapsed to the concrete floor of the warehouse.

Rory turned to see Candy standing there, holding one of the other dropped machine pistols, a look of shock on her face. Rory moved to her side and gently placed his hand on the weapon, "It's okay, you can let go now. He's gone."

Candy slowly realized what Rory was saying. She looked at him, let go of the weapon and looked back at the mutilated body, her voice nearly inaudible, "That's what he gets for killing my father - and for feeling me up."

"I'll keep that in mind," Rory said as he secured the weapon.

An uneven smile crossed her lips, "It's okay, I wouldn't do that to you if you did it."

Rory nodded, knowing she was in shock at what had just happened.

A moment later, Candy turned and looked her sister, lying on the concrete in a pool of blood. She rushed over to her, "Keira!"

Knowing there was nothing he could do now, Rory looked at Skye, "What about the men outside?"

"I took care of them. They're in plastic handcuffs." She set to the task of securing an unconscious Blacker and the others in plastic handcuffs she had in her pockets.

Rory began collecting the weapons as he watched the last moments of the two sisters.

Candy lifted Keira's head gently onto her lap, brushing the hair back from her sister's forehead.

"I'm sorry," Keira whispered up to her little sister.

Candy only nodded, tears falling onto her big sister's cheeks.

"I wish...I could change things," Keira whispered. "I wish–"

"I know," Candy said.

Keira Jossel slowly closed her eyes as her breath audibly left her.

Chapter 49

RORY'S HEART WENT OUT to Candace Ella Jossel. All those years of pain and suffering had ripped her family completely apart. He wondered how difficult it would be for her to overcome the tremendous betrayal she had just gone through. He hoped she wouldn't continue to blame herself for withholding information from her big sister. Sometimes family secrets have a way of biting back.

Skye went over to check on Connor Harrison Lane - skirting the blood pooling under his riddled body - and checked his neck for a pulse. She looked up at Rory and shook her head no.

Rory stood up from the pile of weapons, taking a deep breath and wondering how his death would eventually be presented to the American public. That would be up to others. As Skye walked back, he gave her a nod, "Glad you could make it to the party. Avis said you were diverted." He gestured to the knee pads, "I hope you didn't break too many laws getting here."

"I'll send you the tickets to pay - when they catch up to give them to me." Skye frowned and gestured to Blacker, "We were tracking that bugger's cell phone. I had a shootout with him and his men at our building– "

"What? Is everyone okay?"

Skye frowned again, "No one on our side got hurt. But a security guard and a couple of responding officers got taken out - I'm sure he got the drop on them using some government credentials."

Rory grimaced, "Good news and bad news, I guess."

"Yeah." She glanced back at the body of Lane, "And now I can understand how he was able to divert me away from Washington." She shook her head, "I almost didn't make it in time."

"I'm glad you did."

Skye nodded somberly and looked at Candy, "Do you think she'll be okay? This had got to be pretty heavy on her."

Rory didn't reply as he looked at Candy as well. It definitely wasn't going to be easy for her.

Sirens sounded in the distance.

"Sounds like the police are on their way."

Skye nodded, "Yeah. I called 9-1-1 from the catwalk when I saw what was happening."

"Good." Rory turned his attention back to Candy.

In the silence, Skye removed her armor jacket and knee pads, leaving them on the floor. Then she stood side by side wither her brother, watching and waiting.

Candy caressed the face of Keira for the last time. She finally let her big sister's head rest on the cold concrete floor of the warehouse. Slowly getting to her feet, she wiped tears from her eyes and staggered, obviously overwhelmed by everything that had happened.

Rory moved in quickly, holding her shoulders to steady her. Then he turned Candy away from the bodies, walking with her back to where Skye stood.

Skye reached into a back pocket of her leather pants, "I have something for you, Candy."

Candy wiped a tear from her cheek, her voice quiet, "What is it?"

Pulling a black object about the size of a pack of playing cards from her pocket, Skye held it out to Candy, "It doesn't look like much, but this is a portable hard drive. It's filled with specific information for you from ZongChi Technologies."

Candy lightly brushed the back of her hand under her nose and sniffled. She reached out and took the drive from Skye's hand, "Specific information on what?"

"It has files and text messages that clearly show how you were set up for the murder of your friend, Wendy Symonds."

"Really?" Candy's hands shook as she looked at the object in her hands.

Skye nodded and tapped the hard drive, "Uh-huh. This will prove your innocence. Those Secret Service guys manipulated the crime scene. They used scotch tape to transfer your fingerprints to the murder weapon. You won't have to run anymore, Candy. And our office has several large hard drives filled to the gills with information outlining how China bought the presidency, their spying and how they planned to get *their* president to allow them to infiltrate computers across the free world with compromised hardware and software."

Rory shook his head in amazement at the ambitious plan, "Doing that would have given them a pipeline into every democratic government's computer system. Incredible."

"Yeah. It's hard to believe how close they came–"

Candy threw her arms around Skye's neck, hugging her tightly. "Thank you," she whispered, "Thank you so much."

Skye smiled at the intensity of her emotions and hugged Candy back, "You're very welcome."

Letting Skye go, Candy turned and threw her arms around Rory's neck, hugging him tightly, "And thank you, Rory."

Rory grunted with the force of the hug and grinned.

"But there was even more, big brother," Skye said. "They also planned to infiltrate the systems of major companies, as well as the stock market itself, through their hardware and software. They would have been able to manipulate the free world economy, even siphon money into their own treasury as they waged a hidden, technological war on the world."

Sirens wailed and tires screeched to a stop outside the warehouse, alerting them to the fact the authorities had arrived.

Candy released her hold on Rory and wiped another tear away, "I guess I should talk to the police and clear myself."

"No need to," Skye assured her. "The Attorney General has already been briefed and shown this information by our office as well. The police won't be bothering you."

"Really?"

Skye nodded confirmation.

Candy held the small hard drive tightly in both hands, "I don't know how I'll ever be able to thank you and Rory."

Skye put her arm around Candy and started to lead her to the exit and further away from her big sister's body, "It's our pleasure. Now, you do realize that's a dangerous disguise you wore? My brother is attracted to big boobs like you can't believe. He'll forget all about protecting you–"

"I know," Candy said. "He couldn't keep his eyes off me."

Rory could only shake his head and smile.